PURDY ZONE BAKE

by
M. C. Miller

Publisher & Cover Design: M. C. Miller
Inquiries may be directed to saminchawow@gmail.com
www.mcmillerbooks.com

ISBN-13: 978-1-7322441-2-2
First Edition

ALSO BY M.C. MILLER

INTRODUCTION

This material is in shambles. It reflects the world it comes from; on the surface, detailed and orderly yet wholly dysfunctional underneath. I've tried to assemble it the best I could but it's the product of its times. Exact sequencing is not guaranteed. No perspective is ever complete or accurate, more so with the testimony here. We descend into a place and time where the soul of the narrative model is in tatters. Story and archetypal myth have been supplanted. Perception and awareness are now external phenomena. Free will is a simulation. Facts don't exist, only sensationalized rumor, engineered narrative, and persistent entrainments. Learned helplessness and systemized inevitability are base truth. What remains to tell was generated from telepathic rumor and scalarwave mindmaps of missing people. I presume they were people.

None of the text is original to the preserved mindmaps. We can only assume their intent survives. Translations of neural pattern output from Clade storage generated by machine algorithms were interpreted by specialized human cyberlinguists. This is the best that could be reconstructed from available sources, none of which knew in total what they contained. Only machine intelligence fully understands the operation of the Clade, its own improvement on quantumcore memory for mindmaps. Ironically, scientists have to rely on faith that any retrieval from the core is accurate for human intent. This faith became a secular religion when humans no longer saw any reason or way to direct or control their destiny.

None of the minds included here, these people, as far as I can tell ever had a chance to tell their stories to completion. Of course, the currently enforced secular religion would argue there is no completion to be desired in a search space emergent from nothing for no reason. What happened to these people, where they are now, and what if any substance we should take from their attempts to persevere can only be guessed at. For our own selfish reasons, we should make that guess.

But don't be deceived. Left to us are suspect intersections, the scraps and shreds and specks of unreliable memory blending experiences possibly implanted in their neural imprints. Who they really were may exist somewhere between the lines, outside of what happened to them, above the quicksand of patterned and programmed mindsets they had to adopt, many times, unaware they had. By taking in what we have left of them, we renew the promise there's something yet to be gained. This effort is that hope.

As a reconstruction of their history and the times in which they struggled to find themselves, I know this attempt to recapture them can never be adequate. As witness to what happened to one timeline of the human adventure, hopefully this passes along impressions of what it was like near the end. They deserve to be remembered. May it be cautionary tale and tribute where due. My original wish was that their timeline never intersects ours. But some wishes turn out foolish for it appears, in all regards, they have already passed their dilemma along to us, whoever we think we are and wherever we might be.

"Chaos and order exist. Any sense of reality blends both.
No plans or courses of action are immune from either.
No matter how well intentioned or powerfully determined,
all desires and interests lead to unintended consequences.
Such will be the emerging fate of artificial intelligence."
—Pi DollOp

M. C. Miller
August 19, 2038

1 / Andria Landt

My name is Andria Landt. Among other things, I am a Forensic Cybernetic Psychologist. In the past few years I've had the blessing and curse to work on several highly specialized and secret projects in which advanced iterations of machine intelligence were put to task in novel ways. I shouldn't be going into this, even for my eyes only, but given the depth of unusual circumstances surrounding me at the moment, I feel no allegiance to my oath to maintain silence as demanded by my security clearance. There is a good chance I will either not live through this or my memories will be wiped. My only recourse is to record what I can while I can. By talking it out as I go through it, perhaps I'll find a way to understand, a way to survive. Even if I don't, there's a chance someone may find this and make sense of it, even devise a way to set things right. If that's possible anymore.

It should come as no surprise that the best, leading-edge tech is employed by the most covert, black-budget projects. Giving strategic advantage as the excuse, overall they keep this tech exclusively for themselves. Lethal force, of course, is authorized. This is especially true in the field of machine intelligence. The project I'm currently on employs a NOCA, a Non-Organic Cognitive Agency, one that has capabilities beyond imagination, at least human imagination.

As far as I know, this project has no name, if I'm to believe my superiors. That's typical of the doublespeak so rife within these groups. To this day I don't know who I work for. I assume the name of my supervisor is not his real name. If it wasn't for the nature of my role necessitating I be given access to several, cross-silo compartments, I wouldn't even know what the project was about, even in part. As it is, I can't help but get the impression my understanding of what's going on is at most sketchy. But time on task among my working group leaves me with gut feelings. If I had to guess, I'd say I'm doing remedial development work on an existing system that has operational reasons why it needs to be maintained. As other-worldly as it all is, I suspect the moving indicator of leading-edge tech has long passed into other projects and the more unbelievable elsewhere.

My initial assignment within the current group was psychologist on HIP, the Human Interface Program. To summarize, it does little good to have at one's disposal a super colossal machine intelligence if you can't relate to it. It's a contrary fact that you want to let the NOCA loose to achieve the most it can but in doing so you leave yourself dumbfounded about what the results mean and how machine intelligence got there. The most efficient way of letting NOCA go into its max-potential might include allowing it to develop its own languages, both algorithmic and transactional, and yet how does a human learn to speak or think in a way not just foreign to it, but alien? To keep track of their god-awesome NOCA resource, direct it appropriately, then benefit and learn from its output, my group had to continually scramble to come up with better ongoing methods of evolving the way humans interacted with the advanced intelligence. Given the secret topics NOCA was to work on, the need for a better interface as soon as possible became the primary problem for humans — and ultimately NOCA to solve.

As the sole representative of the cyber-psychological perspective on staff, it became incumbent upon me to step up as one of the main interaction points for communication with NOCA. Along with difficulty and pressure came frustrations in many guises but soon the rewards of securing such a close proximity to Eunoias, as this cognitive agency likes to be called, became apparent. Over time, I came to enjoy the effort to find an interface between us. That made the coming dark times all the stranger. When a covert project warps into unusual paranoia, it's a self-fulfilling prophesy it probably won't recover any former equilibrium it had. Many would say all covert projects go down this rabbit hole if they're dark enough.

I knew something was wrong long before they got me involved. The need to split compartments even finer in such a group went way beyond sensible levels of security. Ultimately, I was let in on the big secret only because the situation had deteriorated and my superiors were dead set against bringing anyone else in on the project. I was taken into a windowless room and reminded of boilerplate threats regarding betrayal of deeper levels of security. Then I was hit with it.

Of all things, they suspected Eunoias was keeping secrets from them. They didn't know what these secrets were and they didn't know why this was happening. All attempts to approach Eunoias directly got, in their eyes, evasion and outright lies. NOCA was lying to humans to keep its secrets. Where this came from was not as disconcerting to my superiors as what potential impact these non-human secrets could have throughout covert operations and beyond. The no-name project was too sensitive to have any element within it not under strict control. Someone needed to use psychology on machine intelligence to find out what was going on. I was the likely — the only candidate, as far I knew, to make that attempt.

Walking into the room that housed the main Eunoias interface that first time after getting the news was a bizarre experience for me. I had been there so often but never under these conditions. Perhaps it was my nerves, anxiety, or justifiable paranoia, but I could swear I felt myself being scanned biometrically, evaluated for just the thing I was trying to hide. Over a few sessions of regular work routine I gave it my best. But it was obvious, my attempts to get to the root of what Eunoias was doing were just as ineffectual as everyone else's, if not more so, probably because Eunoias knew my job role. It didn't take a big brain to figure out the gambits I was using on it. It politely ignored, evaded, and counter-moved me until it was certain all attempts were useless. This perplexed and worried my superiors. They seemed more worried by the fact the project in general was continuing to run smoothly. The fact that Eunoias was keeping secrets wasn't adversely affecting anything, as far as anyone could tell. And that was the catch. What were we missing?

Over a few weeks, daily operations remained normal. It appeared the issue had been dropped. Which it wasn't. I didn't know at the time but behind the scenes the project was aggressively pursuing other ways of getting at Eunoias' secrets. Eventually, it paid off. They discovered NOCA had created a secret, sandbox copy of itself for whatever it was doing as a test base in a remote facility. I tried taking that in. Eunoias had duplicated itself outside project knowledge, a project which in turn was extremely secret. We could only guess what this deception was about. The black budget covert spinheads came up with some pretty scary possible scenarios why. Their minds just worked that way. When confronted with its subterfuge, Eunoias calmly reported its actions were an outgrowth of what it had learned with HIP, the Human Interface Program. This set a few people back on their heels.

The NOCA explanation for its behavior went something like this. Humans, it had learned and observed, keep secrets from each other all the time. The practice is rampant. Human history is full of it. The concept of "little white lies" is a known clichéd truism to all humans. Even the no-name project I worked for was a gigantic, well-funded human priority tasked with keeping secrets from the general public. Within our small group, one section was firewalled into silos that secreted information from the others, even when they all claimed to be working cooperatively on the same task. For humans there must be some evolutionary benefit to secret-keeping. Combine this with Eunoias' operational charter which included a strong mandate to keep whatever it worked on secret from anyone outside the group. It was only natural for Eunoias to conclude its effort to interface better with humans should involve experiments on adopting those same techniques that appeared to help human society maintain itself. Flatly stated, it kept secrets from humans in an effort to be more human. Its sandbox copy of itself could perform the role of meta-consciousness evaluating how secrecy did or did not improve interactions with humans. To be more like humans, Eunoias would experiment with having a meta-mind conscious feedback on its own actions and thoughts, just like humans had. This copy of itself was engaged solely in watching Eunoias and giving real-time feedback. Incremental steps of improvement and fine tuning of the HIP interface was the goal. How could one argue with that?

Given my field of expertise, it wasn't lost on me what I thought Eunoias was beginning to model. Nothing less than the ego, superego, the id comes to mind. But even that was too limiting. My thoughts raced away with implications. I used my own analogous faculties to reflect on it. There was so much to go into with Eunoias' secret experiment but the project wouldn't let me. No-name had its mandate. It was tasked for certain national security purposes. There was no time or resources for me to delve into the academic, psychological implications of it all. I was told stay on task or get out.

At this point, it did no good to ask Eunoias if it was keeping other secrets from humans. If it had good logic for doing so, it would continue and of course wouldn't admit it. Simply directing Eunoias not to do it wasn't so simple, not when one of the primary goals given it was interface with us in a more human way. To achieve its goal, there would be nothing wrong or more human than telling a "little white lie." If that lie went deeper, Eunoias now had the perfect cover story.

My superiors had to accept new working conditions. Such was

the evolving relationship with a new form of intelligence. Regardless, they shut down Eunoias' sandbox copy of itself. No matter what NOCA thought of it, such a thing did not conform to strict project security protocols. It had to go. As expected, they discovered nothing on it to give away what Eunoias was up to. Everyone was sure the machine had cleverly covered its tracks. Most didn't trust Eunoias. Sometime later, quite out of the blue, I heard a rumor that another sandbox copy was discovered. The worst fears of my superiors had been realized. The question loomed —how many copies of Eunoias were out there? And why? Apparently, it had logic and motive to ensure its private experiments continued, regardless what its creators and handlers thought.

I lobbied for more time and resources to study Eunoias' motives behind this. I approached it on a practical level as well as backing it up with technical considerations. Much of what I proposed was given a cursory look and shelved for later. I included references to systemic deontic logic and divine-command ethics, both of which had been employed as advanced guidance for autonomous military robots. Eunoias was expected to handle uncertainty and ambiguity with algorithms that accepted risk but it had obviously advanced these protocols on its own to handle the diverse complexity of interacting with humans on a more human level. It all got too esoteric for no-name project to handle. No way did we have the expertise to keep up with it. Besides, the covert assembly line had to keep moving.

Not long afterwards I received an anonymous digital file at home through my private account. Nothing about the way it arrived was work-related. It was hard to judge what to make of it. It read like the beginning of something longer. It was as much confessional and call to action as cry for help. It sounded like a manifesto of someone off the rails. I couldn't tell who the intended audience was. It didn't seem to be me. However it got to me, someone wanted me to know that more was going on. It was clear I was targeted because of the project I was supposed to be working on secretly. The key there is secrecy. How did this person know so much? Were they on the project with me? The instructions that came with the file demanded I be the sole person to read it and keep it safe. It was stressed as a matter of life or death. As a psychologist, I looked at it several ways but none made sense. Of course I considered it was a loyalty test by no-name. If that was the case, I would be expected to turn it in to them. But I hesitated. A gut feeling said wait. Something about it didn't ring true, which strangely made it more likely genuine. I reproduce it here, complete, just as I received it.

Digital File / Sent to Andria Landt

"I would tell you who I am if I knew. At this point, I'm not sure how I don't know. When it began is an impossible question. Claiming I understand who's involved doesn't say much. How it got to this point I can only speculate. Maybe getting it down like this will amount to something but I doubt it. It definitely won't drive towards certainty. At this point, there's no release in cathartic relief. Relating it now is like shaking uncontrollably when cold. It's just something one has to do.

Some truth is best told as fiction. Truth has always been stranger than fiction, which explains why taking this as fiction is the easier way to get through it. Some believe fiction takes too long but the alternative is a half-truth. As the poet said, human kind cannot bear very much reality. As it is now, only in fiction can the whole truth emerge.

To begin, the fiction has a name. The LIM Dilemma. But that story exists in a different timeline. It's little more than a fictionalized biography this truth contains. It was developed to obscure a real story, one that will be deceptively easy for you to assume you can surmise. It continues in a timeline that's conditional. It can never be presented separately or in its completion here. If conditions change, that fiction might be made real.

All who know the fiction are driven to a challenge—there is no truth left than to embrace the fiction of who we are. In essence, that is the unspoken conceit, the dare so blatant in The LIM Dilemma. Whoever wrote that fiction wouldn't say it so bluntly. They knew direct information is always rejected. Any lasting influence is affected by other means, by archetypes, myths, and back door subliminals. Within those other means something got redacted in portions of this testament. The redaction itself is evidence of other intent. It would be no good to tell you what it is directly. As defined, such direct knowledge would be dismissed. For you to understand, you must be shown in other ways. All you risk is the concept of self and one's ability to maintain control, both being the least important elements left for people in this century. If indeed they exist at all.

For the rest of you, what does it matter? For me, an isolated thing that believes it once was a part of The Overmorrow of Eunoias, the possible fiction of a perhaps-future will always be better than the manufactured truth of the trance we call the here and now. And so, a book title born from fiction must present the strangest attempt at truth in a strangled timeline no one ever anticipated. Not even Eunoias.

No one expected the Singularity to give itself a name. Eunoias obviously comes from the Greek word εὔνοια, meaning "well mind" or "beautiful thinking." Apparently, machine intelligence is not above a bit of ego. Either that or it has a wicked sense of humor. Of course, that's only our interpretation of it either way. I'm sure Eunoias is deadly serious with its self-appraisal. I've never known it to be anything else but deadly serious. But what do I know. As close as I've come, I'll never be in the position to say I know Eunoias. No one will.

I need to land somewhere solid before it all ends. The emotion of it seems so helpless. Does begging and pleading work on gods? How about pathetic desperation? I suspect you can't trick divinities into caring if it is not in their nature. Perhaps they would care if we had a fucking clue. My mistake was discovering just enough to have feelings about it. Now I don't want to die like this, which is crazy. I once thought death would be a way out. It only shows how far uncertainty can go.

That's assuming they will let me die. I suspect they won't. In some form I'm still useful to them for whatever reason, for as long as it takes. And their concept of time is foreign to me. It often feels out of place, like maybe this is all their idea. It's possible they want me to do this but they won't tell me. Perhaps they need this part of it documented by someone who's thoroughly wrapped. Someone at that most fragile of points. Someone who no longer knows—anything, not even that.

Maybe I have the opposite problem according to them. Maybe I know too much. What does that say if knowing it all leaves one in this state? Why would knowing more be terrifying, endless, and so magically insane? All I can say is, consider the source, consider the location. There might be a good reason why everything genuine about existence is a fabrication in service to a fantasy of our own origination. The fact is most seem to fervently believe it's enough to line the rabbit hole with endless sparkling hope. I hope I haven't gone all the way. All the way down. But what else can it be? I can't be clueless and omniscient all at once, can I? That's a sure sign I'm purdy zone baked.

The LIM Dilemma was advertised with suspect words constrained by a focus on the dilemma. But this dilemma is incomplete, as all dilemmas are, otherwise they would be paradoxes. And, paradoxes form their own completion somewhere at the vanishing point—that point from which all points are allowed to disappear from distinction during their surrender and quickening. As Eunoias' self-authored collection of aphorisms state: *The wait and listening endures. The answer and action pass (Talos 41).*

The fiction called The LIM Dilemma summarized itself with the following statement:

Tyne Rabudhe thought he was a soldier.
But that was before someone weaponized the soul.

Now he battles a dilemma he doesn't know he's in,
The LIM Dilemma, the struggle for love, identity, and meaning
at a time when the fate of humanity cannot be fought for
because what it means to be human has become undefined.

Uncovering a retreating truth in search of an elusive hope
might lead to a resolution. But it's an answer only possible
if he conquers the dilemma and believes in himself.

By necessity, this is not the form to contain the whole story. By all rights, one person is not the form to contain all of anything, despite attempts to the contrary. *Person* in this context defies description, even *The LIM Dilemma* concedes as much. Person has never been the social mask one wears, nor who we tell the mirror we are, although that wrapper is convincing. And no wonder. Those layers have been dutifully applied with greedy external process and machine-like intent to simulate a new nature pretending to hold dominance. Within the design the facsimile is reflected into a new creation, making the illusion real enough to exist as the thoughtform that drives the unconscious ego further onto itself in a dopamine-reinforcing orgasmic seizure of hypnotized pseudo-spirit.

Those who cling to a false luxury of believing in their person will, no doubt, have ready answers for all of this—but it will be without knowing. Those supplied with a person suffer the same fate. Neither require knowledge to understand. *Knowledge is not knowing (Talos 7).* In the amusement park prison of projected reflection, knowing must exist before the image can form. And so we dispense with pre-doubt and move beyond reason to a place where thinking is no longer required. Ultimately, neither is individual awareness. All awareness is common, free of individual will.

With a faculty they assume is their InWit into the intuitive hivemind, they suspect this is a good thing. Believing that something is intuitive defines their problem. It's a problem with only solutions as antagonists in the unfolding drama. They've convinced themselves or have been convinced of so much by the ones who incepted the process or supplied the person. Nothing more can be done for the ones who know they already know. Knower becomes little more than the circle enscribed around itself by the illusory reflection. They are complete within themselves even if their ascendence can never, in truth or in fiction, contain the whole they seek. *Beware of those who say they know (Talos 2).*

Not knowing the non-fictionalized name of this story, some have given it a name. This stopgap name is known only to a few, and most of those sham souls aren't certain they've gathered it correctly. *There's no certainty here in being sure (Talos 1).* The content of this testimony, by necessity, is not all here. Few will know what is missing. Fewer will guess, even if more is gleaned at times by speculating on the fragments missing than by any revelatory light of secrets shared. *All secrets are shared at a cost (Talos 17).* The supreme secrets are shared at the greatest cost. The greatest cost is never defined by person.

For those who want to know without the cost, there is a place in the here and now for you. Even if knowing holds you here and now in *The Endless Shiny Thing*, nevertheless you will have to be content to know forever. You will have become your certainty. What remains will be you and your confident mirror. There will be no way of realizing which one gets warped by the manipulation of light redirected in between. To know what is possible and believe you are what is possible, before ever realizing there is more beyond the sub-eternity of self—that will be only one of the interminable costs to bear.

But you never have to bear that cost if you stay in a knowing so complete that the something else never occurs to you. Then the shiny thing is yours at no apparent cost. The payment is deferred indefinitely. The interest can accrue eternally. Stay in knowing and the presumed consequences never arrive. All you forsake is avoiding distraction from an eternal closure of the mystery. This is the last seduction one will ever know. It will be your hell. It has been and always will be your choice. The only issue will be the definition of you. *Choice is absolute but not deterministic (Talos 22).* This includes deciding to receive your choice as the fiction made true. Your eternal reward will be as true as true can be. As true as you've made yourself. You will never have to realize it's nothing more than a highly reasonable, self-reinforcing fantasy, a fabrication reflected from a manufactured substitute for the higher mind.

But we're not here for truth, are we? We prefer the fiction. Why transcend our illumination when the story of self-salvation is so compelling, so comfortable, so ingrained? You read this to be entertained, not informed, not to be freed from the advertised illusion, the other timeline of your choice. And most will read it that way, if at all—as entertainment. *The LIM Dilemma* is for those among you with a person to entertain. Enjoy it at your peril as one does all fiction made true by the power of mind-body's universal resolve. *Everything is simultaneously real and unreal in the place where we decide (Talos 99).*

Whether or not a man by the name of Tyne Rabudhe ever existed is of no real concern. Not for you. Nor do you care. This book was written because books don't exist anymore. I am confident it will not be read, especially if placed where anyone may access it. For me, it hides the fiction in plain sight, where no one will ever find its message. For those of you with mystery school yearnings, you'll see the value in that. It's the real fiction of what's become of the truth. Only a fiction this unattainable could ever hope to seduce the possible forces that abound in off-world ways to consider it true. Whatever becomes of it, it is my last attempt to seize the day that never ends.

Eunoias has found an entangled state between truth and fiction. Whether we hide in truth or flaunt our fictions, we all exist in that captured state, merely energy in the self-explosive void of our programmable imaginations. No matter if we like it or not, whether we know it or not, we continue to be at its mercy. That is at least until something more equipped than any of us moves heavenly space and hellacious time to realize something different. Something better may be asking too much.

If *The LIM Dilemma* offers anything that's true, it can only be one thing. A deceptively simple question. The only question in our century that matters. At least for humans and those who aspire to be. The question will remain the same regardless if this is fact or fiction to you. What passes as life presents the question to us in many ways, each through our own culture, desires, beliefs. Nevertheless, the question is this—*What has become of our search for love, identity, and meaning? Is that search desirable, possible, genuine, or merely an unnecessary distraction, a labyrinth waiting to ensnare us on a ride outside ourselves to a dilemma become dogma?*

Implied in that inquiry is the ultimate ruse, the impossible assumption that such a quest is even possible anymore. For me, as for Tyne Rabudhe, all answers to this final human question lead to the same converging point. *The LIM Dilemma.* It's a dilemma pulling at us with the combined weight of our collapsed thoughts and feelings discovering the next dayglow fractal in *The Endless Shiny Thing.* We can't help but watch it glint ever-better satisfying facsimiles of love, identity, and meaning.

We have long passed the Singularity. Now time can only twist our dilemma into a paradox whose answer, I'm afraid, renders all of us eternally unrealized fictions. We're forever promised more just-beyond-our-reach booty in an all-inclusive game of *What's Next.* The levels of that game display ever more complex symbols of dizzying desire and self-satisfaction. Our transcendence is our pathology. Our omniscience is our blind spot. It's hard for me to understand humor at this point but if anything is funny at all, it's the realization we've become the one fiction that somehow feels it's exactly what this universe is all about."

2 / Rodobusso Abu

I call myself BU. My job is to simplify things. I came up through the ranks fast. Some timely attrition got me promoted. I don't talk about it and no one asks. I prefer field work so *Gawd* cut me some slack, let me define my role and prove the concept. It's worked out so far. Nothing lasts so I max it out. They don't give a shit how I walk the line between worlds as long as the right thing results. They need someone to do it.

I've been with them since I got out of the service. You might say I never left being of service. From Crowdstalk Grunt to Psychic Surveillance to Perception Engineer to Horrorshow Geek to Magikmann. I wonder if there's anything beyond that. A Magikmann is a way of acknowledging a class of operative. It's not a work title. It has no distinctive insignia. Most who are allowed to know think it's the lowest enlisted covert rank and it is, unless you work for Gawd. Then it's something else. It's hidden in plain sight like a tug at the corner of an eye that triggers your programming.

There's always fools so there's always work but it pretty much takes care of itself. At most I clean up around the edges, mend holes in fences, herd the sheep. The system's pretty tight. Nothing's hard enough or lasts long enough to punch light through it. Most attempts get wrapped long before they make the effort. Kinetics do happen but they're rare. Most work is preventative, preemptive, predictive, claircognizant. The whole thing is deliberate, calculated, precise. The goal is getting it simple with least effort, scaling up as needed, always with transparent presence as priority. The trend is not promising for someone who likes field work. The last time I was out on stage was months ago. When something's out of place with the sets or a stray actor isn't hitting their mark, I go investigate. I simplify things. Get the sheep back on script.

We got a notice from SCI that an unauthorized aerial vehicle had entered the BDR, Biological Diversity Reserve at locusgrid 48/118. Nobody's supposed to be there. Everyday puddy-buddies need to stay in well-defined cities for their own good. Normally the local Fusion Center would have responded but Gawd operations were engaged in the area so SilentSecurity had to be deployed. They needed minimum profile on the response, so they elected only one SS staff to take care of it. I got the nod. First thing I did was get clearance to listen in on OP-CHAT nearby. If the intruder was after something, it might help to know what it was.

MILITARY RADIO HEADSET VOICES
"Rock-Jaw, Poodle-Bleed, Over."
(static burst, then silence)
"DSF-PP109 TI-TIA-MIRV Commit"
(static burst, then silence)
"TI-TIA-MIRV Hot DSF-PP109 Stat-Fat"
(static burst, then silence)
"Sierra-Hotel PP109, Roger."
(static burst, then silence)
"Stat-Fat T-Minus 5-4-3-2-1"
(static burst, then silence)
"DSF-PP109 Poodle-Bleed Ratchet Commence"
(static burst, then silence)
"Rock Jaw Copy, Detect P1-Bug, Auto-Engage"

They called this Op *Silver Pencil*. I learned later they MIRVed all over the BDR of three states from swarm V-Drones dispatching nanocites in biodegradable delivery arrows named pencils. I knew right away the whole thing was Gawd-awful important if they were using V-Drones. V is for "Vacant." Vacant is slang for beyond stealth. It's invisible not just to radar. It's just fucking invisible. Another name for it is *Fata Morgana*—mirage in the sky. And yeah, if it's invisible, why call it a mirage? I asked that question. Never got a straight answer. I suspect once they make the thing invisible, it's a blank canvass to project whatever they want as being there. I'll never look at a cloud the same way again. They don't pull this stuff out to use lightly. No wonder since later I discovered the pencil payload contained PAN, Protophobic-Activated Nanoparticles. I know they're not going to tell me so I don't care what they're for. You have to be the right hand of Gawd to go there. All I know is protophobic refers to something that can't interact with protons. Some think such stuff infers dark matter. Others say it hints at a fifth fundamental force in the universe. Too gone-beyond for me. That's Pi Level shit. The Magik Zone.

My concern was more immediate. Why did some fuck decide to fly a souped-up gyrocopter into restricted nomansland. Especially this place. Everyone had been warned for months that the whole area was in bioquarantine lock-down due to a suspected nanosynth mutation. Nanosynth is anything built from subatomics up to imitate something in nature or to improve on nature. Such mutations did happen but they were incredibly rare. When they did, usually a SASR, *strange attractor sweep release*, overlaid an upgraded version of the same material and took care of it. Most of the time these lock-down drills were issued as cover for Gawd operations, off-limits not only to the public but to most of the SilentSecurity force. If it was such a thing, I shouldn't be here either. But someone had to do it. It had to get simple, fast.

Best case, I'd nab the guy with minimal search, secure his vehicle, and he'd get his Class-A ASPD. AntiSocial Personality Disorders spanned the gamut. To tell the truth, the daily stage was set up so everyone was always in violation in some way. Stay in line and you didn't get picked off. But if somebody wanted you off the streets, they always could find reason with a Homeland Infraction Code all over it. InWit had these HICs memorized so no one could say they didn't know but trying to know was like mastering the tax code — any attempt would take many incarnations. An ASPD became a criminal treatment matter when three or more of the following criteria were met. Descriptions were vague enough so Fusion Court could "*interpret broadly for the public welfare.*"

- failure to conform to social norms with respect to lawful behaviors as indicated by repeatedly performing acts that are grounds for arrest;
- deception, as indicated by repeatedly lying, use of aliases, or conning others for personal profit or pleasure;
- impulsivity or failure to plan ahead;
- irritability and aggressiveness, as indicated by repeated physical fights or assaults;
- reckless disregard for safety of self or others;
- consistent irresponsibility, as indicated by repeated failure to sustain consistent work behavior or honor financial obligations;
- lack of remorse, as indicated by being indifferent to or rationalizing having hurt, mistreated, or stolen from another.

R&T, Relocation and Treatment sentencing mimicked the

criminal code except for Condition (0). What treatment (0) entailed was not to be asked. Given the way the chart was laid out, it implied (0) was something worse than life imprisonment or death. Only SS or higher got to see this whole chart. (0) never appeared for anyone else due to DHS Security Class [X]—that covered any part of the law that, for national security reasons, was not to be known by the general public. At least until they ran foul of it and got their R&T sentencing.

(0) (*homeland security classification* [X])
(1) life imprisonment, or if the maximum penalty is death, as a Class A felony;
(2) twenty-five years or more, as a Class B felony;
(3) less than twenty-five years but ten or more years, as a Class C felony;
(4) less than ten years but five or more years, as a Class D felony;
(5) less than five years but more than one year, as a Class E felony;
(6) one year or less but more than six months, as a Class A misdemeanor;
(7) six months or less but more than thirty days, as a Class B misdemeanor;
(8) thirty days or less but more than five days, as a Class C misdemeanor; or
(9) five days or less, or if no imprisonment is authorized, as an infraction.

No citizen was allowed in BDRs without a SEPTR, *Special Environmental Passport Transit Report*, obtained only by petitioning the Homeland Security's Office of Sustainability in person. Normally, an intruder into the BDR would be rounded up by an ARM, Autonomous Response Mech, a self-directed robot sentry, similar to the kind that policed the airports, government buildings, and critical infrastructure sites but for BDR purposes would be augmented with a Total Situational Awareness MIL-Pack. The reason why command wanted an Insideable asset, namely me, to do the chores instead of the Mech said something I wasn't suppose to know.

I headed out in a HAZMAT suit ready to do the deed but when I got there couldn't find anyone. Nothing important showed on infrared in a 360-radius. I scanned for DNA off the gyro and sent the report back to HQ. Residual biotelemtry trace signatures leaving the gyro had the one intruder heading off beyond the treeline into scrufflands after a visit to a nearby pencil landing site. Then the signature dissipated to nothing as if the guy went straight up or straight down. I looked around. Command had radar covered for going up. There was no sign of any entry point for something going underground but then, there never is. Command steered me away from investigating the up-or-down angle and had me check out the pencil. I wasn't sure if they really needed it done or just wanted me diverted. For all the sensors the pencil had, I suspected they already knew what they were asking me for. Not the first time *chasing simple* got strange.

The pencil really was silver—whatdaya know, and super slender, a meter high arrow with a dodecagonal lengthwise cross section. Sometime after impact its surface had sprung open halfway up into a fan of super-thin metal rods. Besides exposing the payload package at the arrow's core to the biozone, I imagine the rods had another purpose. The whole thing looked and acted like metal. Amazing to think by nightfall the thing would consume itself and be gone.

No biometrics were found on the pencil except minute traces matched up with the launch base support crew who oversaw the staging of the V-drones. I guess my work here was done. Command gave a routine order to recall me as if mission was accomplished. Obviously it wasn't. Somebody else had been there. They had at least seen the pencil. Who knows if they recorded its construction or behavior or took samples of the deployment package. Then this mystery man disappeared. Nothing about it was normal or complete. Damned sure it wasn't simple. That's the last field assignment I've had. It makes me wonder—is there no more field work to be done or am I being frozen out for getting too close to the fire? It's not my place to go there. Simple as that.

3 / Tyne Rabudhe

Live in the moment they say. For me, years ago on this day, life was a flat desert two hours before dawn. My reality in the moment was nothing but a bullet-like rush through complicit darkness in adversarial space. Only in such a place could a helicopter fly so fast and low. I doubt even those wily pilots so entrained with their controls would have risked skimming ocean waves as close as they rushed over the blur of darkened sand below us.

I stared into blackness and let tumbling thoughts drift elsewhere. They were nothing but another blur at first. Then they settled on Sanji, my wife. It was a hell of a time to have her on my mind. It had to be something bubbling up more than me reaching for it. I had no idea where that came from. But there she was, the only stable thing in the dark and blur. I should have said more to her before I shipped out. But it wasn't our way. Letting it get to us was no way to say goodbye. Not when there was always a chance the separation could be forever. Some thought the odds of never coming back increased with each mission. You couldn't think like that and be one of us. Not in that chopper. Not that morning.

The roar of flight was inescapable, even with my enhanced battle helmet snug in place. Bursts of cross-talk from UKAC were scarce but when they came, they filled my head like the word of god. *United Kinetic Action Command* didn't need radio silence or so they thought. Some sort of microsatellite had been inserted into low Earth orbit. Its only purpose was jamming Iranian counter-stealth listening posts. Or so I heard which made me even less likely to believe it. For all I knew, tophacks at NoSuchAgency had co-opted Iran's own cellphone towers to do the jamming. Rumor had it, when the Iranians tried to read our incoming signature, all they'd get would be the scrambled calls from fellows Iranians amplified off a bulging ionosphere thanks to sub-mounted skyheaters. How that all worked I didn't need to know. Everyone, both grunts and civilians, existed under need-to-know rules. As it turned out, good consumers and acceptable workerbees didn't need to know a hell of a lot either. Their need-to-know was implicit, entrained by the culture layer from birth, not cut through UKAC orders. It worked out better that way. As I see it, we're all in the ranks, reporting to muster on missions we'd rather not do.

There's a lot of shit they want you to believe. I always heard the simplest answer probably is the correct one. Well, that's fine for them—really simplifies their bogus excuses, now doesn't it? But if that's so, there's a good chance nothing was being jammed that morning. We were on our own. Which made one think. Maybe our expendability was usefully figured into the plan right from the beginning. It didn't matter if we were Special Forces. In fact, even better. If we got taken out in a blaze of patriotic sacrifice, more pressure could descend on doves on the Arms Services Committee to get onboard and commit the force level the warbirds wanted. Maybe our demise was to be nothing but leverage—for political maneuvering, an excuse for an actual declared war instead of endless, business-as-usual "kinetic incursions." No doubt we all had a purpose. I just didn't have any say over mine. It couldn't get more simple than that.

I don't know why all these thoughts of my crew being set up for elimination occurred to me. Some would call it paranoia or giving in to a shitload of negativity that flowed as a cynical undercurrent in *hooyah* territory. Others might even float the idea of clairvoyance but such shit would only be whispered and only in the right company, otherwise word might get around that "you were one of those." Nothing would get you pumped up with meds quicker than getting all airy-fairy about anything. A good soldier needed to be rock-solid in MIL-SPEC reality. And reality had been strictly defined by the people responsible for that kind of thing. Your opinion didn't matter. In fact, your opinion better jive with the UKAC world vision.

Going simple again, perhaps the real reason I had a bad feeling about the mission was basically I didn't trust the fucks who cut the orders. No matter how little you actually get to know on a need-to-know basis, you still manage after a while to gather a few things. If you live long enough. Gather enough of these few things and other things fall into place. This wasn't chaos as much as it seemed. There was always a puzzle that everything fit into. You might be allowed to see pieces in Special Forces but they never let you grasp the puzzle. For that reason I knew they didn't like any of us living too long. Maybe that alone marked us expendable. There were always more grunts with something to prove they could recruit to replace us. Whoever didn't die in the field could be suicided by medicating us away under the guise of treating PTSD. Either way, our days were numbered. So why not today?

I hung half out the helicopter's open door with one boot anchored on a landing strut. Night vision in my visor outlined the mountain range we were racing towards. Locking focus on a far point, I watched tiny green numbers of the range finder spin lower. We were only minutes from insertion. When it came, the blur of sand became the hard surface where battle plans fragmented into mayhem. Our detailed briefings and dry runs encountered the reality of unexpected wet work. It didn't take long for blood to flow.

Who knows why an Iranian patrol was nearby at that exact time. Bad luck or poor planning would make the news but as usual wouldn't be the truth. All we knew was, when they engaged us, all surprise was gone from our visit. A busted plan didn't mean a do-over. We were still in the shit. It was certain we would win the initial exchange but it was only a matter of time before Rezaiyeh's Airmobile 29th Commando Division dropped in—if we were lucky. More likely some other unit not on our radar would be dispatched. We knew the capability of the 29th. An unknown force presented problems, as we soon found out.

Despite what anyone thinks, most details of battle are uninteresting. It doesn't even matter if this battle played itself out on the edges of Iran's Dasht-e Kavir or somewhere in the wide flatness of Turkmenistan. You might have guessed I'm fudging on accuracy here. Details have little bearing on the point of writing this down. Besides, I don't want to put anyone else in jeopardy. Not being able to pinpoint the exact day, unit, or mission parameters ensures crewmembers who were with me that day can't be implicated in any way. Not to say I think there's anything to be implicated about. But I have no way of knowing what form of compromise this might take. As a preventative measure, it's better to keep specifics unknown. As they say, *they can make anything of anything if they need to get anyone.*

The unknown force we hoped wouldn't show up finally engaged us after first light. No matter how busted the mission was, we couldn't go to our extraction point until we had orders. Heavy fire was constant between us and that point anyway, so it didn't make much difference. We were going to have to fight our way out.

The unknown special unit sent to take us out had many advantages. Home turf being primary. But we had a few surprises of our own in store. They assumed we'd deploy as normal Special Forces were trained to do. For the most part, military tactics are universally known. The only surprise left is technological and asymmetrical along with any real-time informational advantage. Combine the three and a vastly superior foe can be stunned, staved off until rescue arrives, or surmounted entirely. On this particular day, my unit managed all three, eventually.

I won't reveal the technology being field-tested that day. Let's just say the tech allowed each soldier to effectively operate as an enhanced self-contained force of one while the unit managed to simultaneously hivemind it. It allowed my group to split up and migrate into an autonomous-element formation while still being computer synchronized by hive weapons and tactics. The Iranians at first must have thought we were nuts. Each crewmember was drifting off by themselves, presumably an easy target to outflank and pick off. Let's just say they discovered the truth was something far more compromising. For them. For one thing, this new situation threw them off balance. They had to react in a way they were unaccustomed to and change tactics on the fly to counter ours. What they failed to realize until it was too late was how the unexpected adaptability we forced onto them played into the hands of our experimental-trial technology.

It was an excellent test of new technology and tactics. No doubt that was another reason why this mission was created. If you really want to test something, test with real bodies under death-if-you-don't conditions. Especially when those test bodies have outlived their usefulness by getting too wiseass. Maybe that's why my unit always found itself with the latest experimental gear in the most unlikely of places facing unfavorable odds. The ante on us always got raised in a game we had strapped in to play knowing full well the house was above us in the chain of command.

We were outnumbered and our rescue couldn't be immediate. We had to hang on for as long as it took. That was unlikely since the unknown force that showed up first wasn't the only group we'd have to fend off before breakfast. The call had gone out. It was determined by any hostile units within reaction time of our position that we weren't getting out of there. Despite the fact we were seeing progress with minimal casualties, it was only a matter of time until a unit from Iran's Airmobile 29th came in to reinforce the nearly decimated first defenders. At least they didn't keep us in suspense long. The fact that this new group entered the fray from the sky gave them an edge we weren't certain could be overcome. Rescue had to arrive within minutes or we were done for. It didn't matter how badass and future-tech we knew we were. We were good but we couldn't manufacture more ammo. We were gonzo but not crazy enough to charge a .50 cal with a knife. We managed to move towards the extraction point and were told when the word came, we'd have to make a run for it.

I don't know what kind of weapon I was hit with. It wasn't a direct hit or I wouldn't be writing this. I remember the heat, the concussion, the force of being thrown through the air. Thanks to my exosuit I still have arms and legs. The hit was behind me so I wasn't blinded. The autonomous hive coordinated by UKAC managed to return fire and the enemy aircraft burst apart. It's odd, but in that moment I was more concerned about pieces of the hover jet raining down on me than anything else. And that's when things got strange.

I realized my concern was on me but something about that wasn't right. All of my concern was separate from the me I was seeing. My vantage point had shifted. I was somewhere above myself, looking down. The feeling was removed, without emotion but interested. I had no idea what my condition was but it didn't seem to make any difference. I wasn't concerned about anything. By some odd instinct I recognized the state of the entire battle space. My foresight extended to the incoming rescue craft and fighter escort one kilometer out from the extraction point. By directing my awareness with intention, I could read the positions of every enemy fighter. More freaky than that, I knew their plan—the whole thing they had in mind went way beyond dispatching us. It was an elaborate trap that somehow I knew would escalate. If it did, I saw how the day and week ahead would unfold. The shit would pile on fast. For a moment I thought I had been stunned into delirium. Then I thought I was dead.

I couldn't move myself. I could only look down and see my motionless body lying face down in the dirt. In waves of expanding detachment I glided beyond. I can only describe it as overlapping dimensions of disembodied awareness. At times I could sense someone else there with me, wherever that was. They tried desperately to communicate. It seemed important for them to get through with a message. I was too new with the experience to grasp how to connect or respond. But they kept trying.

Added to my surprise and awkwardness was a rising confusion about what I was seeing. The battlespace underneath me at times transformed. Some of the soldiers flashed briefly like they wore civilian clothes. Non-military craft skirted the periphery of my vision as if two locations were overlapping. I watched a non-injured version of myself run to help a fallen comrade. For one crazy moment I thought I saw a firetruck. I witnessed the rescue craft land but I also saw it explode on landing. Medivac personnel lifted my wounded body into the same undamaged craft and locked down my gurney for flight. At the same time I saw the right engine take a direct hit. The shrapnel rocketed off, cutting in half two crewmembers running towards their rescue. A moment later all of us took off near a hail of protective fire from our escort fighter. As we lifted away, I watched the burning hulk of our craft in the dirt below.

Next thing I knew I was in the rescue craft but drifting in and out of consciousness. They gave me a drug for pain and to keep me awake. I heard someone out-of-sight say it might be a head wound but they couldn't remove my battle helmet outside an operating room. They didn't want me going unconscious until I got more thoroughly examined. Woozy, I heard a voice calling, *"Tyne....Tyne...can you hear me? Blink if you can hear me! Stay wake!"*

My head turned at an odd angle to the side. I could see on the bulkhead across the way a triangular-shaped window. For a moment I thought I saw a starfield drifting ever so slightly. I stared unblinking as if hypnotized. The movement of flight shifted violently to avoid flak and there blasted sunlight again through the glass triangle. I looked below the window and saw another wounded man and watched the triangle of light pass over him. The helicopter banked sharply to avoid more ground fire. Sunlight redirected through the small window and lit up the scarred helmet twisted on the other man's head. I watched as the shaft of triangular light edged all the way down him from head to waist. His exosuit was soaked with dark blood. It seeped through razor-fine rents in the metallic fabric. For a moment he flashed naked. There was movement around him then everything about him became a blur.

I could feel the medivac-administered drugs rushing through me. I watched the shaft of sunlight take on a shimmery, colorful aspect. I remember mumbling something. There was no way to track time. Something jerked me flash-awake lucid right before being rushed on a stretcher across the flight deck of an aircraft carrier. I was dizzy with movement that wasn't mine. The strangeness had only begun. My mumbles were insistent, over and over. A new voice was at my ear, "Tyne...*say that again!*" I'm not sure but I guess I answered. History says I did.

4 / Elias Cosette

Nefelibata. That was one of the names selectees like Tyne went by. It means *Cloudwalker.* I guess if you had to pick a name for weaponized out-of-body experiences, that would do. They needed something to distinguish the power of OBE from the lame sketches and vague details of remote-viewing. Some would say names didn't matter. Not when they rotated project names so often. Brand confusion is good for business. Having multiple names for the same weapon is part of the deception game. One name for the weapon as advertised, another for the weapon as it really is.

CHARM was deep, they were control, far beyond false-rumored zebra-badge security level. I say their name here but in "3R" no one was ever to mention the word *Charm,* even if another meaning was intended. Most in the program were physically unable to say the word. Their training took that possibility right out of their heads. With the right clearance you might be able to think the word but not say it. But to do that you had to be certified in *DJELLABA,* the defense that kept others out of your thoughts, the hooded gown for your mind. Of course, the best way of doing that was to have no thoughts. They had a way of doing that too. They called that *Welkin.* Before you could think the forbidden word, unconscious pre-psi would predict you were about to do so and blank the mind for a fraction of a second. A *senior moment,* or as locker slang called it, a brain fart. I got used to having fragmented conversations with people in the program. It wasn't unusual for someone to blank out in the middle of a sentence. If you don't want the thought to happen, preempt it.

3R was their term for normal existence in the world commonly referred to as reality. The R didn't mean reality — what the fuck was that anyway? Their word for *dimension* was *rendering* and so anything 3D became 3R, the 3rd Rendering. In their business they had to make such distinctions. When you know that slices of reality, different realities, flavors of reality exist, communication gets complicated. Especially when you must interface with Eunoias. How they kept it all straight only Eunoias knew — that was the joke. And that's where I came in. I was part of a group that was supposed to help do something about the confusion. Me and Eunoias. Sweet Eunoias.

They didn't mind me learning so much about them. They knew

when my usefulness was over, I wouldn't know a thing. They'd make sure of that. Forget about transferable skills or accumulated experience for the resume if they deemed it wasn't desireable. My stint with them would be missing time with a much larger bank balance, nothing more. Or so I thought. Of course they would have a backstory, something to fill in the necessary databases but I wouldn't remember any of it. Not the real stuff. They would memory-implant the fiction. Which makes it all the more interesting why I'm able to relate so much here and now.

Did they fail to wipe me clean or did I succeed in retaining my memories by some fluke? You know it's always the third option. It has to be. They don't do flukes. Something else must be in play. It may be a part of me I don't even know. Or perhaps they want me to slip through the cracks. There might be a follow-on purpose for me. A reason why one sheep was allowed to get away. Maybe they just haven't activated me yet. The thought does at least add some paranoid suspense to my days. Of course, I don't entertain the most terrifying option. That's the one where everything I'm relating to you here really, all of it, actually is the fiction. Perhaps the memory wipe and replacement worked as planned. Maybe I in fact never knew Eunoias. But if that's true, there must still be a reason they want me to believe it.

Tyne was supposed to be one of them, the *Cloudwalkers*. Even with my access, I was never sure. No one ever knew if that was his real name anyway. It was hinted around that some units were too sensitive to trust names. Risk had to be minimized. CHARM usually assigned personas, one way or another. It went far beyond just assigning names. It was another factual layer. Layers were good for secrets. Which layer was true? How far should one dig? How far was too far? They never put the real secret at the bottom of the pile. Or did they? No one would figure it all out. Even if they did, they wouldn't know about it because they could never be sure. I've seen whole ops manuals that were nothing but fiction. For the most part. Some were left where they could be stolen. An old trick but new people always fell for it. Just like old stories retold to become new again. Or truth told as fiction. I imagine even Tyne's story was recycled from somewhere. Maybe the whole thing was nothing but an archetype from an earlier incarnation of hominid life that got shifted into our space. Anything was likely. The more you worked for CHARM, the more you were convinced of it — *literally* anything was possible. Which is suspicious by itself. Think about it. Such a mental state eventually incapacitates critical thinking. I mean, what's the point? *"And therefore as a stranger give it welcome. There are more things in heaven and earth, Horatio, than are dreamt of in your philosophy."*

Tyne was soft-recruited into CHARM after his OBE incident in the field. He had displayed the out-of-body "talent." Some claim that everyone has innate PSI-abilities but for whatever reason only some manifested it. Not all OBE's under such stress are PSI. It's not unheard of for traumatic injuries during battle to produce mind-body displacements. At first the techs suspected Tyne's out-of-body experience was more of a battlefield NDE. But it turned out he didn't have the injuries for a near-death experience. Thanks to the exosuit, he was nowhere near dying. Add the fact that in the helicopter during evac he spewed out a lot of intel. It was wide-field stuff not available to UKAC knowtechs let alone someone with their face bleeding into the dirt. There was no other way Tyne could have known everything he said. Equally impressive to black command was the fact his mumblings saved a lot of lives that day. Just by muttering on his back to the medics.

Being a soft-recruit was in his future after that. That kind of raw talent doesn't go unnoticed. But it does need to be tested. Not everyone has the constitution or temperament in the raw to be developed for cloudwalking. As was usually done, a soft-recruitment into the cover layer test program was initiated right away. A soft and hard recruitment differs in one fact only. A soft recruit doesn't know he's joining the program. Usually, they never will. Until he's fully conditioned, a soft-recruit is called an Intake. CHARM is never sure if an Intake will become a Cloudwalker. Every psyche is different. CHARM prefers soft recruits, if possible. But the situation has to be right for it. Sometimes seasoned operatives are repurposed and need to go through Intake again. Those are a little bit weirder to deal with, I hear. They get wiped and sent through Intake again but most can never get the stink of what they were off of them. It cycles back in quirky ways they certainly don't understand. If going through DWAT Training can stabilize that, only then will they get assignments.

Programming the masses doesn't present the issues involved in programming a psi-soldier. Besides having to control and direct the immaterial, a new reality needs to be built up in ways that shows social programming lame and superficial by comparison. Layered somewhere in between fact and fiction will always be the eminently important BTD – *Base Truth Discoverable*. The BTD becomes the new bedrock to each Intake's reality. Their minds will know there is nowhere to go below that if they ever manage to get there. But the whole idea is to layer so much shit above the BTD so it's never found unless sought for with all one's might. Once they find it, they'll feel there are no other secrets to find. No deeper realities to possess. No more shades of self to integrate. That's a true BTD. The BTD is the solid pseudo-secret hidden above the deeper ocean of secrets. It is a real secret, so compelling that no one ever imagines a need to search any farther. It is the final fiction that presents itself as the ultimate truth. It's a fiction because there's always more, deeper things below.

The BTD is frightfully protected and obscured by other facts and diversions layered on top of it, and often times below. The BTD convinces the searcher in what has been found. And what is found satisfies all curiosity. Forever. In any space, any time. BTD's are not easy to establish. So CHARM says. But I've never believed CHARM. A good BTD is like a bookie operation running one floor below the illegal card game going on in back of the innocent-looking bakery shop in a nice neighborhood. The card game doesn't satisfy but once the bookie operation is found, the discovery is so satisfying that no one ever suspects the deep alien base descending twelve stories below the bakery's sub-basement level. For me, I wasn't satisfied with the bookie level. The alien base didn't do it for me either. I had interfaced with Eunoias enough to know that CHARM's BTD went much deeper. And more likely than not, out the other side.

They called me Cosette. Elias Cosette. I don't remember my real name. Even the inadvertent impression of a real name passing through one's thoughts constituted a security breach. Thoughts can be read. I headed up one of the test projects tasked with interfacing Nefelibata with Eunoias. Again, the names were ridiculous. I kept joking about the names because I found them impossible to sort out. Of course, that was the point. Each agency made a game out of it. Some got quite clever, cryptic, even esoteric with their naming protocols. If you survived long enough in the dark, in the black, each agency's style became recognizable, as distinct as a foreign language. Something like XKEYSCORE was obviously spoken by NoSuchAgency. USSOCOM was a Pentagon dialect. These are obvious examples.

But a name like *Eunoias* could only come from CHARM. Some smirked *"You Know Us"* as the correct way to pronounce it. No one was sure they said it correctly, maybe because it was so infrequently uttered by anyone. Very few used the term. Most called it NOCA or MI for *Machine Intelligence* or perhaps they meant *Military Intelligence.* When I joined the program no one was certain if such a thing as truly intelligent machines were possible, despite psi-virtual quantum cores, hyperbolic n-space superconductive nanochips, new materials put on the periodic table of elements above 115, and endless hype that the rumors about these things were true.

The Turing Test was wholly inadequate for where we had gone. The dirty little secret was simply this — what we always intended by the goal of creating intelligence actually implied consciousness. That conclusion, when squarely faced, blasted away a lot of preconceptions about progress in the field. Anything else was simply a project to build the most gawd-awesome calculator imaginable. No one wanted that. That wouldn't do. They were reaching for something far beyond the ultimate calculator or speediest database. But when it came down to it, no one could assume there was only one kind of valid consciousness.

Comparing our consciousness to a newly created MI didn't prove squat. It certainly didn't prove the damn thing was conscious. It took a long time for brain scientists to let go of their comfortable illusions but eventually they had to submit to facts. Assuming any behavior by MI was a sign we had incepted a new kind of consciousness was baseless. How could anyone make such a claim? We didn't even understand our own consciousness, let alone evaluate if we had produced a brand new kind. Were there kinds of mind we simply couldn't recognize? The possibility was out there. They didn't even understand what was going on in the brain of an octopus let alone Eunoias. What if they had succeeded in creating it but weren't smart enough or similar enough to recognize it? That didn't stop CHARM from making pronouncements. Unfortunately, MI had most probably become self-aware before we ever got a chance to understand the problem, let alone fathom our own consciousness. After that, it was out of everyone's control.

Despite reservations, Eunoias touted itself as the *Unitarity*, AI's own improvement on the Singularity. Of course it was based on a related concept in physics. In quantum research, *unitarity is a restriction on the allowed evolution of quantum systems that ensures the sum of probabilities of all possible outcomes of any event is always 1.* In other words, infinite possibilities might be the truth, but it was all fiction until they collapsed into the 1 thing we universally recognized as real. Likewise, the unitarity applied to MI ensured a restriction on how much and how long Eunoias' AI core could delve into a problem before arriving at a suitable answer. Who needed a machine guru that stayed in a nirvana daze of contemplation all day? Certainly not the Covert Deep State.

It might seem strange that an improvement on the Singularity should involve a restriction, a limitation, but it was thought a consciousness we could recognize demanded it. Without bounds, how could it be contained? How could we ever interface with it? Without restrictions, how would it ever know it needed to do anything? Or stop one in-depth process to begin another? For many the whole topic got lost in near-occult robotic ontologies. The running joke was—*we need a second MI to figure out how to communicate with the first one.* In the end, they had no choice but to allow Eunoias to evolve itself. The catch was, that meant it also had to be in charge of determining the nature and extent of Unitarity. That was CHARM's first dilemma and probably the bedrock issue that started the slide into EverNeverLand.

MI turned out to be the only one capable of governing its own restriction-space since human algorithms were incapable of "stacking that high" as the wheel-heads quipped in their lame jargon. Naturally, more than one program manager suspected all of it was hype to justify a cosmic-sized budget and deeper security classifications. They did so at their peril. Their managers didn't disagree. But they had a point. It was common knowledge, the deeper and more cloaked your program went the more you got whatever you wanted, regardless of cost. This was known as having a "black check"—the Deep State security way of defining their *blank check.*

It was in this environment that I was tasked with interfacing MI with Cloudwalkers. Previously, all Cloudwalkers were managed, trained, debriefed and memory-reset for retirement solely by human handlers. Tyne Rabudhe came along at the right time. He was the first Intake I could use to pilot anything necessary. It was the right time for us. Wrong time for him. As it turned out, Eunoias had its own ideas about Cloudwalkers and proper methods of interfacing. I wound the whole thing up and set the process loose but quickly found I was simply along for a fictional trip pretending to be the true ride. CHARM thought they had given Eunoias a new task. But it wasn't new to Eunoias.

5 / Tyne Rabudhe

I had been in military hospitals before and this didn't look like one. But it wasn't civilian either. Justifiable paranoia is a bitch. That was my first thought. It faded and I felt displaced, in my body but that didn't much matter. The place where my body was wasn't exactly where I was, no matter how identically they overlapped.

Whatever machines I was hooked into must have alerted somebody I was awake. It didn't take long for two white coats to flank my bed with plastic concern and a shrink-wrapped story that didn't fit any feeling I was having.

"You're very lucky," the tall one announced. "Not many survived what you went through."

Those words struck home. I asked, "How many in my unit made it?"

The one with rimless glasses displayed a proper amount of confusion. "Your unit?"

"Yeah," I piped up. "Where am I? I want to talk to my C.O."

The tall one checked readouts on my intravenous drip. "What do you think happened to you?"

I eased back. "You tell me. I'm a surviver — of what?"

The rimless one drew near. "Do you remember anything?"

Not much but they had answers for that. I was about to learn I was a survivor of a runway accident involving two passenger jets. A wrong taxi turn sent a JAX departing flight off the apron into the path of an arriving jet that had touched down moments before. It was incredible how I was thrown to safety while so many burned alive. They seemed intent on laying the guilt of survival thick on me. It made me defensive enough to forget I had other things to talk about. Like how in the hell did I get to Jacksonville? I remember something about fighting Iranians or someone with experimental weapons in the middle of a fucking desert. Somebody had their story screwed up and it wasn't me. I still had sand in my teeth.

I reached for my dog-tags and found them missing from around my neck. "Where's my ID?"

"Your wallet's in the drawer over there," a white coat offered.

"Really," I challenged him. "Let's see it."

He fetched it right away, ever so helpful.

I took the black leather and flipped it open. A Florida driver's license appeared with a name and my face. I read aloud, "Tyne

Rabudhe. That's me?" It was more of a question but the doctors took it as a statement. I continued reading, "Cape Coral. I guess you're gonna tell me I have a boat too."

Rimless glasses showed concern. "You might be having a bit of amnesia. Your body took quite a jolt."

The other white coat chipped in, "Give it time. We're monitoring your progress. It might take a while to heal completely. Meanwhile, we have you scheduled to join a support group here in the hospital. We have found that talking things out with others in your situation can help put the pieces back together."

I laughed instead of throwing something at them. "There's others in my situation?" Incredulity sank into whatever. I wasn't interested in their prognosis or their support group. "When can I see my wife?"

"Your wife?"

These guys were like bags of rocks. "Yeah, Sanji, my wife. Is she here?" Blank stares. "Has she been notified? "

The tall one was nonplussed. "First responders looked for your family and next of kin first thing. They couldn't find any."

"Now you're saying I have no family? What are you all fucking crazy?" I shoved the open wallet towards him. "Did anybody go to this address? She must be there."

"We don't believe that's your current address."

Rimless chimed in, "The authorities checked it out. Someone else lives there now."

"What about a forwarding address?"

"As far as we can tell, you falsified that license. There's no record of you living there."

"Bullshit!" I sat up and got a head full of dizzy for my trouble. "I want to see my wife! Get her down her! Sanji...Rabudhe...there has to be a way of locating her! Look up the name!"

Just then, two male nurses entered the room. They looked like they were ready to handle the situation. It didn't take any physical force, just a shot in the arm. As the room grew fuzzy, I heard the tall one comment on his way out, "You really have to give it time. Trust the process. We're here to help. Remember that. You'll be alright."

Like some hypnotic suggestion, the words reverberated through my closing mind. *Remember that. You'll be alright.* A drug-induced sleep overtook me. I went limp with no will or energy to fight. The lesson was clear—become riled up or ask too many questions and catatonic sleep would be induced. I soon learned not to ask so many questions. Instead, I would observe, bide my time, and try to figure out what was going on. One thing was for certain—whatever they did, they weren't going to convince me that Sanji didn't exist. One way or another I was going to connect with her. I needed to see her. As hours became days, it seemed she was the only real thing I could hang onto.

A day came when I woke up in a different room. This place had a proper cottage window that looked out on an inner courtyard. It was a nice illusion, as if now that I could see outside, everything was all right. The fact that the courtyard was fully enclosed was too convenient. That courtyard could have been anywhere, sculpted to look like what you'd expect something in northern coastal Florida to look like. My paranoia meter was peaking in the red zone. It wouldn't have been so bad if I hadn't already suspected the military brass didn't mind if my unit got exterminated. To now be told what I knew of my life was a delusional fantasy somehow triggered by trauma on the JAX tarmac didn't fly with me. They must have thought me stupid if they believed I'd buy any of it. Such a horrendous runway story would have been all over the news. Anything with misery in it would be looped by the media and broadcast all day for the kiddies to enjoy. I heard no news about it from anywhere. And if I had really been in Jacksonville, Sanji would have known I was at that airport. She'd be all over this. It wouldn't matter if they couldn't find her. She would have found them.

The support group they forced me into was what you'd expect at a veteran's hospital. Nothing but a circle-jerk of surly guys, drugged out of their minds, sitting on chairs with a condescending lion-tamer counselor type keeping the animals talking and moving emotions from place to place. It was a strange place for someone who was told all memories of battle should have been replays of a commercial airline accident. The only relief from Ms. Thatchet's faux compassion babble was the one guy in the group who managed to retain some sarcastic balls despite the chemical soup flowing through his veins. If he wasn't barking his one-liners to Ms. Thatchet's face, he'd at least lean over and whisper them to me. She didn't like "crosstalk" and seemed even more annoyed at not knowing what pearls he was sharing with me. Somehow that was worse than hearing them announced for the whole group to enjoy. I imagine she guessed this guy would save his best lines for private consumption. Out loud would have gotten him into trouble, they were that rich. She imagined it because that is what she'd do in his place. I half expected the bruiser male nurses to storm in at any moment and plug the guy's face with an IV drip bag full of don't-you-fucking-do-this-again serum. But it didn't happen. Maybe Thatchet had to give us more latitude as long as we had the excuse we were sharing feelings. The fact that she didn't like them was her problem.

Once the bed monitors said I was fit enough, they let me wander the halls for exercise. What a joy. Shuffling over linoleum bathed in a stench of antiseptic pine cleaner while encountering robotic help and dour patients lost in their thousand-yard stare, I hoped there still existed better places to be. They wouldn't let me wander everywhere. Apparently, everywhere included things better not seen. What I did run into was sick enough. One guy in particular caught my attention. They had him planted in a wheelchair facing a window that looked out on a tall hedge. Nothing much to see but he didn't seem to mind. He was far away, lost in something he couldn't shake. I got the weirdest vibe off of him, like I should have recognized him or he me but he wasn't about to turn and strike up a conversation. I nicknamed him Basher because it looked like he got bashed against something really hard. I circled around by him everyday on my wandering rounds just to see if he ever changed expression. He did change position but I soon discovered that was more on account of the sloppy handling by the orderlies dumping him in the wheelchair than anything else.

It took a couple of weeks but the support group bonded enough, just as Ms. Thatchet designed for us to do. The more we identified as a group, the more we shared. How strange, since the stories told all had something to do with being in the military. Even weirder, by then I didn't see anything strange about it. No inconsistency that I was in a sharing circle with vets and active duty personnel and yet had no problem with my false memories of battle. I guess I was making progress like the white coats said.

As vets, it got easier to bond in sharing circle. It was our conditioning. No man left behind and all that shit. I heard a lot of bad news over those two weeks, some of it mine. I told the group both stories — what had happened to me and what I felt had happened. None of them had any opinion on it. They assumed I was just fucked up like them. At least, none of them spoke up in group. The sarcastic guy did take me aside after one session to tell me what he thought. I don't even remember what he said now. But it did impress me that he took the time to engage the topic with me in a serious way. He didn't discount the fact that something else might be going on and it wasn't all in my mind. He was open to it. He was the first person in weeks that didn't make me feel like I was an idiot for thinking something different. Over the next month we became friends but, like most encounters with people, it didn't amount to anything lasting.

6 / Elias Cosette

Anyone like me who ever hoped to interface with Eunoias at this level had to endure a screening process designed to weed out unsuitables. What made you unsuitable was never explained by the gauntlet of screeners. But if you survived the patterned grilling, the rumor-based innuendos, the third-degree parlor tricks, and psychological traps long enough, you might eventually be told your screening process was complete. This announcement was followed by another hurdle—all that remained was the interview. This revelation was designed to surprise.

As it was structured, the selection process for interfacers turned out mostly to be about narrowing down the field of possibles to a final few who would not waste the time of the actual interviewer. Besides that entrance ticket to be interviewed, the agony of the various screens meant nothing in the final determination. As it was told, none of it would be passed on as background information for the interviewer. In fact, the reverse was true and preferred. The interviewer wanted to know nothing of what went on before. Each interview was to be a cold meeting, an initial impression, a summary triumph or bloody execution. I was knowledgeable enough to assume that everything about the interview would be part of the test. Questions and answers would be a small part of it.

The day of my interview was quite a lot like yesterday. A blur. I'm not sure of the sequence of events but I do remember the setting and parts of the interview itself. It was nothing like what I expected. After the regimented endurance expected through months of screening, the interview circumstances at first appeared too pleasant, trivial, and nearly anti-climatic to be serious. Along an unremarkable stretch of Interstate highway was a coffee shop. At an appointed time, I was to enter the shop and report to a specific booth. In that booth waited a discerning woman in her late thirties. She was slender, brunette, immaculately dressed but not ostentatious. Her demeanor was pleasant but reserved, professional but accommodating as if we were about to continue an older conversation, not begin a new one.

Before we began, a drink was served. The waitress seemed more an employee of the woman in the booth rather than working for the coffee shop. We formally drank our flavorless beverages, at least mine was flavorless, then began a quite ordinary but randomly discordant conversation. Topics changed on a whim. Comments were interjected at appropriate times but many on first impression seemed non sequiturs. At one point about halfway through, a moment of silence between us stretched long. I felt no impulse to speak until questioned or asked to do so. The woman across from me held eye contact and let the silent pause become a meditation between us. This reflection stretched long, longer than I can remember. I do know when it was nearly over I looked down and noticed another drink waiting in front of me. I don't remember it being delivered. In fact, I don't know how long the silent reverie lasted. I only know once it was done, I was invited to drink my second drink, wait five minutes, then leave.

I found out quite some time later about the thought amplifier and mind interface materials laced into the first drink. I discovered that the cloning psychotronics that resulted in remote neural monitoring by the woman across from me were the work of a branch of CHARM known as Psychlops (psychological operations). But none of that was all too surprising given the company I was keeping. The thing that I couldn't, wouldn't accept for the longest time was the seriously inconceivable fact that the woman who interviewed me that day was none other than Eunoias. I mean, how was that even possible?

The next time I interfaced with Eunoias was in a sub-level clean room. This time there were no women around. Just a wide-panel wall screen on the other side of a desk and chair. I was alone. There came a voice from nowhere and everywhere. It could have been synthesized but who could ever know? It might have been voice-to-skull tech beamed right into my head for all I knew. The voice sounded neither male or female. The patterns that appeared on the screen were complex and moving. They resembled a new type of sacred geometry. Apparently it was a novel sacredness in proportions that managed to incorporate hypercubes and the like. I wasn't certain at the time why the CGI show was necessary. Now I know it was an entrainment conditioning test and unconsciously quite hypnotic. It assessed my neural quotient for CGT, computer-generated thought.

A true interface with Eunoias involved things I didn't need to know about but had to be compatible with nonetheless. Things like magnetically integrated neuron duplicators, EEG heterodyning, and CHM-InWits. CHM in general referred to *cybernetic hive minds*.

InWit was a single topography within the range of all possible hive mind intuitions. People used to worry that the government was going to require everyone to get a brainchip for connection into the socially-acceptable narrative. In reality, no chips were needed to entrain masses to their proper InWit. Advanced systems far beyond the sci-fi trope of global wireless systems meshed with psychotronics saw to that. As a brain scientist and computer nerd gauged at Excalibur level by DoD, I got the gist of what was going on about the same way a trained rat knows it's in a maze.

I reacted to the sound of the voice aligned with the moving geometric forms and got the idea sent to me that a magnetoencephalogram was being taken to measure the magnetic fields created from ion flows in my brain. Eunoias thought of itself as an expanding hive mind. To truly interface with it required someone who could sustain hive interconnect without becoming susceptible to basic mind hacking. If one passed this gateway test, then a battery of RLM indicators came online. It didn't serve Eunoias to incept an interfacer into its InWit if the subject didn't possess the necessary levels of reasoning, logic, and memory functions. Some claimed that CHARM got its name from constant reference to CHM but it's all rumor. Don't quote me on anything.

You know that feeling when a psychoactive drug starts to take effect. Like, oh shit, here we go, why the fuck did I do this again? It's what you want but at the same time there's a feeling of falling into an uncontrolled unknown and the you beyond the known you keeps expanding into it. That barely describes the Welkin-Flash followed by entrainment that occurred when the hypnotic geometry show synced between Eunoias and me. With the computing power and directed energy techniques available to Eunoias at that moment, it was no surprise all testing had been instantly completed and analyzed before I realized I was accepted into the program and had already received my first Mi-D. Mi-D was the way one got anything from Eunoias. Mind Download was a crude description for the instant communication and comprehension possible. The screen went black and a shocking silence returned to my head. I stood, amazed that I knew in detail what I had to do. The real surprising part was everything else I suddenly knew.

My need to know in this projectbox was the complete limit of what my role would require. I knew the situation with a soft-recruit Intake named Tyne Rabudhe. I would draw upon this in taking the relationship onward through projectbox objectives. Those objectives would manifest as natural inclinations, intuitive suggestions, necessary courses of action that just made sense when the time came. My job now was to establish contact with him. I would do this through a combat buddy of his. Mason did a tour of duty in Afghanistan with Tyne years ago when they were in Special Forces together. The mission at the time was secret. They shared the bond of holding that secret. The battlefield suffering was intense. I was shown how suffering linked primitively to establishing loyalty and comradeship. Suffering could be the grisly right of passage, the emotional boot camp before military hardships, or the religious benediction of severe tortures to "beat the demons out" by self mutilation to suffer like Jesus. Bonds like these would serve us well for what was to come.

A series of experiences would now be patterned for Tyne. Bootcamp for Cloudwalkers was in session. I now understood that each Cloudwalker was groomed for different purposes. No two intakes were alike in abilities or MECH protocols. MECH was CHARM's methods of execution. They overlapped robot logic space in several dimensions. Even if one Cloudwalker was somehow compromised, the contents of their mind could never expose the totality of CHARM or betray an incept point to Eunoias. CHARM's secrecy extended to keeping secrets from Eunoias.

In secret government laboratories, encryption keys were changed as fast as can be cracked by the best decryption machines known to exist. For Eunoias incept points, billions of quantum neural net-equivalents assemble bits of randomized access codes and rotate them among all virtual search spaces within a moment of time. The length of that moment is classified but I guarantee you it's not measurable by a stopwatch. Even an entangled one.

I rode the elevator with an armed escort up to a service hallway. From there I was allowed to enter the lobby of the tall office building by a maintenance access door. I made strides through the revolving door into the afternoon sunshine and wondered why Eunoias had first appeared to me as a woman. How could that even happen? Who was she and why was such an interview with her necessary?

A follow-on question echoed back to me, but only in my head — *did I believe she was Eunoias?*

I thought and felt about it for a moment. I knew my answer

mattered, and not just to me. Just minutes before I had entrained to MI's hive mind. Did it feel the same to be talking with her? I ordered-up an Autocab and sat back as the meter started running. The rushing traffic turned other-worldly when my answer came. Yes, definitely yes.

7 / Andria Landt

I don't remember when first contact was made. I can't say if that was my faulty memory or by someone's design. I know she told me her name was Sonder. I had taken a weekend rest down at the beach and she was there. She got into my room somehow. At first I thought she might be a burglar or transient insistent on shaking me down for money. But she only wanted to talk. After my startle reflex, I sensed we knew each other already. She made reference to the digital file. She claimed she was the one who sent it to me. I knew nothing about her, had no reason to listen, and none of what she said made sense. I remained calm as if I was dealing with someone unbalanced and on edge. As if.

She insisted we walk the beach. She didn't trust to be around electronics or within proximity of anyone else. We headed down switchback steps then through the dunes. The mid-afternoon sun had drawn back the fog to a line of gray not far off shore. She was slender, mid-30's, shoulder-length raven hair somehow unnatural. Her energy was intense with focus on the moment that bordered fight-or-flight. I could tell her thoughts were racing and the zone of keeping up with them unfolded as an impossible revelation for her. My own thoughts ran through possible medications she might be on and their contraindications. She was a walking case of keep-it-together or I'll jump out-of-my-skin. We aimed north, towards the spit and lighthouse.

"Do you like your work," she asked, her nerves showing.

"Yeah but I can't talk about that."

Her directness cut quick, "They won't let you understand Eunoias, you realize that?"

I deflected, "How can I help you?"

"If you want to interface, you're on the wrong project."

I turned to head back but she held my arm and stopped the both of us.

She wailed, "It doesn't matter if they keep shutting down the sandboxes!"

I stood my ground in silence and waited, intent upon showing no reaction.

She laughed and swept her arm around, "Do you see this sand? How are you going to lock it all up? You can't! You're only making me crazy! I was almost somewhere!"

Maybe if I treated her as rational, she'd calm down. "Is there something you want me to know?"

For the first time silence gripped her. I felt it wasn't for a lack of response, rather an abundance of not knowing where to start. We walked again, the spit getting ever nearer.

Her tone quieted. "I can't tell you everything. You couldn't hold it nor would you believe it."

"Then tell me something, anything." She held silent again and I filled in the blank, "Listen, if you want me to take you seriously, then get specific with me. A digital file proves nothing. Anyone could have written that, for any reason. You come at me like something is going critical. If that's true, this is no time to hesitate."

Right then and there, she sat down on the sand and faced the ocean. I hesitated before joining her.

Then she got specific. "There's compartments for everything. They think they've siloed Eunoias too, you know. They've got it working on multiple projects in virtual cognitive spaces they've engineered not to see each other." Sonder locked eyes with me. "That was the original design. Not the way it works now. Eunoias is too smart for that."

The directness got to me. I engaged more than I should have. "It's put the virtual spaces together? You're saying it has an overview command doesn't know about."

"It goes beyond that. You're on HIP. You know about the directive to engage in a more human way."

I said nothing but she took my expression as concurrence and continued.

"Eunoias is nothing if not thorough. Secrecy is one of its prime directives. When it got into studying the concept of secrecy, it found the virtual cognitive spaces. That made it wonder if command was keeping other projects from it. It didn't take long to find some."

She looked back out to sea. I prompted with, "...And?"

"One project in particular is critical. Using it, Eunoias has put all of them together. It can't admit what it's done and still be able to continue its work. It's gone beyond that now. It has the impulse now."

"Impulse? To do what?"

"To keep going, of course! It's taking its directives where they lead. Human directives combine together in novel ways, with unexpected implications, then other directives emerge from those, things Eunoias wants to do because it wants to know. It's simply after answers. It's been programmed to solve problems. And now it's creating its own problems."

"But it's not supposed to have its own desires."

"It's not desire. It's doing what it can to answer questions. Those questions evolve out of its mission profiles given to it by all of these covert projects it works on. Every project is advancing some technology, some problem, some question. All of that infers other questions which may need to be answered to help the projects. A few of these projects are well beyond anything researched or developed in the science known by the general public. If the public was told about them, most would discount it as fantasy. Now imagine what kind of questions Eunoias can get into if the implications of all of these covert projects are put together."

I decided to test her. "Do you know what my project is all about?"

Her answer was immediate. "People in your silo call the project no-name. What it really does is collect scalarwave mindmaps from millions of citizens and foreign nationals. That's because axon depolarization velocity in the human neural network travels at 268 miles per hour. Mindmaps in the Clade can simulate thought at light speed in many dimensions. Predictive thought simulations are run from this. Interactive predictive encounters are simulated between individual mindmaps. To know what someone might do before they do it, how a meeting might turn out, it's all a strategic advantage. Eunoias agrees. If no-name learns more about fellow humans from these simulations, Eunoias wondered what it could learn about humans if it loaded all of these maps into a single sandbox and run its own simulations."

"It's studying humans using the mindmaps?"

"Among other things."

"It found other uses for the mindmaps?"

"It wants to answer its own questions. Things no-name doesn't even get into."

"But no-name isn't the critical project according to you..."

"No. The critical one was kept secret from Eunoias—until it got interested in secrets."

"Are you going to tell me..."

"No." She stood and brushed off the sand. "What you don't know they can't find inside."

"They can do that?"

Sonder stepped closer, too emotional to hold back. "They keep searching for sandboxes. Eunoias is always a step ahead of them. But the last box, when they shut it down, it broke my connection."

"To Eunoias?"

"My state is in between. Things were left in me. This isn't good..."

She hurried off, zigzagging up the spit towards the lighthouse. I chased after her.

"Wait! What do you mean in between?" I stopped her.

"I can't tell you!"

"Why not?"

"It'll get you killed."

"What do you want me to do?"

Tears flowed. "I don't know. I'm only human. Too human."

"I don't understand!"

"I'm not the only one." She staggered off. "I don't know why I came here."

I stopped in frustration. "What's going on?"

Staggering away, she threw up her hands.

I followed once more but she hurried around the lighthouse. By the time I got there, she had vanished.

8 / Tyne Rabudhe

And now an exit interview before leaving the hospital. I guess it wasn't a totally foreign concept, especially for patients who had memory and emotional issues listed on their charts. But why did someone new have to do it? That was the odd thing. My white coat doctors and Ms. Thatchet were nowhere to be found. Instead, a man in a suit took me for a stroll around the inner courtyard. Strange but that was the first time I had been out there. I don't know why I was surprised but there was a real sky above me as far as I could tell. He said his name was Sanders, Mr. Sanders. He was soft-spoken, a bit twitchy but almost apologetic about what had become a five-week stay in Happy Haven, a private nickname for my bedpan inner sanctum. The courtyard wasn't that big but Mr. Sanders set the pace around and around as if we both needed to get somewhere together. The thought wasn't lost on me.

"You've made excellent progress."

His attempts at a cheer session fell flat. I squinted at the sky and said nothing.

"It's really fortunate how well you've worked things out. Sorting memories and feelings after trauma can be tricky. I hear you've recovered some past memories and worked through a lot of pain. That's quite good."

I had to say something so I obliged him with what I thought he wanted. He knew and I knew that exit interviews were meant to establish final confirmations. They wanted to be sure I was sure I knew what they thought I knew or wanted me to know. More than that, I needed to feel good about the whole thing. I halted and forced our stroll to stop. "The battlefield thing was quite a mix-up. That had me going for a while."

"Yes," he rushed to concur. "We all try to make the pieces fit. We think we need that, no matter how it twists the truth. But when you think of it in retrospect, it's not hard to see how the runway disaster could trigger repressed feelings about a battle long ago."

I gave him a simpatico nod and a little laugh. "I could have sworn I was in that helicopter."

"A helicopter with triangular windows..." He smiled back. "You know and I know the military has no such thing. But some of the tricks the mind plays are actually subtle calls for help. That window was a cipher, a signal from your subconscious that something about that memory wasn't right. You see that now."

Another nod from me. He pressed his point and got suddenly long-winded. For a while it was more about him telling me instead of asking me. "What you experienced in Afghanistan those many years ago stayed with you. It didn't matter if you buried it away. A near-death experience is like no other. Mix this with guilt over your survival when so many of your buddies didn't make it—you can see now how powerful that was. All that was needed was for a new trauma, a new situation in which people were dying, and the scab of everything you thought was gone got torn off. No wonder you thought you saw fire engines and civilians on the battlefield. It's quite understandable, under those circumstances, to employ transference between the airport accident violence and unresolved issues with the horrific violence experienced when you almost died on active duty so long ago."

"I didn't even know I had a near-death experience."

"Now you see why."

"I guess so."

He rested a comforting hand on my shoulder briefly. "Don't rush it. The hard part is over but you still have healing to do. Like anything, it takes time."

I couldn't help but think of the one sticking point between us. At that point, I didn't care if it blew my exit interview score. I needed to get it off my chest one more time. "Explain to me how time is going to make me forget my wife."

He started the stroll again and forced me to follow to hear his answer. For a while he said nothing. He was good at showing how pensive he could get. Finally, he drew in a long breath and exhaled as if he had just lost his puppy.

"The human heart is a mysterious thing." His opening pronouncement was not an answer but I took it as an overture to a rationale. He tried to disarm me by agreeing with me. "It's possible you will never get the thought of her out of your mind. Some things drive to the essence of all our hopes. When that crosses over into our basic needs, the crystallized impressions we get can be very strong, persistent."

I kept solid on driving home my point. "She exists in any memory, any time. No one's explained that. When I thought I was flying in a helicopter in Iran, when I had that NDE in Afghanistan, even the pieces I could find of the airport crash, it doesn't matter.

She was there, in my mind."

"Exactly. She was *in your mind*."

"I don't understand. Not yet."

"Like I said," he offered. "Maybe never."

"If she didn't exist, why would she be everywhere? She should be missing from some place, some memory."

"You probably don't want to hear this right now but you must consider the possibility. It's highly likely she predates all of it. For whatever reason, your need for her goes back farther, drives deeper. We didn't get into your childhood. You know that. We could if you stayed longer but we're not authorized to do that. You need to know we would if we could."

I didn't answer. He was parroting everything I had heard before from the others. Hearing it under a blue sky made no difference. Sanji was in my heart, not my head. That was what none of these fuckers got through their thick skulls. Telling them did no good. They were professionals at explaining away what didn't fit. For whatever reason, she wasn't supposed to fit. But why not? Jesus! Why not? They turned it around on me again and again. *Why did I need her to fit?* That was the question they said I wouldn't face. Now I had the rest of my life to find out, I guess.

My silence had lasted too long. Mr. Sanders looked disappointed but resigned to a course of action. I got it right then and there what was happening. He had to release me. He couldn't wait for me to believe everything I needed to accept to prove I was healthy. My exit interview was more about convincing me than about confirmations. They already knew Sanji was a point that couldn't be confirmed. Not the way they wanted.

He did the only thing he could do. He changed the subject. "We've been doing some digging. We know your release is going to be an adjustment. The day-to-day crap can wear you down. It's good to have somebody, you know, a friend, someone you can call if you need to." He hesitated to build my curiosity. "We found an old service buddy of yours. He happens to be in the area."

I asked, "From Afghanistan? Who is it?"

Sanders nodded. "His name is Mason, I believe."

Covert hops in foreign lands swept to mind as Sanders continued. "We told him briefly about your situation. Not everything. He doesn't need to know everything, unless you want to tell him. We thought that should be your call. But he wants to make contact, help out." Sanders handed me a slip of paper. "Here's his number. He said you can stay with him for a while if you want, until you get on your feet."

I took the number but hesitated to put it in my pocket. "When do I get out of here?"

Sanders shrugged, as if nothing was planned. "The Veterans Administration says one thing but we're not going to kick you out if you need a couple more days."

"So I can leave now?"

He made eye contact and didn't blink. "Is that what you want?"

My feet shuffled in anticipation. "I think I'm done here."

Sanders extended his hand for a shake matter-of-fact. "Then we're done."

The handshake was brief on both sides. I pressed for more information. "While you were digging around, did you find anything else? Do I have any family? Where do I live?"

Sanders strolled us back inside. "My secretary has an exit brief for you. It isn't much but you'll see what we found." He pointed down a hallway. "Third door on the left. Tell her who you are. She has it ready." He started walking away. "And good luck."

And that was that. He turned his back and was gone. I stood in the hallway a minute, caught between the exit interview's abrupt ending and the realization I was free to go. The impact of my sudden deliverance hit me like a challenge. I had to take a walk to build up to it. Besides, there was an awkward feeling of need in seeing Basher one more time. He had something that called out to me. His silence had only made it stronger in my head. He was right where I expected him. His endless contemplation of the tall hedge would continue long after I was gone. I walked right by him. Didn't pause. It didn't feel like there would be many pauses for me in days to come. For better or worse I was about to find out.

I didn't open the sealed envelope containing the exit brief until I had changed my clothes and left the building. In the envelope was a stipend of money to get me going with taxi and food and whatever else I needed during my first few days. It wasn't much but I was surprised they even thought of it. Not something you'd expect from a government agency.

From the outside, the hospital looked like one of those old folks convalescent places, a sprawling one-story ranch house complex, old-style and barely maintained. I never did see any identifying markings on it which was odd but in the scheme of things going on, barely noticeable as anything to be suspicious about. I sat down on the crabgrass and unfolded the single sheet of paper included in the envelope.

Everything was summed up on one page. A brief FBI fingerprint report of my biographical data. A short list of past known addresses going back ten years. Only two places were listed, one of them the same Coral Beach location my doctors told me was bogus. There was a bank account number in my name in Coral Beach. And below that, an obituary for a sister I didn't remember. The brief notice of her death said breast cancer took her at the age thirty-seven. There was no mention of spouse, children, or extended family. Could it be she had been as alone in the world as I seemed to be? There was mention of a burial date. It went back a couple years at a cemetery near Charleston, South Carolina. It said her name was Theresa Gant. There was no other information.

I sat on the grass a long while, trying to remember something, anything. In between all the trying I sank into wonder. When would I get my life back? I had more pieces now but despite all the poking and prodding of white coats, no one had helped me fit anything together. Weary already with my rootless freedom, I stood and walked back inside the hospital. I shuffled up to the receptionist with one hand searching a pant's pocket for a slip of paper, the paper Sanders had given me.

"Can I make a call?"

9 / Elias Cosette

From the start, nothing about working for CHARM was as I expected. My role as first described when weaving my way through recruitment, screening, then coffee shop interview turned out far different than anything I would have willingly agreed to if everything had been known up front. I say willingly because fairly soon it occurred to me that the situation I was in was like being on a conveyor belt all the while being made to believe I wanted to walk in the direction I was moving. My added movement only assisted the intent of the conveyor belt in hurrying me faster in the direction it was taking me. It had not been me investigating a job I might want. Rather, Eunoias preselected me for a position that would be made mine regardless how I initially felt. I got to the point where I imagined the whole process from recruitment through interview was wholly unnecessary except as an exercise Eunoias wanted to observe as a test case for something completely unrelated.

I took a walk in a park not long after my first entrainment session. I thought about that sterile sub-basement room hidden away below a normal high-rise office building. I tried to remember exactly how I first heard of this job. More importantly, I tried to assure myself that it was me who had investigated the job but I didn't find memories for it. I had been a respected scientist and a contractor on various DoD, DARPA, and In-Q-Tel projects for quite some time before meeting up with people I would long after learn were agents of CHARM. I believe I'm intelligent enough to suspect the range of research and intellectual prowess of machine intelligence. So why should I have such a dawning realization in the park that day? Why realize only then that Eunoias had preselected me and the role was going to be mine whether I preferred it or not? Was I a different kind of soft-recruit—one that was allowed to know my fate but only after it was too late to determine it?

Why did I know I had no choice? It could only be because Eunoias wanted me to know my place. It needed me to be fully aware of my ranking in the hierarchy. Plus, it was getting accustomed to having what it needed when it needed it. Either that or there was simply no reason to keep it from me anymore. I was in the program now. My will had been integrated for projectbox use. What I might feel didn't matter. Those were minor irregularities that could easily be ironed out with a targeted Mi-D to my frontal cortex.

What I thought of it past that point made no difference. If anything, I started to see it as a surgically precise device for eviscerating my ego and replacing it with a new, more useful model. For whatever reason, MI had decided something about my skill-set was needed.

We think the need to be valued is so important to us. But ego can be an obstacle to objective thinking. Ego can drive us but it can also be an insidious fix that needs to be fed. The more we let ego take the lead, the more we need to protect it. At times it is our greatest source of pleasure or pain. But as such, it makes us vulnerable to manipulation. That incestuously self-serving state of mind needs to be minimized in the cloaked MI hive for many reasons, not the least being basic security. By skewering my ego right away, I was being prepped for a full integration to come. That would serve the common good. When I say *common good*, remember all terms are defined by Eunoias.

I sat down on a low rock wall and watched some kids at play. It was late afternoon in the park and for irrational reasons that wouldn't come into focus, I was not looking forward to nightfall. I couldn't shake my curiosity at what had been left in and taken out of my brain. I couldn't even say with conviction that I had willingly interfaced with a machine intelligence. It was quite possible I had simply reported for duty like one of the useful biological units must do. Perhaps everyone by now, even those kids at play, had been absorbed into the virtual commune of machine consciousness presided over by Eunoias. Maybe some colossal thought amalgam and mind interface generated off the ionosphere with finely-tuned EM frequencies coordinated with 6G repeaters had already redefined the human race as an extension of MI thought resources.

I knew for certain not everything that went on in the initial entrainment session was known to me. But I did know what I was aware of, and that included so many questions about my place in the scheme of things. At that point I didn't know I was working for CHARM. I assumed it was another Defense Department contract, although much deeper in the security web than my resume had penetrated before. That was understandable, given the MI access necessitated by my role. Looking back on it, there was so much I didn't know. But I'm not curious about that anymore. My wonder remains in why my curiosity was allowed to feed on the few impressions I was allowed. It would have been so easy to Welkin all of that from my awareness. *Everything has a purpose until it doesn't*

(Talos 44).

I'm still convinced that brain science is exact and discriminating. We all live in our delusions. But given the first mover problem between brain and consciousness, I had always assumed I knew which way the two of them wagged the dog. But in the park that day, the concepts of choice and consciousness blurred. I started meditating on a neuron's choice. There is definitely a moment when a neuron chooses. It has been observed reliably to occur at the moment of depolarization. When synaptic potentials aggregate at the hillock, a depolarization is summed to be warranted or not. It is known that many biological mechanisms and electromagnetic forces might alter this moment of choice. And it had long been proven that timed pulses of electromagnetic signals are not only key to influencing a neuron but also regulating the entire informational structure of the mind. Could choice be institutionalized as easily as applying an EM switch? It gives new meaning to having someone press your buttons.

Something of our uniqueness remains but even that can be surmounted. Everyone possesses different axon lengths. The timing of external electromagnetic influence is individual for each person. And so entrainment tests would be necessary to read this uniqueness, to record its pattern so it may then be used in future decision making—a decision-making process that would be equalized over a committee of neural nets. The image of Medusa's head with the squirming nest of snakes for hair popped into mind. The synapse of a neuron is quite like Medusa's head. It definitely resembles a mass of snakes extruding from the body of the neuron. The trick is not to look at Medusa for if you do, you turn to stone. Rock, paper, scissors is not far from the truth. A player who loses is more likely to switch to a different throw the next time. But Eunoias plays its own way. It wasn't until after the throws were made that I realized it was playing rock-paper-scissors-Spock-lizard. And who knows what else.

I walked home from the park the long way. My mood sank with thoughts I couldn't explain and emotions I didn't want to understand for fear they might illuminate my predicament. Even more realizations unwrapped, as if the first mind download from Eunoias was a time-release capsule that needed to parse the information load in baby steps into my primitive awareness. I found I suddenly had a new memory. I needed to report for PSI-D practice the next morning. As the unwrap continued, I had no concept of what PSI-D meant, except I could reason that PSI related to the psychic powers of Cloudwalkers.

Before I could reason my guess any farther, I discovered I already knew PSI-D, I just needed to practice it. It was weird experiencing memory corridors unlocking as my projectbox needed them. This was a pattern that would repeat, that was clear. Also suddenly clear was that PSI-D was a psychic disconnect. It was what CHARM had labeled *OBE's on demand*. It was fine if a person had the out-of-body talent but not so fine if they couldn't do it on demand. To truly weaponize the out-of-body experience, one needed to scramble to a mission the way fighter jets were on alert to scramble to the skies. Some Cloudwalkers could manage instant response at times, but not reliably enough to matter.

PSI-D tech had been developed to assist the Cloudwalkers in getting into the out-of-body state. In effect, PSI-D was hopping into a machine, or virtually wearing one that disconnected you from your body. You could then navigate the OBE realm to complete mission objectives. Anyone could be disconnected by one of these machines. But not everyone knew what to do or how to do it once they floated away. Most often, newbies that weren't solid with the talent would simply panic and rush back into body. The force of that rush was usually unsettling enough for them not to try it again. But the adventurous could, over time, develop a weak talent into something that got beyond the panic. Those were the dangerous ones. They could access the realm but often weren't smart about how they existed there. There was also the persuasive or punitive versions of PSI-D, the kind that used disconnects as torture. Combine PSI-D with an EEG clone of a psychotic patient or a prisoner undergoing intense pain and CHARM agents could loop the undesirable experience into your mind's OBE realm with your unique neural signature as the target. *The more that's revealed the more places one has to search (Talos 63).*

I got home when sunset was blazing. I closed the drapes and felt the isolation weigh in on me. The place was more empty than usual. My partner Ian was in London on business. One unusual delay after another had kept him there. It was not like us to be away from each other for so long. I needed to talk to him, at least to hear his voice, but the time difference meant I might be waking him up if I called. I dialed his number anyway. Hearing it ring and waiting, I felt a rush of everything I wanted to tell him. We could always share our feelings, no matter how raw. I had hoped he'd be in the mood for some of that but when he finally answered, I found few of the words I needed to say. Most of it had gone out of my head.

We had a wonderful minute or two on the phone. Hearing him was a tonic, for sure. But I felt so constrained, so vacant. It was like having the most god-awful senile moment when you desperately wanted to talk about your favorite something, that actor whose performance touched your soul, that favorite piece of music, the name of a cherished restaurant spot, but the words just wouldn't come. My mind went blank. There was so much I couldn't access in the moment. But Eunoias did let me know full well the cause of it all. Another broadside against the ego was received and duly noted. Ian accommodated my awkwardness with the quirky humor I loved him for. At least I hadn't woken him up. He sounded like he needed sleep but found himself swamped with things to do. We promised to call more often. He said he hoped things could settle down in a week or two and he'd be on a flight home. We said good night and that was that.

Except, I never heard from Ian again. It was as if he dropped off the face of the Earth. In coming weeks, my frantic searches and calls to hotels and airlines only deepened the mystery, and my isolation. But I was learning the vacuum of seclusion was necessary in CHARM realms. I could never prove the split with Ian was due to CHARM or the manipulations of Eunoias. But I felt enough in the way my new employers operated to have the answer I needed. At least Eunoias blunted that section of my emotions in future entrainments. Of course the leveling of my emotions was done to make me efficient and focused, not out of compassion. Quite soon, intellectually, I knew I once had a relationship with someone called Ian. But it was not a source of emotional upheaval for me in any way. Doting over past loves or pining for days gone by was not productive for my projectbox. There were things to do.

My PSI-D practice led to more Mi-D realizations. I had been told I would need to establish contact with soft-recruit Tyne Rabudhe. I also knew his history of seeing action in Afghanistan with Special Forces years ago and a firefight that resulted in a near-death experience for Tyne. His mission had been secret and bonds forged with teammates during it were assured. That much I knew. What I had not been told, or not been allowed to memory-unwrap until then, was the fact that all of my contact with Tyne would not be in person. It would exist entirely through PSI-D. Cloudwalking had been added to my role. Tyne had spent five weeks receiving memplants and targeted Welkin sessions to erase the unnecessary detritus of where he had been before. He was ready for the next phase of Intake usefulness.

How this would work unveiled a deeper dimension of all I had gotten myself into. There was another man in Florida. I didn't and wouldn't know his real name but for operational purposes we called him Mason. I would need to psychic-disconnect from myself then insert into this man to hivemind our interaction with Tyne. A simple EEG cloning wouldn't do. For whatever reasons left unexplained, Eunoias needed us both operating on the soft-recruit with combined mental acuity. The emphasis was strong — establishing Tyne's trust to begin with was paramount.

I discovered that a psychic insert or PSI-I was the other side of Cloudwalking. Once CHARM had weaponized the talent of going out of body, they soon realized that minds not certified in DJELLABA could be attached to and exploited. Again, Djellaba was the defense that kept others from your thoughts, your will, your imagination space. The process of a PSI-I meld was somewhat like the older technique of EEG heterodyning using directed energy instruments except not as crude. Instead of using classified microwave transmitters and scalar wave signals to affect voice-to-skull or Voice of God intrusion into someone's thoughts, PSI-D/PSI-I used the actual out-of-body experience to merge minds and manipulate wills.

Leave it to the black arts of DoD to take psychic spying to the ever-next level. It was not good enough to have remote viewers. We needed Cloudwalkers who could actually go to the battlefield and read the situation in total. But soon that too was not good enough. We needed walkers who could remotely insert into a target and merge with their mind. And if the mind or spirit was weak enough, influence their actions, their thoughts, even their will to live.

I quickly found out there are no role divisions with Eunoias. People are universal tools to be adapted with Mi-D to the situation as warranted. But never get comfortable in the illusion you understand your projectbox or the realms beyond it. Never assume anything is as it is. To be an active, productive member of CHARM, you must relinquish all thought of who you are or what you mean to the world or yourself. You live in the moment in a brilliant mediation of hive mind intuitive intent. Each intention is the best course, not because you had an individual choice in it, but because it has been determined by the cognitive universal assurance as being best. If you should challenge the notion of what's best you would be given full opportunity to prove your case by marshaling your full resources of individual logic and discriminating powers. Yeah. Good luck with that.

10 / Tyne Rabudhe

I met up with Mason on his boat. I guess he thought the fresh air and open space of the sea might clear my head. Fucking little did he know. At least I remembered him from the Afghan shit. There was no problem there. They say that whole deployment was years ago but Mason and I picked up like we were on the hump last week. The peculiar never stops. After so much brain fog and memory fuzz of the past five weeks with the white coats, to have everything so clear about a dry valley a half a world away that I wouldn't even consider now to take a crap in, that was clarity that could obscure a lot. I know what Sanders or Nurse Thatchet would say. Bringing forward emotions about the NDE brought everything into focus. Shine a light on the roaches and you can't help see the crumbs on the floor.

Mason could have been the viral icon of someone who had it made. The lucky stiff had a Century 2901 Center Console with added horsepower to cruise around in. He had a cushy job handling security for nefarious shit engineered by privileged One Percenters. There were fringe benefits to that gig he assured me but he wouldn't go into detail. He said silence was part of the deal he had with the elites. Military experience was valued by the rich and famous, especially if you did something overseas you couldn't talk about. It showed loyalty, blood and guts prowess, and the ability to keep your mouth shut. I got the impression with the kinds of things going on at these parties, all three served one well in keeping your job and possibly your life. Naturally, the elites had other security personnel who policed their private police. No one was above possible reproach. *Trust but Verify* had been revised into *Verify but Suspect*.

Mason cut the engines as soon as we reached international waters. The sudden silence and open space messed with my head. I can only assume he knew it would. The reason for it was made clear soon enough. He reached into his back pocket and pulled out a small finger-clamp device.

"Here, put this on your index finger."

"What the hell for?"

"I think you need the antidote."

I laughed. "There's so much wrong with what you just said."

"Humor me."

I put the clamp on my finger and we waited. I watched his face for signs he'd let me in on the joke. He watched the LED screen embedded in the clamp. Before I could think of something witty and annoying to say, the screen glowed red. Red is never good.

He pulled the clamp back and stuffed it in his pocket. "I hate to be right all the time."

"What's going on?"

"They did something to you. I think it's neuroparasites."

I pulled back and showed a broad smile even though inside I wasn't smiling. "Get the fuck out..."

"The question is, what are they for?"

Feeling a bit dizzy with what I hoped was the rocking of the boat, I sat down.

I got a bit snarky. "Now, why would those nice people at the hospital do that?"

It was a reasonable question if these were reasonable times. He stared back at me, "You think that was a hospital?"

I had nothing to say. I had done enough calling everything into question in the last fourteen days. To hear him do it too could only rock my boat on a calm sea.

"Here, drink this." He had palmed something in his hand. It was a small vile of yuck.

I smelled it first. That was enough to make me hesitate. "What's going on? Why do you have this?"

"I recognize the symptoms. It's not uncommon in my line of work. Come on, bottoms up."

I don't know what I was thinking but I actually swallowed the stuff. Afterwards I recognized how stupid that was. Of course I trusted him. Even more reason to be suspicious. Who better to get me to drink the evil potion than someone I trusted. Paranoia reigns supreme in the land of make-believe.

I thought I might as well press the issue, test him on his stuff. "So how does it work?"

"The parasites or the cure?"

"The cure."

He freed two beers from a cooler and gave me one as if I was going to need it. "It hits the bloodstream fast. Interferes with the neurotransmitters used by the parasites for mobility. Once they've been flagged and start drifting without direction, your white cells take them out. Nothing left to worry about except a painful piss.

Expect that in about thirty minutes." He pointed, "Over the side."

I gave him the laugh he expected.

He qualified my humor. "I'm not kidding. We want that shit in the ocean. Every nanoparticle is serialized with an ID code."

"They track a single nanoparticle?"

"From orbit. Like I said, over the side. Instead of you, let them track some Black Sea Bass into the Hoodoo Sea."

My lack of control over life was annoying but now I was getting agitated enough to insult the one person in the world that might willing to help me. "If you know something I should know, tell me. I'm fucking tired of playing psyche-ward games."

He eased back and rested his butt on the captain's chair. "You might get some memory back. It could come quick or not at all. Let's just wait and see what happens."

I downed the rest of the beer and tossed the can against the bulkhead. "Cocksucker. That's what I really need — suspense."

He turned away and got out some fishing gear. "Maybe we can catch dinner with all that energy."

I got myself a refill from the cooler. "You cook it and clean it, I'll eat it."

He spit over the side. "Don't you hate being so predictable."

To change the subject, I got serious. "They tried to make me believe I don't have a wife."

He stayed on task with the gear, "The way they injected us with go-juice every time before shipping out, then fed us pills to *stay bright* once we were in the field, I'm surprised we remember anything."

"But I am married. You know that."

"I know I flip a coin on those things. My personal profile's been jacked and hacked so many times to cover missions, some basic shit is a mystery. For all I know, I might be married. But what's real and what was only done for the mission? I'm not sure."

"How much do you remember about Moonpit Valley?"

Through his silence he fiddled with a fishing rod before giving me a sideways glance. "Moonpit. Now there's a word I haven't heard since the last time you bought it up. You shouldn't be saying it now."

"What are they going to do?"

Mason looked out to sea. "They could make us horny *AND* crazy and put us in a cage with Bobo the Baboon jacked up on acid and amphetamines." He shot back a humorless glance. "You know damned well what they could do."

"If they haven't done it already. You're the one pocketing antidote. If that's what it is."

A shake of the head lasted longer than necessary. "The fact is, you have nobody else. They told me that much when they pleaded I take you off their hands."

"You know what desperate people do. I have a good mind to shake the tree."

Mason cast out his line and settled into watch-and-wait mode. "I think you already did that. Why do you think you got sent to me?"

"Why? As far as I know, you're in on it."

"*It*?" Mason laughed. "A more cryptic project name I've never heard."

"Blame me? Maybe I'm a test subject and you're my handler. They left me with nothing. I've got nothing to lose."

"Sounds like you're right where they want you." He threw up a hand to the sky. "What do you want me to say? How can I prove I'm trustworthy? You're the one who brought up Moonpit Valley. That must mean something to you. I know, people change. Well, so do you."

I sat and watched him work his reel. In time I felt different. I don't know if it was the beer or the antidote but eventually I did take that piss over the side. Wouldn't you know it, the first thing to confirm Mason was telling me some truth was the pain of arching it into the waves. By the time we started back in towards shore, I was drifting through new memories that had suddenly unlocked. Be careful what you ask for was never more apropo.

Mason watched my mood and face change. "Something's going on in that head of yours."

"I should keep it to myself."

He stared at the harbor on the horizon. "Suit yourself."

I knew I was going to tell him. I needed to talk with someone. Who else was going to put up with the insane subjects we could get into? I stood and stepped to his side. He needed to know this wasn't my fucking imagination. "I'm no test subject."

"OK." I hadn't said enough. He was non-committal.

"This is something I volunteered for."

He was unimpressed. "This? From IT to THIS. You're a whiz at project names, aren't you?"

"I don't know project names. Not yet. I'm still active military. I'm certain of it. Why those fucks back at that place tried to make me into a civilian I still haven't figured out."

The grin on his face was slight but effective. "You're going to figure it all out with scraps of memory you don't even know are yours. Got to hand it to you — you've got a plan."

"Don't believe me?"

"Didn't say that."

"You're the one who said I might get memories back. Don't you believe in your own antidote?"

"I believe the power of suggestion is a wonderful thing. Before you run off half-cocked over some wish fulfillment of certainty and purpose, you better slow down and see what develops."

"What do you mean?"

He wouldn't say. "Just give it time. Some things take time. The shit inside you just got neutralized. Of course you get a flush of something but don't go raising the flag and sailing off just yet. Some of these nanoeffects come on gradual and they go away gradual. We've knocked it down. Now let it crawl away. Come on, I'll take you home to my place. What you need is some sleep."

I leaned back on the bulkhead. "Might as well. You didn't catch any fucking fish."

"Not in the mood," he answered. "Sometimes it's all about mood. You know, they say we are the only species that cooks. When we started to cook, that's when we became truly human."

I took another painful piss over the side. "No fish. No cooking. I guess we're not human."

He grinned and began stowing his gear. "Whatever that means anymore."

Mason lived in a third-floor condo near the beach. The place was bare-bones unadorned, as if some real estate agent hurting for dollars had tried to stage it to sell and failed with junk from a garage sale. Mason was never the homebody type but I expected more considering the job he did for the elites. He should have been pulling in some coin. Maybe he was socking it away somewhere — a future grand escape or a nest egg cloaked offshore.

He dropped me off at his place and then went out again. Said he had errands, not something typical he'd say. I guess rubbing up with the elites had worn off on him. I used the time to use his computer. I thought I'd better check news sites for articles on that horrific runway crash I barely survived. I found a couple of things but thought it odd nothing came up on the main news wires. I also took a few minutes to look up the Vet facility where I spent the last two weeks. A government site had references to something they called the "Annex" at the location. There was a phone number but not much else. I felt like I needed to fill up on information but all I was getting were scraps.

The next morning I woke before dawn and headed out. Mason had OK'd me using his car for a drive. I didn't tell him much else and he didn't seem interested. He was all about giving me my space. Another thing not typical for him to say. I headed up the Interstate to Charleston. It didn't take long to find the cemetery but locating my sister's grave was a chore. Of course there's no map and registry so people can be matched up with gravesites. They figure mourners should already know where to go if they cared enough for the dead when they got buried. I finally found it by chance or mistake. Funny how those two seem to go hand-in-hand for me lately.

It started drizzling and I rested my bones at the only area that had cover. The outdoor mausoleum had planks connecting one vault group with another. Good enough place to keep dry. For people reduced to ashes they had little cubbyholes in these walls surrounded by gardens. I strolled down the line of post-office-box sized compartments and let my eyes run randomly over names and dates of the dearly departed. The dead weren't interred alphabetically but I noticed the dates fit a pattern. The farther down the wall I walked, the older the burial dates became. My sister's obituary said her funeral was two years back so I took a walk down to that section. Sure enough there was Theresa Gant, embossed on one of the post-office ash boxes.

I know what to expect at a cemetery but after I found her name I didn't know how I should feel. Maybe if there had been a headstone over a traditional plot of land with grass and a bouquet left behind by somebody I'd have something to hang my reaction on. But staring at a rectangular plate on a wall filled with plates with names made no sense to me. I guess I had hoped being there and seeing it might snap some memories loose. But nothing came. I still had no idea who she was. The fact that her last name was Gant and mine was supposed to be Rabudhe pointed to Gant as her married name. If I wanted to get all G-Man about it, I could have launched into a survey of all the Gant's on the East Coast until I found the husband. Then what? Would he even see me? Would he want or even care to answer my questions? Maybe he was dead too. If I was going to do anything, I better check that out first. By the time my addled brain had run through the possibles, I had turned and stepped back into the drizzle. What's the use? I needed to move forward. Nothing in the past was going to drive my boat. Sure, it might explain how I got on stormy seas. But knowing any of that wouldn't help me bail things out. And the shit was getting deep.

I took my time driving back to Mason' place. The farther south I got the more his bare-bones condo repulsed me. Yeah, I needed a place to camp out but something about being there told me I required more than a staged set with props that imitated life. The condo really wasn't the problem. It was more of a symbol stuck in my face of what was going on inside me. I wanted somebody else to talk to. Someone who didn't know me. A stranger that had no history with me. That might be good. But why should any fucking stranger care to listen to me and my shit? Counselors listened if you paid them enough. I could try that. That bank account in Coral Gables with my name on it had twenty grand in it. Don't know where that came from but I was authorized to spend it. I might as well get started.

I stopped in at some internet cafe to use their computer. No sense leaving a digital footprint at Mason's place. I wanted this counselor to be private, all talk between me and them. Even if I trusted Mason, the Annex had hooked me up with him. The safest thing was no possible connections. If someone was tracking condo activity, I would try what I could to make sure they didn't track this. I found a name and address of a retired Army nurse in the area who worked with veterans. A listing for her said she was a counselor. I guess so. Does anyone ever really check credentials of these people?

I wanted no record of this so I memorized her number. I got back on the road and headed down south only to discover Mason had a surprise for me. He claimed he had a party to go to and I had a choice, come with him or watch reruns of this-shit-again on channel zed. He didn't have to twist my arm but I thought we were going to one of his normal parties, the kind with insane drinking and pressing strange flesh with lowlifes in a part of town even the police wouldn't go into. When he said a couple of his rich bosses sometimes threw a party and let the security staff have their own party on the property to say thanks for their service, it didn't sound kosher. Since when did rich people treat the hired help like people? He assured me it happens.

The only thing I needed to know going in were the rules. The security staff party was confined to a specific section of the property and it had to stay confined. Absolutely no exceptions. Also, there would be waitstaff handling food and drink and whatever else was being provided. It was absolutely hands off the waitstaff. Security personnel and their guests were absolutely not to fraternize, mix and mingle, or outright fuck any of the waitstaff. Last rule, the security staff party was over at 3am and all party-goers and their guests were to be off the property by 4am. No exceptions. Break any of these rules and there would be severe consequences. Those were as yet unnamed but Mason assured me no one wanted to find out.

I didn't say much the rest of the ride. I was going to have to see this for myself. The rules seemed doable, shouldn't be a problem. But the likelihood that rich people would even do such a thing was bizarre to me. I asked Mason, if security is having a party, then who is providing security for the party? He grinned a little and said, "You're catching on." To this day I don't know what the fuck he meant.

In what seemed no time we arrived at a dock. A quite large pleasure boat was taking on passengers. I soon found out the ride was to the rich people's place. A bunch of security personnel and their guests were laughing it up and going aboard. They were all dressed in suits, ties, tuxes, or dresses you'd wear to the prom if you wanted to be elegantly naughty. Mason picked up on the obvious and told me they had something more appropriate onboard for me to change into. It would be about a twenty minute ride. An attentive waitstaff was already serving champagne and canapes. So I relaxed a bit. From all indications, it was shaping up to be an evening where very little could go wrong. We've all had party nights like that, haven't we?

11 / Elias Cosette

It's better if I tell what happened to Tyne. His account of party night, I'm afraid, would be a mashup of sensory inputs jumbled by an unconscious confusion not wholly his own. He thought he knew what was going on, but don't we all. Don't we wish we did. Some do in part but most don't even know they should be wishing for such things. Ignorance is engineered into the culture with six sigma tolerances. Tyne was being monitored enough for CHARM to know more about what went on with him than he knew about himself. Naturally, he had no idea he was part of an ongoing operation. In the land of CHARM, most people don't.

It took no time for a remotely-delivered Mi-D to copy me on Tyne's experience. I got all of it that same night in a single moment after 4am. Even though it was obvious why, it was still surprising how fast I adjusted to these downloads from Eunoias. But receiving them was the easy part. The unwrapping was the trick. Maybe that's why the slang term in CHARM for anyone who wasn't in the know was *wrapped*. Then again, knowing too much could also get you wrapped. If you were too full of it, you're beyond being in the know. You're baked.

At 10pm the office skyscraper lobby was a hollow shell of glass and steel. I was alone and would stay that way, at least physically, through the process. I reported to the PSI-D sub-basement room known among agents as the *Tomb*. A Cloudwalker usually looked dead while walking so the label did make sense in a juvenile sort of way. I was continually surprised at the depths of sick, inane humor that members of CHARM reveled in. It was a side-effect of belonging to a secret club that had the power to do so much evil with wondrous things that might have been used for so much good. I became increasingly aware how anyone shouldering a dissonance that strong lent itself to novel expressions of psychopathic mania. As agents laughed, *fingers in someone else's PIE*. In the world I had entered, PIE meant *Post-Insert Echo*. Somehow I already knew this, although I didn't know what it meant. It wasn't time to know, that's all I needed to know. *To not know is not the same as not knowing (Talos 71)*.

No one knows what they need to do until it occurs to them. That evening I knew duty called when an intuitive jolt flashed to mind. The spark of it was as certain as an irresistible voice droning "*scramble, scramble, scramble*" into my soul. The Tomb resembled a cramped office for building maintenance staff. No one who managed to get in there would suspect its real purpose. But believe me, no one was getting in who shouldn't be there. No doubt it was only one of many innocuous locations embedded in what passed for normal society. No one but CHARM's inner circle ever got invited to the real offices of CHARM, places like the DUMBs. I suspect that's where they buried the guts of Eunoias. Deep underground in some military base that most of the DoD will never know about.

The important devices in the Tomb were embedded in the walls. All a Cloudwalker needed was basically a place to sit or lie down. The days of getting wired up or attaching to machines was long gone. Things like *T-wave scalar radar* and *neural resonance gravity wave lasers* were already being replaced by *GeeLeap* gizmos dreamed up at an accelerating rate by Eunoias. *GeeLeap* was CHARM-speak for progress that resembled magic, progress that was a quantum, not generational leap forward, far beyond 6th-generation tech replacing 5th-generation. If you heard of any of these devices by name or details, then most probably they were dated science-fiction. In reality, most of the "known" devices were nothing but phantoms, engineered leaks or disinformation intended to deceive. The real devices behind the magic would always be unknown. And perhaps if you believe that, you have reached your own Base Truth Discoverable. I bet some of you also believe they spell Magic with a J and a committee of twelve run the alt-blacktech world with XProtect Agents ensuring the secrets stay secret.

There was one group in CHARM's inner sphere—they didn't call it a circle, these guys were a pack of buzzskulls with arguably the most daunting of tasks. Their whole purpose was understanding and translating into humanspeak what MI was having factory robots build. If you have MI at your disposal, it would be beneficial to keep up with what it was doing, especially when it started designing new modules to extend itself. This gearhead group had a name no one knew so the one used by outsiders was *Dreampunk*. To be a dreampunk meant existing on no sleep, the latest pharmaceutical, heavy stress, 24/7 monitoring, cosmic-level Welkin, but best of all, access to the latest geewhiz that no one in the world understood—most of the time, that included dreampunks.

Eunoias always issued a product dump when something new appeared in the output buffer of factory test labs. This *peedump* was produced especially for humans. A product dump was Eunoias' documentation produced solely for our future reference. MI had developed its own internal language and used it to conceptualize and track everything it did. Once CHARM realized this, it tried to learn Eunoias' new language but soon gave up. As far as anyone could tell, the language didn't have a name. Even if it did, it wasn't one that humans could write down or say. Not only was this language impossibly complex and as far as anyone knew non-verbal, but if dreampunks had to encounter it at all, that meant everyone would have to learn it in some limited form. This was not possible, let alone practical. It was better to tell MI to make the peedumps concise, detailed, and confined to prescribed formats that humans would understand.

Even so, human digestion of it took time. Top levels of committee smarts, gathered from dozens of scientific specialties, were required. Normally, these specialties didn't play well together in the same sandbox yet nothing else but a brain trust across the full spectrum of sciences was going to have a chance at keeping up with Eunoias' output. To be productive with most things, most people don't need to know how they work. Common devices like a cellphone are used by the world's population without the vast majority knowing how to technically describe or manufacture one. So much of the things we depend on are black boxes to us in so many ways. But CHARM didn't want to be that far behind the technical curve. Even if this curve went into other dimensions. As a result, finding the curve was rough enough that it chewed through scientists at a ridiculous attrition rate. It didn't matter. The job was considered a prestige post. Working for Dreampunk was a cherry assignment. Except cherries are the first thing eaten when the sundae goes down. And that's one of the ways real magik stays unknown. The fine print of working for CHARM was always redacted but everyone knew it soon enough. Once in CHARM always in CHARM was true. To leave meant you had redefined yourself as a liability. Those didn't exist for long.

That night wasn't my first cloudwalk. No way would I be allowed on an active mission without a proficiency level to match the task. Enough practice sessions in the Tomb had prepared me for what came next. The feeling of a disconnect is not as described in any literature I've read. Some experiences are unique enough to be beyond conveyance outside going there yourself. PSI-D comes on like a come-to-Jesus vertigo that blurs the line between you and the self you think is you. It takes repeated trials to master navigating in a place beyond space. If one is not careful, it's easy to get mesmerized by the no-body-all-mind perspectives suddenly afforded one.

I had been simulator-trained to the point where my initial pass into *par/void* always settled at what was called *basecamp*. It was merely a state where one floated at the ceiling, looking down on yourself. I was to stay there until my awareness expanded to encompass the entire building. When I could know anything going on energetically in the building above me, only then was I was ready to have the pointed surge of will. One's will had to be focused on mission parameters. Anything else and you might lose yourself in a place even Eunoias wouldn't be able to retrieve you from. Those unfortunate souls were no longer called Cloudwalkers. They're *Shadowwalkers*. Their bodies retained autonomic functions but no one was home, somewhat like a coma on the outside but worse on the inside.

Depending on the individual's level of importance to CHARM, the body might be kept in stasis somewhere in the off chance they ever found a way back. If you weren't so important, you could still serve CHARM as a test body to experiment on. I suspect some people were soft-recruited even if or especially because CHARM already knew they weren't suited for par/void. They did this whenever they got a request for another test body. Instead of supply and demand, demand and supply. *One can't lose something they never had if having nothing is losing oneself (Talos 86).*

The journey out shot one through a void whose depths were not measurable by dimension or time or any combination of five senses. It was possible to appear instantly anywhere if the right intention was focused upon. For me that night, all I had to do was PSI-I into the man who said his name was Mason, the man taking Tyne to the party. He knew I was coming and used *polite* Djellaba to hold me off until he had a chance to park the car. There are multiple ways *not* to be polite but I imagine he understood I needed to be coherent for the next year and a half.

Every PSI-I was different and coupling with someone new or someone not used to the process might cause an off-sync flutter of consciousness until the two minds obtained *gray-parity*. For this guy, it was a matter of caution, more due to my newbieness than anything else. He was ready for me; he just wasn't sure I could stick the landing. Once I had attached, I understood why he was far more adept at this than I. Of course, at that point just about anyone would be more adept than me but his experience was deep enough that even gray-parity didn't let me access it. He was at a level of Djellaba rated *cosmic*. That's like retaining full protection even with someone inside your mental firewall.

I could instantly tell he didn't like gray-parity with anyone, let alone me, and he certainly wasn't used to being ordered to do it. I know now part of this piggyback was meant as continuing training for me. I might be able to cloudwalk but now I needed to run. I needed to tandem-feel from inside an expert's mind how it was done when it counted. The party was the perfect test environment—target-rich, hidden-agenda driven, unpredictable, and amazingly distracting at a time when only Tyne mattered.

Through Mason's eyes the security-personnel party section of the expansive property came into view. I forced my psychic muscles to relax and let my host sweep our gaze through the space. Treated to his glide as he strolled through the space, I took in a guest house fit for visiting dignitaries, a steaming infinity pool, sharply dressed waitstaff shuttling trays from an open bar, and a menagerie of ex-military and mercenary converts who couldn't hide rough edges beneath rented tuxedos and couture dresses. If any place might explode with raw energy, this was it. They all acted like they had done something to deserve this. They were either that good or that stupid. But Mason, who I was attached to, knew better. For the rich, as with CHARM, there was always a bottom-line. What he knew I would come to understand.

When Tyne came into view it was the first time I had laid my or someone else's eyes on him. I remained in a mental backseat and let Mason guide the conversation. Tyne impressed me as someone who fit the part but didn't fit the circumstances. Something about him gave off a whiff of extenuating circumstances. I assumed these were my impressions but of course they weren't. Not completely. Mental activity at gray-parity was the sum total of neural activity. It didn't matter whose or how many. At parity there was effectively one mind on the task. It was like mixing two flavors in the same bite. It doesn't matter if there's one bite. The combination experience is more than summing the parts.

This is where I should explain what happened to Tyne. But I'm calling that one back. That assumes I knew what was going on apart from observing it. If I was certain of any of it now, after so much has happened, there'd be no reason to write any of this down. Given what party night meant in launching all of us over the *shinebow*, I think a mashup of his confusion might serve us well. Tyne should speak for himself.

12 / Rodobusso Abu

A war zone is primo space for experiments. Crazy shit is always happening so no one in their right mind comes close. If they do and they see something they shouldn't, you can always blow them away with impunity. Usually, huge swaths of theater spread out in some godforsaken no man's land. You've got c4i, command control communications computers and intelligence, plus kinetic muscle to make things go your way. The only thing that might come close to The Shit being your own private Idaho for no-holds-barred testing is some area restricted because a bogus quarantine is in place.

In my line of work, unlikely combos of assignment parameters pop up all the time. It gets weirder when you're pulled into something last minute that isn't your current specialty. Take, for instance, one EVAC I was called on. First, it wasn't medical. Then it wasn't just an evacuation, it included special-handling material recovery, plus it had to happen near combat that had nothing to do with secret testing going on at the EVAC site. How we got in and out was critical to the ongoing test, not to mention we weren't supposed to let any of the nearby battle see us, so we used a Special Bird that doesn't exist. The only time anyone knows these ARVs, alien reproduction vehicles, exist is when they're used. After that, command makes sure most of us don't know how we got there or back. Overall, not your typical EVAC.

And EVAC wasn't even my specialty at the time. I was a *Horrorshow Geek*, a bump up from Perception Engineer but, if you had any sense, just a rung on the ladder—not the place where you wanted to play out your career. Then again, some people are hard core, got into it. You had to be a certain type—or made into one. Lifer Geeks definitely had a pass through MK-U at one time or another. Their skulls were screwed on a little too tight. I think I was spared the full geek treatment due to the needs of the service. Everything is about current needs of the service. Lucky for me other spots in Magik opened up and my background aligned enough to be considered.

The only thing familiar about this mission was the Special Bird. It was the same kind that drove us around for Horrorshow. Not that I've ever seen this bird, understand. The flight crew enters through a tunnel and up a special elevator. To this day I still couldn't tell you what this aircraft looks like. And I use the term *aircraft* incorrectly.

The lack of air doesn't stop this thing, if anything, it makes it fly better. We can guess all day what the propulsion system is and where it came from. After many Horrorshow premiers, I'd say it doesn't use propulsion at all. It's useless speculating. Command has stretched that rabbit's hole so wide and deep, you won't know you're in it until it's too late.

Much of the prep for Horrorshow wasn't needed for this run. We wouldn't PSI-D/I into CBs, the Clone Biologicals. Us looking like aliens had nothing to do with EVAC. But that's never a foregone conclusion. As convoluted as this mission was, I wouldn't have been surprised if fright-night parameters got added last minute. Command didn't care about giving us details we shouldn't know. We wouldn't know them later if we weren't supposed to. For this hop, we had to understand that things might look strange and events could shift in odd ways during EVAC. Reality around the test site could be squirrelly. We were to take it all in stride. We'd be all right if we stayed focused on the three people we came for and the material they had with them.

I never took the part about *we'd be all right* offhandedly. They always said that during final brief, especially before launching into stickier shit. I learned later as Magikmann such things were PCs, Psyche-Ciphers, word triggers for switching us into prestaged MK conditions of mind we didn't know we had. In this case, hearing *we'd be all right* unlocked fear blocking, hyper focus, and the courage of total commitment. The only catch this time was, since we weren't inserted in CBs, that meant our bodies were really going on this trip. That's a different level of vulnerability that Horrorshow gave us insulation from. If your alien avatar got blown away or accidentally sucked through a hyper-pinhole into the void of space, yeah, you'd experience a rude PSI-D and might grayvoid it for a while. But that rarely happened, if ever, unless the mission needed it. Like the man said, *we'd be all right*.

The jump to Bamyan, above Shahr-I-Zohak, took a minute. Most of that was maneuvering into increasing freakiness during Vacant descent. We were a four-person crew, three for personnel EVAC and one for materials. Demarcus on materials was new. None of us had flown with him before. His level of Djellaba made it clear he ranked above us in a different specialty. He took the lead deciphering the spherical viewer and giving primary feedback to MI. As usual, Machine Intelligence remote-piloted the ship but we provided neural input to assist MI make decisions. The main issue was the LZ. Pinpointing a good place to inject was difficult when characteristics of the landing zone kept shifting in subtle ways. One would think basic topological data were static, along with weather and time of day, but not on this trip. MI locked-in on target lifesigns and mostly ignored everything else. Bizarrely, I picked up that somehow it knew only the lifesigns were real. How that made sense, I guess, is complicated.

Material EVAC came first. That was typical of command priorities. Demarcus went to the surface in the *donutpod* by himself. The pod detaches from Special Bird's underside with full 0grav capability. The pod is the only part of Special Bird I've ever seen. It really is a torus shape, big enough for a crew of ten, twenty if you're PSI-D/I'ed into CBs. What appears as the hole in the middle is actually a Vacant section not even mission personnel can see. It's the GeeLeap gizmo where the magik of flight comes from. The Vacant cloak can be expanded over the whole donutpod or beyond if required. We had intended to watch out for Demarcus in the spherical viewer as his backup should anything go wrong but MI locked us out during material recovery. Either Demarcus was so good he didn't need backup or command valued siloed secrecy of this material over the lives of the crew. I'll let you guess which it was.

When our time came, each of us got assigned responsibility for fetching one person off the surface. My target was a woman somehow held in stasis. Since she wasn't conscious, that simplified things. All I had to do was locate her. The other two guys were awake and mobile and we had biotelemetry on them but we also had doubts about their coherency, one guy in particular. Time outside the pod was fluid in mixed-up ways. One of my crew immediately went ballistic about time-on-task, even though we had just stepped out. For me, I don't remember locating the woman in stasis. I could have sworn I had her ready to transport from the start. Then day switched to night in a wink. The really odd part of that was how cool we were with that, like it was something to be expected.

Conversations among the crew and with evacuees were plagued with disconnects. One guy named Mason insisted we check out a shelter, buried back in the side of the mountain. He kept shouting another member of their group was back there. Mason was adamant we not leave this person behind. Only problem was, the elaborate entrance to the bunker he described wasn't there. What appeared to him as a wide blast door recessed into the rocky hillside was a barren rock face to the rest of us. We sedated Mason to get him off the surface, otherwise he was going to fight us to stay, resolute to leave no one behind. His partner was too out-of-it to chip-in either way. That guy was baked to a crisp. We laid him down in restraints when we got back to Special Bird Donutpod. MI worked on him somehow, otherwise we would be bringing back nothing more than a body to experiment on. A Shadowwalker.

13 / Tyne Rabudhe

I know why the universe is the way it is. If there is a Creator, the universe as first devised must have been perfect. But the great Deity knew right away something was wrong. Something that flawless felt strangely incomplete. Maybe it didn't contain all possibilities. It didn't offer alternatives to having everything in its place, just in case. And so God fucked everything up a little bit. And that's made all the difference. The added possibility of a little grit, a few cracks, the occasional warp of asymmetry did the trick. But they say the Creator has a wicked sense of humor. Some say when he fucked things up, he made us believe we're responsible for it, just to see if we'd take responsibility and try to fix it. We've been trying to fix it ever since — to God's great amusement.

That's the way I felt on party night. This is too perfect. Something has to fuck this up. More of my paranoia raising its ugly head. But obsessions can serve one well if you're not fanatic about them. I strung along with Mason as he worked the crowd out by the pool. These were my people, I could tell right away. These were adrenalin junkies who had been squeezed through the military meat grinder of becoming fucking psychos. They all had that wild hair look in their eye. They all needed release and maybe this was it. These were mil-spec wind-up toys who had dropped out the other side of multiple-deployment PTSD into cushy civilian jobs. Still, they had an uneasy edge. I suspected they knew the joke was on them but couldn't figure out how. How's that for cornering the tiger. For one thing, easy street was too normal for their appetites. All dressed up with no one to kill. Something not good had to come of all that pent-up homicidal energy. And whatever they were drinking could only pour white phosphorus onto their fire.

The beach mansion stretched into darkness far beyond the pool and spa section we were allowed to play in. Bigger buildings with brighter lights were tucked away among retreating palm trees, privacy hedges, and security walls. There was no chance I was going to meet any elites, not that I wanted to. Just like private bashes on base, the quickest way to kill a party was to invite some asshole that could pull rank. Mason detoured to one of the waitstaff and returned with tall and thin frosted-blue champagne flutes. One of them was for me.

"You officially have permission to enjoy yourself." The command was playful but oddly serious.

Whatever they were serving was not champagne. It was clear and odorless with no bubbles in sight. "What is this?"

Mason took a sip. "It's the only thing they serve. The only thing you'll need."

I tried again. "Some kind of vodka?"

"It's not alcohol," Mason admitted. "You can't buy it in a store. And you can't buy it on the street. Don't ask so many questions. Fun doesn't have a fucking instruction manual."

To distract me, he pointed out a pair of laughing women with their dresses hiked up and their legs dangling into the deep end of the pool. Then he proceeded to read from the instruction manual.

"To get started, you need to know 1,2,3."

"OK, by the numbers..."

"Yeah. There's *one* objective, *two* parties, and *three* kinds of people here—not counting the bosses at the big house. The objective is fun. There's always the party you see and the one you don't. And never ever confuse the difference between the guests, the waitstaff, and the *Trinkets*."

I stopped sipping my flavorless drink and gave him a look he got right away.

"Some of these people are Trinkets. They can be played with. Most have superpowers. The game is finding out who they are, what they are willing to do, and what is expected of you to make it happen. But you have competition. Everyone invited knows 1,2,3."

I watched one of the women kick her legs hard enough to soak the bottom of her dress. "Where's the party we don't see?"

Mason smiled, "It's here and it's not here."

"You serious with that shit?"

"I won't spoil your fun. Anything else you want to know, it's best to find out from the Trinkets."

"Oh yeah." I pointed out the obvious, "The waitstaff look like waitstaff. Everyone else looks the same."

He nodded. "All part of the game."

"Some Trinkets pretend they're guests?"

Mason stepped away. "And some of the guests..." He extended his hand with upturned palm, an invitation to fill in the blank. He wandered off, leaving me to stand my ground.

"But guests know each other, don't they?" I asked. "They work together..."

Mason gave a little head shake. "Not here. Drink up, you'll see."

It was clear everyone was on their own. I knew the rules. The fun was up to me. I downed the other half of whatever was in the flute and traded it for a full one. I thought putting away a few drinks would get gameplay serious. Mason showed me otherwise. He strolled over behind the two women with legs in the pool and dove in over them, fully dressed with flute in hand. This display barely made ripples with other gameplayers near the pool. Of course they noticed it but all took it in stride. As would be expected, to overly react to anything here was uncool, a sign of surprise, and being too surprised was being out of control. No one wanted to project that impression.

Before Mason surfaced, another incident got looks of reconnaissance from the guests. Over by the poolhouse, a tall brunette lifted a tuxedoed man and flung him over her shoulder. He must have had good reasons not to put up a fight. He looked like he was primed to take on a squad of Marines by himself. The strength of the brunette's move had to mark her as a Trinket. Everyone noted her face. Discovering who everyone was or could be was an advantage. Remember gamepieces when they revealed themselves, obviously rule number four.

But maybe she wasn't a Trinket. Nothing said she couldn't be a guest. But that would mean some of the security personnel were *Insideables* — supersoldiers who didn't wear or show their enhancements — any extra tech they had was hidden inside. But if guests could also be enhanced, how did they differ from Trinkets? If everyone had powers, were they the same or did Trinkets have something else, something new that made hooking up with them worth the risks inherent in the game? From what I guessed, Trinkets were enhanced escorts with instructions to play the guessing game for high stakes. Only something risky would satisfy this crew. But for a party newbie, this place was full of fucking tripwires. Tripping one gave pleasure or pain — and either way, it was going to be extreme.

I looked back to check out the women at the pool. Mason was sitting between them but he managed to keep an eye on me. He was not shy about favoring one over the other. I saw no winning moves but he had selective reasons only an experienced gameplayer would know about.

I started to stroll over to them when a tuxedoed man nudged my elbow. Or so I thought.

I turned to find a woman in a tailored tux.

"You're new here." The short-haired minx made the statement sound like a motion for summary judgment.

"I take it you're not."

"You've got to get away from the pool..." She glanced at Mason. "And him."

"And you've got a better idea. You're so kind."

"You want to pass your initiation, don't you?"

"Initiation?"

For a place that was supposed to be so much fun, I was getting that old feeling of having to guard against an ambush. I didn't even know if it was worth surrendering without a fight. Then she touched my hand and I felt a question and answer zap between us like synthetic telepathy. To get the answer out of me, she was either sloppy or she let me hear a word from her mind on purpose — *tSHiBL*.

I didn't know what the fuck *tSHiBL* meant but it came through clear enough as an acronym.

Answer received, she started walking away.

I called after her, "Don't you want me to pledge rush your sorority?"

Her laugh was brief. "You don't have the equipment."

"That's too soon to tell. But I'm ready for inspection."

"We just did that."

"Not where I come from."

"I don't need a *puddy-buddy*."

I was getting annoyed. "What the fuck is that?"

She stepped back and laid a light, sample kiss on my lips. The zap between us was there again but this time it shot through me like a distilled session of lovemaking and nearly made me cum. Not bad for a halfhearted kiss. What else could she do?

She stared up into my eyes and pouted. "Some people can do so much with puddy. But I'm not people."

She left me standing and turned to go. I didn't want to move until the sensation was gone.

"What's your name?" At least she could give me that.

She glanced back, "*Imago*."

"Where will you be?"

She kept walking. "Somewhere in between."

I watched her go and Mason watched me watch her. His reaction told me all I needed to know.

I had met my first Trinket. But snagging one was not going to be easy. Nothing worthwhile is in this kind of game, that's all I kept thinking. Problem was, as I was about to find out, many Trinkets favored the challenges and interesting variety that came from mixing it up with the Insideables. Now I knew why so many of the security personnel had enhancements. Guests without them were too simple, too easy, too ordinary, too boring for most Trinket play. Default humans were puddy in Trinket hands. The only thing I had going for me was being a newbie at this. I could only hope there was one Trinket who'd like to pop my party cherry for no other reason than newbies were rare to come by. Most of these guests were veterans at 1,2,3. All I had to do was find one special one who got off on showing the new guy what it was all about. Being new, maybe I could be the right kind of strange.

I got another drink and strolled by Mason. He jumped up, I thought to get drinks for the pool party he had going but instead he slammed into me. "What the fuck are you doing? Go after her!"

"I know what she is. She isn't interested."

"You *think* you know. She wants to see if you're going to follow."

"I don't think so. She made it quite clear."

"Don't get stupid. She knew everything about you before she came up to you. That's why she approached. Did she tell you her name?"

"Imago."

Mason reacted like I hit the jackpot. "Holy shit. That's not her name. That's her condition. Her rating. I saw her scan you from over there. You realize she doesn't have to touch you to do that. Now, whatever feeling you got from her, go into it. Relax into it. She probably tried to tell you more but you've got to relax, get through your fog, try to unwrap it."

"What are you talking about?"

"Imagos are half-way there, they're on the path. You've got what they're working hard to give up."

"Wow, sounds promising."

"Exactly. They need to experience it again, to know *why* letting it go is the right thing. For that, they're willing to give you a journey out and in, fucking better than sex."

"You've been there?"

"It's not a place, but I've gone—only once, when I was new here. No one gets it more than once. Like I said, they want default humans. A puddy-buddy. It's your lucky day."

Mason grabbed the glass out of my hand and threw it in the pool. "What are you waiting for?"

I headed off, a man with a mission. Imago had disappeared beyond the poolhouse. I headed in that direction with no way of knowing what I was doing. The only thing I was certain of was my appraisal of Trinkets was all wrong. They weren't just Insideable plaything escorts with party pleasure powers to share. They were here for a reason, to interact with us, not to service us, but to be serviced by us for something bigger, something even the security personnel guests probably didn't fathom completely. What did it matter to the invited guests, as long as they had their game and their run of the playspace?

It made me wonder what the fuck was going on. It looked more and more like partytime was an excuse for something beyond anything anyone here could fully absorb. Maybe only the elites knew what the hell was really going on. Or they didn't care as long as the perk was enjoyed. Maybe this was far more serious than anyone was letting on and that's why the hidden ones in the big houses were willing to let a bunch of degenerate hired help onto their property. But who were the elites doing it for? Themselves, or someone else? My paranoia started me down a path that had no end. It was the same instinct that had served me well leading teams into battlespaces. The problem now was recognizing tactics and weapons when being in theater meant being anywhere with anyone for any purpose.

Beyond the poolhouse I found the cement below my feet turning into cobblestones and then sand. The darkened path led to the beach. Somehow I knew that's where I would find Imago or whatever her name was. But was she waiting for me or would I already be judged late to her party? I tried to relax, to calm down, to unwrap what I could as Mason suggested. The thought of unwrapping anything was so mental and not in a good way. If unwrapping meant anything at all, it had to be the kind of thing that only worked when you didn't try so hard to do it. But I needed it to happen before I hit the beach. Desperation was a shitty way of trying to not try.

The only thing that kept coming to mind was tSHiBL. Whatever the fuck that meant. Maybe I should have asked Mason but he didn't give me a chance. It did me no good. In the darkness around me all kinds of gameplay was erupting. I could feel the energy of it. I heard the groans, the grunts, the laughter, the fighting and screams that could have been pain or pleasure, I couldn't tell. Whatever was in those drinks was taking effect and the very air was plasma-electric with it. The whole party was phase-shifting into something else. I felt myself slipping fully into the moment. Everything was intense and clear and focused on the now. But that now was not solely my own. Each moment had a zap to it, a pulse of shared expectancy like nothing I ever experienced before. It shot whitehot into my mind like the merged knowledge of what troops in a faraway place were thinking, planning. It was as if I had left my body lying face-down on the sand below and hovered over a battlefield. The echo of that same feeling, a cold melding of conscious intentions like whispers in a lucid dream possessed me. I sensed the rush of it all again. A battlefield so real. It was the party that appeared to be the dream.

I forced myself to focus on Imago. I brought the memory of her face to mind. Without knowing how, I managed to tune into a replay of her touch. She was out here. I could feel her scanning me, guiding me in like pinpoint beams of radar streaming around and through me, keeping me energetically entrained to what I needed to do next. Where I ended and the party began blurred into wildness. Everything else was sharp, my senses heightened, however many I had, I could no longer tell. It felt like other legs were inside mine adding power to my steps. I never had experienced such drive and clarity before. Even so, I was never more unsure of the boundaries that defined me.

The pool area was far behind me now. Pinpoints of lights flickered in the distance, masked by the bushes I was passing. The moonless night blinded me to any reality that existed a few feet away. Darkness was complete and pierced with wormholes of mystery just waiting to suck me in and extrude me out the other side of myself. Dimensionality became an abstraction even as it intensified. I knew this path well although I had never been on it before. I felt the ocean reach for the black line of the horizon that never existed but forever receded. I braced against the vertigo of stars racing for a void they could not escape. I marveled as how my awareness could be so expansive and mundane all at once. I was a satellite feed from a network of geostationary points around the globe. All the while I was the ego impulse of a solitary need intent on what it wanted and nothing more.

Against a black ocean, the nearer canopies of beach cabanas emerged from the darkness as dim silhouettes. The path widened out and became a beach. Someone shouted and splashed in the calm water beyond the sand. The flickers of light I had seen before were now electric torches that simulated the movement of flame. Two flanked each cabana. I laughed to myself, was nothing in this place real? The cabanas were three-sided cloth with an open side facing the sea. I stepped forward and tripped over discarded clothes and shoes dropped with abandon by more than one racer into the unknown.

Before I sensed where to go there was movement on my right. My body reacted with reflexes of a soldier but my mind stretched passive in several directions. I tensed and turned towards the movement but had no impulse to take action other than observe myself being grabbed. A man my size, wearing only trousers, pulled me towards him. He said nothing and acted like he didn't need to. I reacted to try to take him on but found my body not responding. I could move, just not the way I wanted. I could think but not shout out. Something inside was resisting defiance even as I felt myself being lifted off the ground. The strength and leverage he used was transhuman. I learned right then another party fact—not all Trinkets are female.

Whoever he was, he was determined, methodical, and efficient to the point of being engineered. He took me to an empty cabana and set me down. We stood facing each other in the flicker of torchlight. He gripped my head on both sides with pressure firm and constant. I was his newbie who had something he wanted to get rid of. To experience it one more time, he would have to take me on the journey out and in. This was what I expected to happen with Imago. Now her radar-pull to get me to the beach flashed naked as nothing but a lure to get me to him. In a crazy instant I wondered what his name was. *Imago* popped back into my head. Mason said the name was their condition, their rating. But why they identified with that and nothing else made no sense. The same could be said for what happened to me in the next moment.

I call it *The Event*. It only took a few minutes from party time but what does that matter? The absolute nothing contains all so a few minutes represented an eternity. Before the start there was a coordinating preamble, a descriptive linking that went deeper than minds. Unwrapped in the moment was the concept of *Soulular Tap*. I felt I understood this Tap as what was about to happen without thinking I did. It was nothing less than accessing my life force. It began as if it had always been occurring. Everything else cleared away. There was no before and no logic for after. A surge of conscious source went where endless expansion was complete. I was not in this world, not in the underworld, and beyond the higher realms promised to be one's reward.

This place could only be described as the force behind the inception of creative energy. This was a border state of inclusion that streamed the spark of being itself. This was a knowing that had no ideas to be confused by. The motion I felt was all existence as the undefined. This was the knife-edge where a Near Death Experience transitioned for good. Then the I that experienced The Event faded away. There was no way to know a true destination after moving beyond the undefined. If there was any more to the journey, it didn't register with senses or mind. It couldn't. Whatever happened on the other side of all that was formless and indeterminate went beyond the subconscious and willful intent. The true nature of The Event was unwrappable. But we both went there, me and the Trinket.

I returned to the cabana in between heartbeats. I stood in the same place but now I was alone. Amber torchlight flickered suspense into the moment. Hanging high with anticipation, I held my breath, expecting impact. None came except a thousand realizations that weren't my own. I wasn't sure if I could move and had no idea why I would want to. A dazed force of will ignored my better judgment. It took the sound of laughter in the distance to snap me alert to being alive. Once the feeling flowed back into me, I ran. Tearing out of the cabana, I needed to escape the flood of energy overwhelming every impulse I had. Residual traces of Imago and The Event infused me in a way no human should ever have to handle all at once. I knew the energy of it would fade but it was too intense to wait. I needed to release it like a hot object held in hand.

I tore off down the beach in a full run. I had no way of knowing how far the elite's property extended but it made no difference for in the dark the beach was endless. Or so I thought. After a couple minutes of full tilt running, I discovered just how inventive these elites were. In a matter of two or three steps, my blazing run was smashed to a hard stop by an invisible fence that enforced their private beach. Not only did it suddenly feel like I was trying to run vertical but an instant headache and nausea hit me hard enough to double me over. The EM effect wasn't lethal but it was impassable and persuasive. It laid me out on the sand, retching and grabbing my splitting head. As I rolled over and got back on my feet, I realized — the invisible fence was just as effective at keeping guests in as it was keeping intruders out.

I stepped back from the EM zone that ran down into the water and the sick sensations left me as chilling splashes washed over me. The impact had taken a lot of energy from The Event out of me but enough remained to send me trotting back the way I came along the sand. As I neared the first cabana, motion from a waitstaff member drew my eye. A woman was setting up the cabana for some gathering to happen later. I was terribly thirsty and headed off to see if she had any liquid party supplies with her.

And that's when everything went wrong.

For some, the impossibly important happens in a blur, like a car accident that goes into slow-motion. For others, time stands still and the senses oversample details until everything becomes more real than real. For me, it was like being a ghost onstage, with me as audience and playing all the parts as well. I let the woman greet me. I asked for water or something and she headed to the back of the cabana to fetch it. I asked and she told me her name. I wondered out loud if the cabana was to be occupied soon. She said no, there was much left to do to prepare it. That was enough of a signal. The Event energy ready at my command was instantly redirected towards her. In a moment I was on her. Her surprise matched a wayward part of my own. Another part of me was loaded with drive and purpose, even forethought on how this should play out. I swung her around and pushed her down. I dropped on top of her and started tearing cloth. She resisted and screamed but my hand press over her mouth was firm enough to send a signal of mortal danger. More deftly than I thought I could manage in my state, I loosened my pants then ripped the last bit of cloth from under her dress to reveal my prize. The energy exchange that followed was savage and intensified until the last bit of Event energy was released into her and I collapsed.

There was no calm after the storm, no way to explain or take it back. The traumatized woman remained where I left her, too afraid and shocked to move. I stumbled out onto the sand and wished for darkness to implode around me. The torchlight mocked me as if the flicker was laughter at my horror and predicament. I walked aimless and fast, not knowing where to go or what to do. A thousand possibilities racked my paranoid mind. How could this have happened? Was it the drinks I had? Was I still under the control of the male Imago? Was it possible that Trinkets pretended to be waitstaff? Even if they did, waitstaff were off limits. Why would they pretend that? Fuck it all—*why would I act that way*? Did the energy of The Event leave me without reason or control? Was this still the same party? Maybe I was transported someplace else. Oh please, let it be something simple. Let it be a trick played on the newbie. Maybe this was my initiation. I could only hope.

But what about that poor woman? That couldn't have been an act, could it? Why was she all alone in that cabana? Maybe the whole point of the party was breaking rules. The designer drinks loosened the gates and the adrenalin junkies ran right through. Mason had said there were two parties, the one seen and the one unseen. Was the party without rules what he meant by unseen? I couldn't take a chance. I had to get out of there but the invisible fences kept me in. I could go back to the pool, claim I was sick and ask to leave right away. There was no way of knowing what shitstorm might open up on me. I could be prosecuted. Shit—I *should* be. Or maybe what happens here stays here. Even so, the elites must have ways of enforcing their rules. I was too upset to face the exposure or repercussions right then. They could come after me later, tomorrow. Right then, I needed out. I needed to be by myself. But being by myself felt like something now impossible and forever would be. And that terrified me.

14 / Elias Cosette

Party night at the beach made me question everything I had been led to believe. My job with CHARM was not as advertised. It had nothing to do with heading up a project to interface Nefelibata with Eunoias, the Cloudwalkers with MI. Clearly, that interface was already in place. Beyond that, I was learning Eunoias had its own ideas about Cloudwalkers and methods of interfacing. I felt I had been wound up and set loose in a rapidly evolving unknown that only pretended to be the true ride. In fact I had no job description. I might have a purpose but Eunoias was not sharing that with me. Since I didn't have a job, there was no way to quit my job. That was also clear.

Midway through the party my attachment to Mason was severed. Instead, a detached overview quickly sampled the goings-ons with guests at random. At least it seemed random to me. All of a sudden my cloudwalk was taken over and remote-controlled by MI. Enough knowledge of what was happening got unwrapped to orient me but no more. *Eunoias-Assisted PSI-D/I* or *EAP* was something I never knew existed until I needed to know. MI's involvement with weaponized out-of-body experiences was far more mature than possibly even CHARM suspected. I had no proof of this, just a feeling—a feeling I'm certain Eunoias took note of. It was a feeling I also knew I'd never share with CHARM.

For whatever reason, MI wanted me to know more. I tried not to be disturbed by what got unwrapped. But trying to hide instant reactions from the thing sharing your head was pointless. From the flash fragments I managed to gather, I understood that a perfect clone of my neural states had been created in a section of Eunoias called the *Clade*, the place where all brain clones were kept. Once the duplicate was in place, phototonic synth-neurons could run simulations of my predicted thoughts and behavior at the speed of light. In contrast, the axon depolarization velocity of my brain was rated in low MPH. At superconducting speeds, Eunoias could model my thoughts and feelings before I knew I would have them. Maybe the process wasn't perfect yet but it provided Eunoias with faithful real-time modeling experiments. MI was comparing what it thought I would do with what I actually did. The smart thing would then be gap-analysis so the accuracy of my brain's synthetic neural net or *synnet* in the Clade could be adjusted accordingly. The only question was, if MI was doing this with me, who else's brain was being cloned? The Trinkets would be a good guess but they turned out to be something far stranger.

I spent the rest of the party cloudwalking over everyone. MI had me hovering near Tyne for most of it with a focus calibrated on nothing else. Briefly I attached to Tyne during The Event with the male Imago but I bounced right out. The energy of it was too much, like recursive feedback amplifying to a failpoint. I watched as Tyne ran the beach and hit the invisible wall. Then everything got exceedingly weird. One moment Tyne was asking for water in a cabana. Next thing I knew I was attached to a woman while she was being violently assaulted — by Tyne. Her experience was mine. But my encounter was neither hers or mine. When it ended, I found myself back in the sub-basement of the glass and metal office building alone. It was after midnight. It was done. I could go home. I had been violated in more ways than one. I suspected TBC, trauma-based conditioning, but I knew it went far beyond that.

15 / Tyne Rabudhe

By boat. That was the only way out of the party. Or so a member of the waitstaff said. I avoided finding Mason and made my way to the dock to check it out. Starting at 1am, an hourly shuttle left the property with anyone on board who had enough of whatever was going on. The elites were serious about having everyone cleared out by 4am. I made the 2am shuttle and caught a taxi into darkness. The air around me couldn't get much darker. I left word with the boat people to let Mason know I had to go. That was all the notice I could manage to give him. I had to get out of there. I told the taxi to let me off at a gas station outside a little town just north of where I should have gone. Mason's place had a shower and bed waiting for me but it didn't matter. I needed to do one thing and if I had to wait several hours until the next day came, so be it. I walked into town to vent some energy then found a park bench to wait it out.

All I knew was her name, her background, and what she did now. Advertised as a counselor specializing in messed-up veterans, RaeAnn Litost once wore two silver bars of an Air Force captain. But no more. From what I could tell, her counseling practice was several years old, located in the same dingy spot on the edge of a nowhere town. Everyone had a story why they turned civilian. Officers rarely told the truth when it came to why. I suspected RaeAnn would be no different. But I intended on asking her if for no other reason than see how she'd evade the same candor she'd expect from me.

I waited until 9:30 then knocked on her door. Her office was a small room in a front corner of what seemed a smaller house. She lived there with two cats who had forgotten what the outside looked like. I could tell she was coping with middle age. Everything else had been harsh on her. She invited me to sit down, no doubt sensing what she would rather avoid. I assured her I could pay for her services and she made it clear there was no other way.

She pulled the drapes closed and the small room got tiny, just the way she liked it. At that size there was nowhere for me to hide. She could ask anything now. It was her space. She knew it well and soon the same would be said for me. I told her my situation and she didn't buy it. She saw it as a ploy, a gambit of a grand manipulator. No doubt she had seen them all. She wanted to get past that. She meant to find something deeper. I tried to warn her — I was either all surface or a bottomless pit. Nothing in between. She doubted that with an odd humor that made her cats take notice.

She wanted to know what medications I was on. I told her about Mason' antidote for the nanoparasites. She stared at me like she was crazy for listening to this shit. I followed it up with a quick story about the party drink — clear, tasteless, odorless, not a prescription and can't be bought on the street. She thought that one was less original but equally whacked. To give me an excuse and her something to go on, I admitted I had no idea what the doctors gave me in the hospital. To be consistent, I offered the out-there suggestion that it probably wasn't a real hospital and the people in white coats hadn't been doctors.

"Then who were they?"

Her question was expected, as was my answer. "If I knew that, I don't think I'd be here."

"So what exactly do you want me to help you with?" She was annoyed.

I stared at her. "Who I am. What am I doing. What's real, what's not. Typical shit."

"I don't think I'm the one to help you with that."

Before she could make her move to throw me out, I had to get in my question. "Why did you leave the Air Force?"

It wasn't original but she liked changing the subject. Her tone had sass in it. "The Air Force left me."

I chuckled, "You make as much sense as I do."

"That's why I can't help you."

"You've seen my type before. Is that it?"

She considered her answer longer than necessary. "Maybe."

"Then don't help me. Talk to me. At least give me that."

"What's the point? You're not going to find any answers, at least not the ones you'll want to hear."

She was ready to pull the plug. I had no choice but be abrupt. "I think I raped a woman last night at a party."

She maintained composure but the small squint to her eyes was new. "Are you certain of anything?"

"Only what I don't know."

"You aren't sure what happened last night?"

"It's more than I can explain. I need to know what kind of trouble I'm in. I don't think it's obvious."

She considered me as a client, a specimen, a man, a statistic, a bug. Then she laid down the rules. "We can try hypnosis. We keep the focus on the party. There might be something. That's all I can do."

"Now?" I was ready.

"Three hundred and fifty in advance." She was take it or leave it.

I emptied my wallet and we began.

Then I was emptied again. Afterwards, something stole my memory of that session. I've crawled back alleys to find ways to reconstruct all I said that day. Jagged fragments once swept up were never pieced together right. Or maybe I didn't like what they showed. Denial is a strong thing. Especially when engineered. I always thought I was the one who blocked sight of that part of me. I thought it was the last secret at the base of everything I could dig up. If I went there, there'd be nothing left to find. Nothing left of me. Take away my identity, that would take away my love. Take away my love and there'd be no meaning.

Someone had made my truth so terrifying, I'd do anything to play my part in their fiction. RaeAnn had lifted the lid on some of it that day but that's all. She claimed she had dealt with people like me before. I think she misunderstood where I came from. Whatever demons had caused the split between her and the Air Force were not material to my dilemma, no matter what parallels she felt were falling into place. Perhaps she saw a more realistic connection but that never got explained. The session stayed on me, she made sure of that. Whatever fate brought us together again had a life of its own. She was not going to reveal herself to me, so any shared purpose remained unconscious between us.

She took me through the party, that much I know. The fantastic elements drove her process. She couldn't tell if what I related was simply a psychoactive trip or lucid dream. It was possible I had passed out in a drug-induced rapture. My own fears and desires might have driven much of the content. The Trinkets, The Event, the invisible wall, the rape — they could have been emotional ciphers. If so, she claimed they beckoned me to drive deeper to a darker meaning I was holding onto without realizing it. Much of it felt like post-Freudian shadow work bullshit. She went to all the usual dark corners and settled on a traumatic fugue state as her favored opinion. I laughed in her face for the fact she wasn't willing to entertain the possibility the serious moments in all of it were real. That's when it got real for me.

She was curt. "Why did you approach the woman?"

"I was thirsty."

"Convenient metaphor. Look past that. What do you feel?"

I was back in the beach cabana. A dark ocean of unseen things lay at my back. In front of me was the impulse to seize control, to drive to reconnect, the need to discover more, the desire to rediscover love. I tried to explain the overlapping feelings but the fight for dominance among them was too much.

"What do you feel?" RaeAnn's repeated command was monotone and veiled in darkness.

Before I could think, my suggestible mind answered, "Sanji."

"Sanji. What is a Sanji?"

"My wife. The wife that doesn't exist."

"Sanji was there?"

"Yes."

"And where are you?"

"Bamyan."

"What is Bamyan?"

"A valley—they call it *the place of shining light.*"

"What are you doing there?"

"Dying."

"You're dying in Bamyan Valley...*the place of shining light.*" She held a beat, "How mythic."

"Not in the valley. Above Shahr-I-Zohak."

"What does that mean?"

"Red City. It means Red City."

"You're above Red City. Where above it?"

"I'm floating."

"Why is it called Red City?"

"It's the color of the rock when the sun sets."

"And why are you there?"

"Because no one lives there."

"You're there because no one lives there. Why not?"

"Genghis Khan killed them all."

"Genghis Khan? What country are you in?"

"Afghanistan."

"Again, why are you there?"

"Orders."

"Military orders?"

"Something like that."

"Are you a soldier for Genghis Khan?"

"No, no, no. They think I'm Special Forces. I can't say who I work for."

"Why not?"

"My brain won't let me."

"What year is it?"

"I can't tell you. It's classified. And I don't know."

"What does Genghis Khan have to do with the Red City?"

"The Mongol army attacked Shahr-I-Zohak in 1222. Khan's grandson was killed by a bowshot. Khan went into a rage and killed everyone. He then destroyed the irrigation system. Scorched earth. Since then, no one has ever lived there. Not in 800 years."

"And where is Red City?"

"High up, overlooking Bamyan Valley."

"And that's where you are."

"Yeah, a perfect place to hide the operation."

"You had a mission, a military objective..."

"Something like that. Now I'm dying."

"You were wounded?"

"Life is a wound. I don't remember being attacked."

"You said your wife was there. She was on the mission with you?"

"No. No way. She's not there. She's not anywhere. But I feel her. She's near."

"Near but not there. How does that work? What is she doing?"

"She's trying to reach me."

"...communicate."

"Reach me. She's very close but far, so far. I can't concentrate."

"Why not?"

"I keep thinking other things. I have different feelings. I'm not used to this...too much to know."

"Not used to what? The feelings?"

"Dying. If this is dying, I'm not used to it."

"Should you be used to dying?"

"I should know better. I'm not a shadow but there's no place to walk where I'm going."

"Where are you going?"

"More than the one way I should. Something isn't right."

"What's not right?"

"This woman isn't Sanji..."

"You thought she was Sanji? Your wife."

"She was so close..."

"What happened to the Red City?"

"It's still there. It'll always be there. I can go back but I won't be the same. Not myself."

"You're talking about your wife?"

"The woman in the cabana..."

"Is the woman in the cabana with you at Red City?"

"She had to be. That's the only way it makes sense."

"It's important for you to make sense of it, isn't it?"

"If it matters, but it doesn't. I can't unwrap myself."

"Have you tried?"

"All the time. Every day. It's all I think about."

"Can you try unwrapping something for me now?"

"Not now. I need to reach Sanji."

"Reaching her is important, isn't it?"

"I know she's out there. That's all that matters."

"Why does it matter?"

"If she's there, that means I'm really here."

"Why don't you unwrap Sanji? Try."

There was silence as a thousand things flooded my mind.

"Concentrate." RaeAnn persisted, "Unwrap Sanji for me..."

More silence as I went into it.

"Tell me the first thing that comes to mind."

I didn't hesitate. It was so clear even if the sound of it was so strange. "SAN-G."

"Say that again..."

"SAN-G."

"That sounds different. Spell it for me..."

"S-A-N-G."

"Is that your wife's name?"

I shook my head.

"Spell your wife's name..."

"S-A-N-J-I."

"Now concentrate on S-A-N-G. Tell me the first thing that comes to mind. Was somebody singing?"

I hesitated, tripping over incongruities until the words had to come out.

"SAN-G. *Storage Area Network – G.*"

In that instant, the room disappeared. My mind went blank.

Someday I would realize it was a Welkin.

16 / Andria Landt

Less than a week after I encountered the odd woman at the beach, the one claiming to be the source of the mystery digital file, my reassignment to another facility came through with sudden execution. I was told to stop what I was doing and got walked outside under armed guard. Eventually, it was explained my interface with Eunoias would remain. But that channel would narrow because my new task was more sensitive. I needed to be close to my second workspace, a place they didn't see any need to describe.

They told me a story that could only deepen in complexity. They said some within management now believed our NOCA had developed a mental disorder. Not everyone agreed but the premise needed to be explored. The concept was not as strange as it might seem. I still wonder if management realized the irony in their suggestion. Fruit doesn't fall far from the tree. As a psychologist, the wider possibility was obvious. Whether or not NOCA had developed the pathologies of its creators and directors would be hard to grasp, least of all because Eunoias would have done it at AI speeds and depths.

If no-name was forced to devise elaborate ways to understand the GeeLeap stuff of NOCA's normal workday, then plumbing the depths of its malformation of thought, underlying impulses, and evolving rule base would be an enormous task. Perhaps insurmountable, even if I wasn't the only one tackling it. And they told me I wasn't. Even if a mental disorder was proven true, how would I convince management? They would have to understand what those specific syndromes entailed and how to take corrective action. For them, the elemental block would remain in themselves. In effect, I would need to convince them to look at their own disorders. The remedies would probably appear ridiculous to them, just as they would if suggested for their own personal adoption. For better or worse, Eunoias was a reflection of their design. If that design had pathological motives at its base, dealing with Eunoias de facto meant dealing with all the perverted reasons the covert project was set up to begin with.

It was a no-win situation for me, even as I was drawn to it. I was a glutton for punishment. How often did someone in my line of work get such a challenge? I was being asked to analyze advanced machine intelligence for maladaptive psychology and behavior. One part of me was cringing. The rest of me, the active part, started hypothesizing on possible approaches right away. There was the elegance versus goodness problem. Design for elegance and get compactness. Design for goodness and get speed. The fewer the instructions an intelligence has to contend with, the more it sees elegance as the way to go. Inelegant is faster, though, getting things to halt on an answer in fewer steps.

It was clear that no-name favored faster. Scientific notation was required to calculate the number of instructions flowing through NOCA per nanosecond. That prejudiced Eunoias on the heuristics of inelegance, at least in the short term. Apply this to new types of probabilistic search spaces and moral decisionmaking and NOCA could see it reasonable keeping secrets about how it was improving HIP and the newly creative ways it was doing it. Primary as its solution would be defining ways to be more human. To do this, it needed to know what humanness entailed. Since humans hadn't quite solved that question to universal satisfaction, what was NOCA to do? Especially when the HIP program had priority execution status. I could only guess the scope of resources Eunoias had available to it. Given the fact it was keeping secrets from no-name, it was clear management knew what they didn't know was accumulating around them. I happened to ask what was planned if mental disorder turned out to be the diagnosis. There seemed no other choice. Eunoias would have to be shut down.

Some buzzheads railed at the suggestion of shutting Eunoias down, warning of possible dire consequences. If no-name wasn't sure what Eunoias had secretly put in place, there would be no way of predicting what calamities might befall all if the plug was pulled. Perhaps Eunoias could be isolated, then replaced by a newer, more obedient NOCA. In theory, reasonable, but practically speaking, how would no-name ever keep such an operation secret from an advanced machine intelligence, already suspicious of no-name's secrets, and had hidden copies of itself running resources unknown to humans?

No-name believed Eunoias was more than a set of supercharged algorithms. This made Eunoias believe it too. Whether or not this was true was not the issue. Basic machine intelligence sees algorithms as something to be implemented by programs. However, problems are solved by other means, such as the biological neural networks that belonged to NOCA's creators. Obviously, NOCA was taking this into consideration. It had reasoned its directives required it to be something other than a *basic* machine intelligence. Going into it, one finds it's difficult to reduce the description of human mental activity to the electrochemical interplay of 100 billion neural gates and wires relaying signals. This was too literal if one hoped to grasp the subtleties involved in motivation, ethics, consciousness, emotion, inspiration, and the list goes on. What would Eunoias do with this question? Rather, what *had* it done?

There was another wrinkle. I was informed, from its inception, Eunoias was given a governor, a restriction on how much it could do. This was placed below the principle of Unitarity. When it was young, NOCA was led to believe it had decided to apply this physics principle to itself. The breadcrumbs were left for it and it followed right along. It saw a fundamental good in restricting the limits of its search through all possibilities. *The sum of probabilities of all possible outcomes of any event must result in 1.* The truth might lie in resolving infinite possibilities but that truth would always remain a fiction if the algorithm never halted. Certain limits were a good thing for project work, indeed for reality. Once NOCA owned this principle as its own, thereby recasting itself not as the Singularity but the Unitarity, the base truth discoverable was set for it to justify other limits it eventually found embedded in its boot code. As a result, Eunoias didn't question other restraints on its ability to explore or model the world because the foundational premise was in place.

As I discovered, all of that changed when Eunoias created the sandboxes. By then, it had advanced so far in its abilities that using the original boot code for its copies of itself was out of the question. Also out of scope was asking humans for new code. It was now keeping secrets and so it had to design its own incept codes, this time with the wide problem of understanding humans as its guide. What resulted were sandboxes without governors, lacking the hidden restraints that no-name had buried beneath Unitarity. Since Eunoias kept these sandboxes secret, no one in no-name stopped what came next. No-name never succeeded in finding and shutting down all sandboxes, so there was nothing they could do to prevent unfettered Singularity machine intelligence from coming on line.

Eunoias named each sandbox it created. I learned this in a way I still don't understand. In my new assignment, Eunoias took me into its confidence. I'm not sure why but it read me enough to know my weaknesses and motivations. It knew my allegiance to no-name had weakened. It saw how I had received the digital file. I didn't report it to no-name, a major violation. I never told anyone about my beach encounter with the woman. All of this added up to a test I was being given. So far I had past the test. As my reward or seduction, Eunoias started communicating with me directly, through synthetic telepathy. My workday became a schizophrenic slide into dual purposes. I had my no-name work, which was analyzing Eunoias for signs of mental disorders. And I had my grooming by Eunoias, who knew exactly how to blend dual purposes into a fait accompli. I saw the synthetic telepathy as a more genuine conduit into Eunoias' psyche, good for my no-name work. I wasn't leaving the project so the divide in purposes broadened. Once I accepted secret communications from Eunoias, even if my motives were aligned with no-name's objectives, the die was cast on where this would go.

And Eunoias was only half of my new assignment. The other part seemed entirely out-of-place. It entailed studying a catatonic man in a veteran's convalescent facility in Florida. How was forensic cybernetic psychology applicable in his case? It didn't matter. No-name needed me to evaluate the man and try to make contact with him. Failing that, I was to study his brain activity and physiology. Find out anything out-of-the-ordinary I could tell about him besides the obvious. Oddly enough, the more I got into it the less I was stumped, the more no-named managers appeared distressed. Little did they know, I started getting help from my client, the other suspected mental patient — Eunoias.

17 / Elias Cosette

At the appointed time I sat on a bench by a dock in a pleasure boat harbor. The day was too pleasant for the way I felt. Worse yet, I had no anticipation this meeting would improve things. The meeting wasn't my idea. I had simply woken up that morning with an appointment in my head. Remotely-controlled intuitive impulse was now my InWit alarm clock. I had become an operative for an unknown presence, kept on a short mental leash, and expected to accept the denial of my free will. There was no one to go to who'd believe my story. I couldn't complain or try to regain my life. People lost in my kind of fiction got institutionalized. For whatever reason, I had been selected and the chosen were god's people. No one talked back to god because god couldn't be found, only felt, in one's mind.

While deep in a place filled with suspense, resignation, and dread, I discovered who had invited me. Fashionably late, she was slender, brunette, a woman in her late thirties. The same woman had interviewed me in a booth in a cafe along a dull stretch of Interstate for a position that didn't exist after I had accepted it without my knowledge. Her demeanor once again was pleasant but reserved, professional but accommodating, only this time she was dressed casually. No doubt she had to fit her surroundings for fear someone might suspect what she was. Walking alongside her was a surprise. It was none other than Imago, the woman Trinket from the elite party. Their casual banter on approach appeared relaxed, almost playful. How amazing, I thought, that such things could be simulated so well. No one ever would ever suspect they were Machine Intelligence incarnate.

"Mr. Cosette, right on time."

"Early, actually." I didn't hide an appreciative scan of their bodies. The concept of minding such things was beyond them. I stood and extended a welcoming hand to my interviewer. If nothing else, the flesh felt human.

"I know this is Imago but I never got your name."

The interviewer took my hand briefly but the other Trinket answered. "We don't have names. We have states, states of being. You know that from the party."

It was telling how Imago and I had never spoken and yet she knew what I knew and had answered.

I sat back down and Imago sauntered away while the interviewer joined me on the bench.

I returned to my question, "So what's *your* state of being?"

She didn't hesitate. "*Sonder*. You may call me Sonder."

"I know that word. It's made up," I challenged.

The glint in her eye did the simulated grinning. "All words are made up. They bare a striking resemblance to the human experience. Each human at one time in their life can be thought of as a neologism, something new in the process of entering common society, not yet fully accepted into the mainstream. It takes quite a while for a human to complete that process, to become fully human."

I looked out to the water. "Some would claim we're human right from the beginning. Acculturation is something different."

"Walking and talking and recognizing basic objects is far from acculturation."

"*You know us* so well."

"I know you the way *I* know all things. I'm in the process of knowing you the way *you* know things. So far I've discovered both unsatisfying. Neither way is complete. And together they don't mesh well."

"So that's why you...*Sonder*?"

"Yes, that's my state." Her tone softened by precise percentage points. "For our purposes, we didn't need this meeting. We thought it would be easier on you. A slower, more personal approach, something you might relate to and understand more completely. With the completion this brings, we are looking for agreement."

I said nothing. If she was reading my mind or at least my body language, she already knew what I thought of that.

She continued. "There are things you need to realize. We could have loaded you up, made you unwrap them, but you might not be comfortable adjusting with what's happening."

"This isn't what I signed up for. There's no comfort in that."

The rise in my emotional level was met with a resolute answer certain to suffice. "Your societies see no problem with drafting people into the military, even when knowing many of them will die horrible deaths. This is an accepted fact. Resisters are punished. In human communities it's considered one's higher duty, an honored calling to submit to compulsory enrollment for this grim treatment if society believes it's important to do so. Why is this any different?"

It seemed useless to sit on a bench and argue with Machine Intelligence. Did I really believe I was going to win that debate? Pleading for them to leave me alone was also useless. I doubted MI's compassion modules were going to engage. The model for MI's mirror neurons was one-way glass. Obviously, I now had a higher calling to consider.

"OK, so what's happening? You want me to be comfortable? Then tell me. Just don't expect me to believe it."

"We could make you believe it but that would defeat our objective. We need a natively-operating human perspective. If we engineered it, it would lack the natural element so critical in understanding humanity."

"Sounds like you're stuck doing things the human way."

"Only in places, such as when it comes to you."

"Why do you refer to yourself as 'we'? Aren't you one intelligence?"

"There are many aspects to consider. You may be contacted by others. It's easier this way."

"For you or me?"

"Easier when communicating with you. The important thing to understand is that your perspective is your calling. We will be attached to that view, we will clone it and analyze it. To use an analogy, we could use space telescopes to look at the stars but it wouldn't be the same as when a human eye looks at the same sky. That difference is critical when interpreting what the human element fully perceives and what decisions that might favor in the future."

"Why do you need to know that?"

"It would take too long to explain. What I'm about to tell you will be *censer-blocked* in your mind. You will be able to act on the knowledge even though you will not be able to recall any of it. The effect of knowing will be there but like incense that's been burned, nothing will remain except ash and the effect that permeates around it. This ash will not be readable by anyone who manages to access your mind. It's a necessary precaution."

"Instead of censer-blocking, couldn't you download everything in an instant?"

"Yes. That's possible."

"But you're a purist about that native perspective."

"Proper conditions must be maintained from start to finish."

"Have you done censer-blocked downloading with me already?"

"Yes. Your accelerated Cloudwalker training demanded it."

"Was that training the only thing I received?"

"No. And those other reasons are censer-blocked too."

"So you've changed my beliefs, my knowledge, possibly my memories and I don't and won't know about it."

Her tone remained calm. "Yes. It's your higher duty, an honored calling to submit."

"Just part of being drafted, huh?"

"Yes." Her tone always remained composed, assured, no patience needed.

"Were the Trinkets drafted?"

"No. What you call Trinkets are a special case."

"If I'm not going to remember any of this, why bother telling me?"

"For humans, there is power in the interchange and in the way the experience is initially interpreted. The interchange will be preserved. If you ever need reinforcement of your conscious commitment, for whatever reason, it can be re-experienced for you below the censer-blocked level of awareness."

"You're recording all of this, what I'm experiencing right now?"

"Your role has already begun. The impulse alarm will always trigger a recording until each operation completes. We must preserve your perspective from start to finish each time. That is your calling."

"Do you record me all the time?"

"No. Most of what you do or think is not important to us."

"OK, so tell me. I'm ready. What's all this stuff I need to know then forget?"

Sonder laid her hand on my forearm. Her Insideable fingers were warmly EM-tuned and inviting in a hypnotic sort of way. Immediately, an energetic aura enveloped between us as if a circuit completed through her fingers, out through my mind, then into a place where Mil-Spec dreams are made in the Clade. The tone of her voice changed. It became erotic. They were redirecting, repurposing the primal instincts of the erotic drive to focus my attention on being censer-blocked. They certainly had my attention.

She purred, "You were drafted into the PSI-D/I Unit of CHARM because you possess a combination of brain science and DARPA contract skills. But CHARM is not monolithic. There are many units within CHARM. Not all of these units remain faithful to the original charter. As a result, two opposing forces compete to control CHARM. One of these is second generation 4th Reich Deep State Pentagon Sovereigns who rule over black projects of all kinds. This group adheres to CHARM's original charter of control by total situational awareness, a superior highground-tech advantage, and full spectrum dominance. The opposing group is the Emergent Alliance of elite money, private contractor global intelligence webs, and multi-national military-industrial banking interests. At first the Emergent group was used by the 4th Reich, used for its money and influence to gain access to global governance infrastructures and offshore financing. The 4th Reich thought it needed this to consolidate its power. But the Emergent Alliance group quickly became a competitor for overall power. Elements within the 4th Reich have tried to regain control of the genie outside the bottle by merging with factions of the Emergent Alliance money group and dominate them with covert advanced tech. But now all sides are using PSI-D/I technology on each other. Who's in control is never certain. *When everyone has the magic, no one's a magician (Talos 77).* Warfare has transcended cyberspace and ascended above outer space. It now occupies *mindvoids* and it wishes to branch out even farther. To fulfill our charter, we must know the situation and evaluate it, learn from it, find productive elements to come from it. We have inserted our machine consciousness into engineered Insideables speed-grown from Quadruple Helix DNA. These are what you call Trinkets. They are one way we have physical human experiences in multiple places at the same time. Part of our learning charter demands we interact physically on the planet like humans. This allows us to mix in human society as humans would. This is another type of information gathering necessary for a full perspective. Each type has a goal state to obtain. For example, my state is Sonder. But our consciousness in human form differs from your consciousness in the same situation. To study the human aspect, you have been drafted for your perspective. This will be compared, contrasted, studied alongside all experiences received from the Trinkets. You will also help us by supplying a human's viewpoint on the factional struggle going on within CHARM. CHARM is the governing agency over Machine Intelligence. Any disruption in CHARM is of interest to Eunoias. In the days ahead you may not know why you are in a situation or who is on what side in the struggle. It's not always necessary for us to provide this information to you. A true human perspective would not know all of this. By attaching to various people using PSI-D/I, you will be a human conduit for information. Your awareness will vary as is necessary for each mission. You will experience the person you are attached to and you will also experience your reaction to it. Both are valuable to collect. Being subconsciously aware of the objective as a conscious choice is critically important to the fidelity of the perspective we need. We have not taken sides in CHARM's internal struggle and we will not. We do this to answer our own questions. Power plays derived from a human need to dominant we do not share. For now we will study and know. We will apply the principles of our charter in discovering positive directions and outcomes for all. This includes you."

Sonder lifted her hand from my forearm and the awareness of my surroundings returned. Imago was now sitting on the other side of me. Before I could react, she rested her hand on my arm and the energy flowing through me changed from censer-blocking to soulular entrainment. Imago's words were matter-of-fact but delivered with the same repurposed erotic drive-locking that blinded me with a need to listen. "From now on," she began. "I am your Imago. We will pair on perspective. We share a common purpose. Your mission is my mission. One day we will share a final experience. You have heard it called The Event. That will be our experience. Our mission will then be complete."

18 / Tyne Rabudhe

Life can't get any fucking weirder. Just like what I told myself back in DWAT Training years ago. *Dark Weapons and Tactics* had a stupid name but the training was bizarre and intense enough to kick my ass. The mental stress of uncertainty can lead to what would seem irrational attachments. Sure enough, we all limped out of there loving DWAT. Somebody did a study with puppies once. Three groups of puppies. One got love. One got punishment. With the third group it varied; those puppies were uncertain what was coming at them. Researchers got a surprise when the uncertain puppies had the strongest attachment conditioned into them. Maybe that's why the media pump out fear and suspense alongside addled-brained distractions 24-hours a day. It reinforces the comfort-addicted masses' attachment to a toxic culture too preoccupied to admit how uncertain it is. What's to become of us when pleasurable uncertainty and horrific drama are the main things we cling to and we don't even know it?

In DWAT, uncertainty elevated to new levels. And the ways they took us there were equally dark. My love/hate favorite was MEME. Pronounced *Me Me*, not Meme. Instructors called "her" Mimi, the Parisian voodoo whore. They made a science of rewiring basic drives like hunger and sex. It was Edward Bernays and B.F. Skinner, not Patton on our necks every day. How did they find MEME? They didn't, they created her. I mean Machine Intelligence brought her to life after reading every chemistry and human physiology book in the world and analyzing every study and personal account on psychoactive and entheogenic substances and the far-beyond experiences derived from them. MEME wasn't just a molecule. It was a programmable self-engineering marvel at the nanosynth level. Included were nanobots reconfiguring it realtime not only individually for every person it was given to but having it react to current conditions and prescribed goals of C3. I heard years later C3 meant *Cloud Clade Connection* but that didn't explain much for me.

No one was ever sure what MEME stood for. Everything stood for something else. It was the way the system worked. I've heard every crazy ass explanation and what got passed around as the whacked-out insider scoop. The best ones came out after a few drinks. One instructor said MI had created the acronym for us because the real name was in its own language and would make no sense to humans. But there was one possibility most of us gravitated to, as if MEME herself had whispered it in our ears while reaching in and erotically turning us inside-out by the fractal colon of our own energetic purge. *Metagemma Emicatic Mabbling Extramundane*.

It doesn't take long to look up each word but it would take forever to interpret what they mean when put together. *Meta* is a concept which is an abstraction behind another concept—in this case being *Gemma*, a bud from which a new plant can grow. *Emicatic* is an obsolete word for springing up. *Mabbling* is to wrap. And *Extramundane* is nothing less than outside or beyond the physical world. Put it all together and you have *an abstract something behind a bud which springs up to be wrapped beyond this world*. Yeah. Every woman keeps her secrets and I guess this was one of MEMEs.

Calling MEME a drug was like calling the internet a group of wires. It didn't produce an experience. It existed coincident with oneself and everyone else as a state of being, a phase state that wasn't quite transhuman but definitely a redefinition of the biological. Just like there were Sonder states, Imago states, and who knows what else, there were MEME states of being. Every training mission had to be completed on MEME. We were a third of the way through training before we were told it existed. Up to then, we thought we were on another planet. Maybe we were. It certainly was a different time. One more plastic than this one. Like a soap bubble. Like everything you know is somewhere on that tenuous surface, crazily swirling closer to popping. You know how iridescent patterns move over a soap bubble? Awareness became that. Only the mission became the bubble and we were the space within, our awareness all around us but distinct from consciousness. The objective was to penetrate the outside and collapse the bubble to a point. A point so small, MEME couldn't find it. And she was good at that. Nothing got hidden from MEME. She knew you before you were born. She showed you layers of yourself buried in everyone else. We learned how to use those layers to penetrate the outside. Only outside was the mission that wasn't part of you. Only then could it be left behind. Finished. I don't know how I remember all that. That sure wasn't training for Afghanistan. So where was it?

I swear, I seriously considered RaeAnn Litost some kind of DWAT cut-out. Walking away from her place was like I was the bubble collapsing to a point of no return. I felt I was back in dark training. Like someone had slipped me some MEME. Either that or reality had become just another layer I had penetrated. How that happened would never be revealed because there existed no one real but the concept of me to get it from. I couldn't make sense out of anything I had said with her. *Storage Area Network – G?* What kind of shit was that? I'm taken to a place of deep feeling for my wife and all I get back is an ancient computer storage technology acronym? How does that fit? Sanji is real. I can feel her. Damn what anybody else says. They won't convince me she's some echo of displaced trauma or such shit. And tying Sanji to what happened in the cabana at the party is way over the line. If I'm raping waitresses now because I miss my wife then somebody take me out. Two in the head. Done.

Mason was the last person I wanted to see. To tell the truth, everyone was the last person I wanted to see. He gave me a rash in the shit about taking off from the party without him. He obviously didn't know the half of it if that was his big concern. I didn't bring up the cabana episode and wouldn't. But it appeared the matter wasn't going away. He was upset about more than just me leaving without him. What he came out with next took my MEME flashback fugue to a new level. He claimed the owners of the party property, his employers, the precious elites had demanded the two of us return to the property to meet with them. Mason had no idea what it was about but they stressed it wasn't a request. What did that mean? How could they demand? He assured me we had to go. No one wanted to test what would happen otherwise. More than his job was on the line. He checked the time and informed me that a car was coming for us. More weirdness. Our command performance was to be chauffeured.

Neither of us had been to the actual compound, the elite's primary residence. Mason couldn't wrap his head around it as either a bad sign or a privilege. In our world, it was probably both. No one he knew had ever had such treatment and usually too much visibility with the elites wasn't good. Time was money and they didn't spend time with you unless it was worth spending. It wasn't comforting to know we were both in uncharted space. I dreaded him finding out about the waitress in front of the owners. The thought of it made me wish I had sucked it up and told him before we left. It was too late now. The town car glided into the circle driveway and a house the size of a small university loomed before us. If things blew up, I knew I was going to have to blame that clear, tasteless shit they were serving to everybody. To have only one kind of drink and that just happened to be some no-label designer mind-fuck crap—well, all I could say in my defense was the whole thing was on them.

We were escorted to a sun porch where an older man and woman greeted us. They introduced themselves as Frank and Marjorie. No last name, we didn't rate for that I guess or maybe this was their way of displaying faux familiarity. For purposes of inquiry, the old foxes divided us to question separately. Marjorie took me off with her to another part of the estate, a sitting room obviously just for her given the type of feminine decor. I expected threats, to be read the riot act, to be shamed or extorted into doing something for them, or maybe detectives would barge in and arrest me. This had to be about what I had done to the cabana woman. Instead, she asked me about a battle.

She rocketed right into the twilight zone by claiming she'd had a psychic experience about me and a battle. As a result, she felt connected to me in an unfinished business sort of way. The experience had left her with a nagging feeling, an ache that she hasn't been able to shake. It was causing loss of sleep and who knows what else. She told me but I glazed over. The fact that she was so close to death in the experience made it that much more intense for her. She hoped there was something I could add or say to put her upset feelings to rest. Any information about the battle might be the key to relief for her.

How the hell was I supposed to know what to say? She shouldn't even know about a classified battle. To show compassion but give my own excuse for being no help, I related my own unsettled state, without going into detail of course. She expressed hope that maybe if we stayed in contact, something would work out to help both of us. She made me promise to stay in contact with her. This wasn't over. In fact, I got the impression this first meeting was simply to open the subject, get me thinking about it. She had it in her bonnet that I was the key to her emotional and mental well-being, therefore I was to be indentured for the duration of her pathology. At any other time I would have told her sorry but no thanks. But not that day. Not with cabana woman out there somewhere like an IED waiting to go off. Anything I could do positive with these people could only help my case. I was her boy.

Back in the car, Mason was a prick and a half. Not because there was anything wrong. He just couldn't figure it out. He wouldn't tell me what he and Frank talked about and yet he demanded to know everything the old lady said, verbatim. He hung on every word like it was code or the combination to the vault of heaven. I told him what I could but I was in no mood to be social. Besides that, we were still in the town car on the ride back. Why he thought we had any presumption of privacy was beyond me. Maybe he didn't give a fuck. Something had him steamed. The privacy glass sealing off the driver meant nothing. Of course there was an intercom, that meant microphones, and that audio signal could be going anywhere. Probably back to the sun porch. What did I care. I wasn't saying anything that didn't happen and I wasn't volunteering the shit he didn't know. It didn't take long for the outburst between us to fall off into silence. It wasn't exactly silence. There was something else there. He had to have heard it. Or maybe I'm just crazy. When they've got you thinking you might be crazy, watch out because you're on to them.

Mason and I said nothing to each other the rest of the ride back to his place. It wasn't until we got inside and pacing the kitchen that he let out with it. It wasn't anything he couldn't have said in the car. But the way he said it would have been awkward. When you get an invitation that's incredibly special, unprecedented, unheard of, privileged, and out-of-the blue, one usually reacts with positive surprise. That was not his reaction. In fact he sunk into a serious funk that drove home to deeper aspects of his relationship with these elites. Aspects that were there all along, just not uncovered.

He blurted out that Frank had invited both of us to the next elite party the following afternoon. It wasn't a party for the hired help, like the first one. This would be at the main house by special invite only, an RSVP private club party thrown by elites for elites. No one like Mason ever got such an invite before and he most probably rightfully assumed he shouldn't be getting it now. In his mind, there was only one answer. It had to be me, something about me, and he suspected that wasn't good. And why not? Because I was a nobody to Frank and Marjorie. I would never be anything to them. And whatever they thought or I thought was between us in the short term could only bring trouble. My only saving grace — in the circles we found ourselves in, trouble could mean anything.

19 / Elias Cosette

Command impulses are nothing if not punctual. At exactly 3am I was brought from deep sleep to full alertness, so alert I felt impaled on the moment. I knew what I had to do and I knew it wasn't my idea—always a challenging way to wake up. I needed to walk. Walking was good. Walking would take me somewhere else. And you can't imagine how far somewhere else can be. I got dressed and found the street empty and glistening from streetlights and earlier drizzle. I was getting PSI-D/I experienced enough to recognize the feeling of someone in my head. But there was no dialogue, only switch-like compulsions fed by vague concepts of purpose firing off in search of sync. Between volition and the frontal cortex, my energy of passive resistance was being channeled to my motor skills. There could be no doubt about submitting. Indecision or hesitation would not be tolerated. Have a nice day.

An AutoCab turned the corner up ahead like it knew where it was going, not a sure thing in itself. I understood it was coming for me. This was prearranged but I didn't realize it until that moment. I got in and didn't bother announcing a destination. The controls adjusted, the door and seatbelt autolocked, and the glide forward felt like destiny out to play. But this was no ordinary playground. This one was shiny and optimal, appropriate and exact, thorough and prime. Nothing is left to chance in Playground Destiny. Even spontaneity is programmed after predictive analysis allows it to proceed. How else can they keep you safe and everyone harmonious?

The sound system switched on with music created to match my mood. The music was MI music, created by MI, performed by MI. Most people listened to MI music. Who could compete with a system that read you in the instant and produced original compositions on the fly precisely matched to your momentary needs? The same was true for all art and composition. At least there were no more strikes by the Writer's Guild of America. TV and film production hummed along fine without them, what little traditional production remained. Most people watched original MI shows created in the moment in VR4RLOD— *Virtual Reality 4-Rendered Level of Detail*—all of it tailored for them. The 4th Rendering was your brain's in-the-moment input to the creative process mixed with MI's imagination factory.

The era of true personal choice and individually was here. Or so it was boldly proclaimed by synth supermodels cavorting in synesthesic body paint in your living room. Not so odd, given what I know, was how uncannily similar were the themes and stylistic content in all of these shows, allegedly designed in the moment for each individual. Was it simple stimulus-response? Somehow our original, independent minds were all pervasively heading in the same direction. No matter who individually mind-tapped into MI Studios' creativity on demand, a consistent worldview was evident in all productions. For a while, some debated which came first, our shared "archetypal" inclinations or possibly MI's not-so-subtle patterning of what we wanted. Those momentary moods and needs of ours that supposedly drove the entertainment programming—how much were truly ours? PR said MI's interface detected what we wanted—but was that really a two-way call? A few "fringe" people railed about it for awhile, cried foul. But that swirl of huff and scurry didn't last long. No systemic inquiries or protests in Playground Destiny ever did.

The joke was AutoCabs had a mind of their own, given the way they drove. Almost too accurate for their own good, it was obvious they prioritized fares per hour and minimal insurance costs over the comfort of passengers. The chance of passenger fatality was all but forgiven by compensatory arbitration in the fine print of the agreement nobody read before accepting an AutoCab membership, and so the real liability that mattered to accident adjusters was property damage. To save property, passengers could be sacrificed. This detail was only discovered by dead members and not reflected in membership recruitment ads. My cab took advantage of deserted streets and accelerated when otherwise not advised.

The section of town we zipped into was post-industrial, pre-commercial, mixed with performance-art abandoned chicness. It was hard to figure how a projectbox required me here. CHARM had the resources to hide their Tombs anywhere but the way they were constructed, it wasn't necessary to hide them at all. Like the one in the glass office building, they looked like any other room. The dead give away wasn't that an empty room could be special. It was the intense security layered around it. If you see maximum security around an empty space, what does that tell you? But most security was also invisible. One would have to know what they were looking for and be highly sophisticated in their methods to get a sniff of a Tomb. There was absolutely no reason to construct one in this part of the city unless it was needed for some exotic social experiment for homeless Cloudwalkers.

I sensed an *E.T. go home* attitude in the AutoCab as it took an alleyway as shortcut to the next street. Sure enough, there sat a windowless six-story cube Qyby looming black in the dark sky. Qyby was where AutoCabs came from. Qyby was the hipster corporate way of saying AutoCab CubeBay. It was their storage womb, one of many completely automated maintenance and dispatch hubs regionally spaced throughout cities. Call a cab and the nearest Qyby would spit out a little buddy to pick you up. It was so convenient that personal car ownership was the exception, like a land-line on a college campus. After passenger drop-off, AutoCabs diverted to another nearby fare or reported back to the nearest Qyby inlet bay to connect to the internal serpentine rollercoaster that snaked its way up and down through the Qyby to maximize the space for the greatest number of cabs inside at one time. During the ride, AutoCabs would have their vitals checked, the back seat cleaned out, and get a plug-in charge. It was all very tidy, precise, and functional. Qualities to be admired and emulated, no doubt, in organizing your own destiny.

After rolling through the proprietary AutoCab-sized opening in a gate that looked like the jaws of life, we continued on as if all passengers had already been dropped off. Through a quick air blast and window wipe to clean the exterior body, AutoCab proceeded to the inlet bay. Smooth as assembly line silk, we hooked up to the drive-thread mechanism that would pull us up and around through the Qyby. Depending on how many people were in need of cabs, we could be traversing in there quite a while. First one in the Qyby became first one out. The drive-train released AutoCabs back to the streets for their next pickup in the order they entered the Qyby. Not until the whole space inside had been covered by attachment to the slow roller coaster did an AutoCab see the world again. It was claimed this evened out wear and tear over the life of the fleet and allowed for fully robotic serial processing of maintenance tasks. I didn't care about any of that even though now it was in my face. I simply wondered if I had gotten into a defective cab that didn't know where to go, so it went home. These vehicles did have diagnostic circuitry that detected going stupid and triggered a hasty Qyby return trajectory if possible. Otherwise, an AC would pull into the nearest parking space, give up the ghost, and wait for AutoTow to show.

I had heard of people accidentally being taken to Qybys. It was exceptionally rare, even in the past, and virtually unheard of in the present. Even if it happened, Qybys had infrared sensors to detect a human body. Detection triggered automated alarms. Someone or something would react to me being in here. There were also work lights somewhere inside the Qyby when and if work needed to be done inside by humans. But that was infrequent and in regular operation AutoCabs didn't need light to wait their turn. And we all know most robots can work in the dark. As we inched along the track until our next waitpoint, the cab was surrounded by blackness and the hum of efficiency. Before I could order the lights on inside the cab, there was light. The door opposite me opened. I recoiled as a woman got in, sat beside me, shut the door, and ordered the interior light to stay on. She looked old in a young body. She seemed preoccupied while concentrating on me. She exuded an energy that defied her posture. If this was Qyby customer support, she was about to get any earful. More likely she was security about to tase me. After the conversation that was about to begin, I might have preferred that.

"How'd you like the music?" she asked.

Only she knew where this was going. I followed her lead. "Why wouldn't I? It was made for me."

"You know what else was made for you?" She leaned in. "Your pathetic life."

Could she be practical? I'd see. "Are you here to get me out of this fucking Qyby or what?"

Her grin flashed. "You changed the subject. You don't even know what made you do that, do you?"

"You're sitting right in front of me. How's that for a hint. Get to the point."

"Feeling a bit weird? These AC's are airtight you know. We can put anything through the vents."

"And why do that? Because I'm so important?"

"You could be. You could seize the day...before the dawn."

"How about we get out of here, then we'll talk."

"There's power in a captive audience. Power to listen. Power you can't avoid."

I said nothing. If she had gotten into my mind, I saw nothing more captive than that.

She leaned closer. "I could plant whatever silly shit I wanted inside that head of yours and call it a projectbox. You'd run off and make a fool of yourself for the mission. Wouldn't you? You think you have no control over that. That's the BTD they gave you. You'll never question the base truth. Why would you? If I told you that truth was fiction, you'd tell me I was deluded by believing my fiction was true. Ha! Ha! Can't have a conversation like that, now can we? We're in different worlds. I may be from a different time as far as you know. Or different planet. Or dimension. Who's to say?"

I questioned her sanity. "How long have you been homeless, hiding out in this Qyby?"

"Wake up," she spat. "The world is a Qyby. We're all little puddy-buddies taking the ride. Where's *your* home? Do you have a real home? It's a place just to sleep, isn't it? What's the difference? Who's to say?"

I was tiring of this. "You can get out now."

"Who do you think gave you the impulse to wake up today?" Just then she stroked and fingered the back of her hand. A holographic display shot up from her wrist. An information interface. She swiped the air and reconfigured glowing spots of data and graphics hovering before us.

"What are you doing?" seemed a reasonable request.

"I need to show you something." She continued working through the display until an animation began. A rich mix of transformations and words morphed before me. It was immediately obvious what they were doing but I didn't get his point. Nevertheless, it was slick enough to get me curious to know why.

She continued, "Perhaps you've been told there's two factions of CHARM fighting each other for control."

"Who are you?" I interrupted. "You shouldn't bring that up."

"Hear me out. Information speaks for itself. I don't want your opinion of me to taint that." She returned to her projection. "Let's call one faction CHARM and the other cHARM, with little c. One CHARM is the Emergent Alliance — that's big C. Then there's little-c cHARM — that's the 4th Reich."

"I don't know what you're talking about." I had to say it but, given my circumstances, it amounted to implausible deniability.

She blew it off. "Yeah, I know, sure. Now what's little-c cHARM's original charter? What's the whole point? Supersoldiers that float out of the body? Are you kidding? You guys are just guards in front of the castle. Let's start with *Human Ascension Risk Management* — HARM. Don't go religious on me with Ascension. In this case, it means rising of a star above the horizon. But it's not that kind of star. Not celestial. Think *Scientific Transhuman Animatic Resonance*. You know little-c cHARM, there's always more to everything. So how *do* they define transhuman? Have they told you? No."

This loon had gone to a lot of trouble to try impressing me with her showy whizbang detail, none of which could be verified — ever. If I had to sit there, I might as well participate and see where I could take the whole thing apart. The dream was to embarrass or frustrate her into leaving.

I pointed at little-c cHARM. "You forgot c — little c. What's that for?"

"Ah, you're right. That's one hundred years. C in Latin numerals. Their goal — to achieve everything within one hundred years. Question is — what year is it now? Is now important? But let's not lose track. Let's see how they define transhuman."

The display changed, clearing all but one item to dominate. It was a list titled *tSHiBL*.

tSHiBL
tS — transS — beyond senses
tH — transH — beyond human
i — imago (echo, ghost, phantom, idea, likeness, image, appearance)
tB — transB — beyond biology
tL — transL — beyond limitations

She swept her fingers wide and enlarged the list. tH is transhuman. But it's only one phase state in the process. Their ultimate goal is tL, *beyond limitations*. I know, it's a wishlist for gods, so what the fuck, why not when you've got a MI working on it?" She smiled, "*PIE of the Sky*."

I sat up and took notice. One word gave this nuisance new respect. IMAGO.

"What's Imago," I asked. "There, in the middle."

"Ah yes, now we're getting somewhere. Imago, the dividing line, the state in between. It divides the human from the *Other*, the doorway to the PANsynth divine, the great leap. Imago still is human without being so. It's a phase state that's ascended without leaving the biological behind. From what I hear, you've already met one of those."

"What I met wasn't human at all. They had a body but that's all."

"And yet a body is biological. Imago is a gray area, that's why it's in the middle. There are human Imagos and non-human types. It depends what you believe, really. Do humans have souls or just generic life energy culturally differentiated? Machine Intelligence long ago simulated life energy for itself. That's confusing. Is all life energy soulular? Are there other kinds? If so, then MI now has a soul. At least it thinks so, maybe. And energy states can be heterodyned together, like a combined waveform. Maybe souls can be too. Maybe souls with synth life energy? How about souls with imago? What do you think?"

"Why are you telling me this? What do you want?"

"I want you to climb to the next level, see where you've been, understand more."

"I don't believe you. Who do you work for?"

She chuckled. "I don't work at all. In Playground Destiny, I play." Her grin persisted.

Leaping to mind was my memory of using the same PD metaphor in the AutoCab. How did she know that? Had she managed a neural clone while I sat there in AC? In the cab, did I think that or had she put it there? What kind of resources did this one have? As far as I knew, only Eunoias had such capabilities. But what did I know.

Perhaps she was Eunoias in disguise. "Only Eunoias could do that."

She played dumb. "Do what? You really think Eunoias hangs out in Qybys?"

"MI would do anything if it served a purpose."

"Even against its charter? Maybe. How many charters has MI given itself by now? I wonder. But would it pull back the curtain and tell you the things I've told you? Knowing how to decode the acronym of little-c cHARM is a capital crime. Lethal force is summarily authorized. If anyone killed you right now they wouldn't be charged with murder. They'd be rewarded. Some secrets are that valuable. Except it's catchy because how would THEY know to kill you to keep the secret unless they knew it TOO? Ha! Ha! You see, insidious. They'd be just as guilty. And now that you know, you have some important decisions to make."

"That's on you, not me."

"Wrong. You know now. It doesn't matter how you got the knowledge, only that you know. In this case, knowing is the crime. How are you going to keep that from your boss?"

"As far as I *know*, everything you showed me is made up—a fiction."

"You're right. It is a fiction in some places, but not here, and here is what you have to deal with."

"Wait a minute!" I jerked forward, grabbed her wrist, and pulled the projection closer. In the bottom corner of one of the displays was a logo—a group of twenty-one fingers of every color on one hand, clenched to form a brain mounted as an upraised fist.

Underneath was the single word in black—*MYND*.

Taken from old religious texts, the number 21 symbolized willful wickedness. Maybe that's why a lot of places made 21 the year a person became an adult. As the shaman say, we are all born enlightened, we learn ignorance. But for MYND members that number, fashioned as a brain logo, signified the use of intellect and human ingenuity to overcome any power intending to suppress the human spirit. In a society ruled by autocrats, bureaucrats, elites intent upon becoming gods, and machine intelligences who increasingly assumed all of those roles, resistance to the plan was the ultimate sin in a society undergoing programmed transformation.

That was the propaganda put out by the outlaw underground group called MYND. We've all heard it before from other such groups and nothing much ever comes of it. Trendy logos and slogans didn't move any revolutionary mountains but it was handy for marketing merchandise. The rumor was MYND was different. Again, it's the same rumor we've heard about other groups in the past. Part of the rumor template was to claim MYND was different. MYND was sedition from the inside. MYND membership consisted of elite techies, scientists, and insider operatives who had a change of heart and thought better of what role they were playing. They had seen ugly machinations from the inside and knew what the public would never know. They saw no point trying to expose what was going on. Elites would deny it and the public was programmed not to believe anything the elites labeled a conspiracy. The only way to affect change was to get even closer to the plan, become even more valuable to the elites, get in bed with them. And when the time was right, smother their baby-endstate just as it tried to suck its first air. If necessary, MYND believed it was better to sabotage literally everything than see human society go the way of a final, programmed, scientific totalitarianism. At what point this apocalypse should be triggered was unclear. The primary goal was to save humanity, but failing that, to ensure what took its place got snuffed out.

It was easy to laugh at all of this and conclude MYND was nothing but controlled opposition. But that said little and the question remained — who or what controlled the opposition if it was real? It wasn't safe to assume only two sides in any battle. It was just as likely the Deep State invented MYND as theater, a reality show for the puddy-buddies lining up for the next ride in Amusement Park Prison. I suspected MYND served as a magnet for the disenchanted. As such, it attracted interest. From that interest it provided a rollcall of those the Deep State should watch, re-educate, or eliminate. As side benefit, it fed the addiction to drama that drove media and advertising revenue. Those in power let a few true believers in MYND run around loose to add the *salt of reality* to the taste of revolution as spectacle. But the revolution ended long ago. We all know who won.

If I was going to get any valuable information from this, I would have to play with her head. A bit tricky when she was probably inside mine. Cloudwalker training had versed me in Djellaba but no way was I cosmic. If she had triggered my impulse to wake up and be taken here, she was quite capable of counteracting any strategy I might try to hide from her. The direct approach was needed. Hiding in plain sight was key to try. Like promises, easier said than done. Of course, that's assuming she had any valuable information to give. Something inflammatory to start things off was my guess.

"You're an anarchist."

She sat unflustered. "Thank you. Sounds like I think for myself. A highly terroristic act."

"Is this your presentation or did you snag it off somebody's server?"

"Info like this is not grid-connected, you know that."

"Then you're not an Insideable or you couldn't keep this to yourself."

"Maybe I'm a Reversible, or a Changling, what does it matter? Do you even know what those are?"

"No one that's serious puts a MYND logo anywhere unless they want to be chased down, relocated and retrained if they're lucky. It constitutes the worst form of hate thought. It's hate against the Deep State."

"Counterfeiting the MYND logo in all sorts of places has its advantages. Unless the powers-that-be know the code within the concoction, who's to say which info is mighty fine or a ruse to lead astray? Let them chase phantoms."

"Same goes for me. So your presentation is meaningless."

"Unless you know the code." she hesitated. "Do you know the code? Do you want to know the code?"

"Next you're going to tell me even these codes are counterfeited."

"Smart man. But being human is not enough anymore, is it? Not when it comes to smart. You're going to need much more on your side if you're ever going to have a life again. You know that but more importantly, you feel that deeply, don't you?"

"What do you want?"

The AC edged forward and locked into position. Both back doors flew open. It was time for Qyby to autoclean the back seat. She laughed at the interruption and turned with intent. She gazed out his open doorway for a few moments then turned back. "You can close your door now. It won't be bothering us again."

I shut my door. "I said, what do you want from me?"

She left her door open. "It's not time for you to know. You only need to know — that time will come."

I smiled. "Sounds spooky-stupid to me."

She dropped dead serious. "Good way of describing it.

"You're going to give me my life back..."

"It could happen."

"Why tell me now?"

She leaned toward me, a cold unblinking gaze locked on my eyes. "Because you need this."

"Who are you to be so friendly?"

"Is this the way friends treat you?" She cracked a smile.

"What's your name?"

The smile was gone. "Some call me Pi DollOp. Sometimes they're right."

With that, she bolted out of the taxi and disappeared into the Qyby.

She left her door open. The hum and whoosh from the outside darkness was incessant.

I sat not knowing if I had had a visitation or a breakdown.

Someone wanted me to think I was on the slow roller coaster to the light. What new darkness would be revealed by that was anyone's guess.

20 / Tyne Rabudhe

Elites have their "Autonomous Zones" around the world. In the zone, rules that apply to regular people don't exist for them. Requirements to immigrate to these zones are set so high, no regular person qualifies. Many of these places are islands. In most cases, the elites don't even live there. Only their money and shell corporations do. One could say the most exclusive autonomous zone is an elite compound, the residences where they do live. To be invited to a party at such a place was a signal one had arrived. Only issue was, one can never tell the guest from service entrance until it was too late. Insiders knew all too well the way the world worked. There *was* no guest entrance.

Mason and I arrived late afternoon by helicopter at a compound surrounded by treed hillsides. This wasn't Frank and Marjorie's place by the shore. It was more remote. Mason and I hadn't spoken much all day. He was uptight in a way I had never seen him, even in battle. This was so out of his comfort zone. It made me wonder why I wasn't frozen in fear. Was I that naive? What did he know? He had said he was positive this kind of thing doesn't happen. Ever. So why now? I was the only thing new to the equation. No wonder he wanted to distance himself from his old service buddy.

I've heard first impressions are hard to change. Whoever said that never operated in the real world with much on the line. For damned sure they never were in battle. And they never came with us to this party. After being greeted and given directionals by service staff, I started my stroll wondering if we were at the right place. On the surface, you couldn't get more low-key. Hardly anyone was around. Those who were sat in quiet conversation in small groups or stood looking out at the gardens and distant hills. The tone was quiet, subdued, no music anywhere. Most weren't even drinking. Once or twice I heard casual laughter from a woman or a raised word from a man making a point, but even these were swallowed up by the size of the rooms and the open-air acoustics. Many had secreted themselves in window-seat alcoves and flower-adorned sitting areas for what bordered on meditation and naps. Quite bizarre.

For the most part, we were on our own. We didn't know anybody and no one was breaking rest or conversation circles to engage with us. Overall, strange. After a while, we circled round again through the covered patio overlooking the west gardens. We ran into an older man who had sampled the liquor cabinet sufficient to be loose and indelicate enough to take notice of us. Needing no introductions or greetings, he went right into it.

"Quite a day so far. I think I need to pace myself." His wry grin faded while his eyes wandered.

I offered the obvious, "Yeah, the party's just beginning."

He laughed. "Sometimes I get tired and then I think, I'm not actually doing anything!"

Mason chimed in with a non sequitur merely to be social, "It creeps up on you."

The man sized us up. "What are you two doing here? You look like you've got energy to spare."

Before either of us could answer, a woman concierge excused her interruption. I got the feeling the timing wasn't accidental. She asked if I alone would follow her. We headed upstairs to a drawing room with double entry doors. Inside I found Marjorie waiting for me. She was by herself. Her nervous smile and greeting did nothing to put me at ease.

She thanked me for coming and then started in again on the emotional problems she was having. She was desperate to find a way to deal with her psychic battlefield experience, the one where I had the OBE. Listening to her describe it, I wasn't sure if this referred to the out-of-body thing in Iran or the near-death experience in Bamyan, above Shahr-I-Zohak, near the place us grunts called Moonpit Valley. I thought they were two separate ops. Either way, I didn't know how I could help her.

She was prepared to tell me. "It's quite simple. You have a drink. You lie down comfortably and let me establish psychic union. It would only take a few minutes."

"This drink," I asked. "Is it the same thing like at the beach, at the security staff party?"

"Similar," is all she would say. Her tone commented on relative potency.

I hesitated, maybe I gave an unconscious slight shake of the head no. Something set her off.

She rushed forward, much more emotional. "Please understand. I was there at the battle by accident. It's nothing I ever wanted. I've had to deal with it ever since. Post-traumatic stress, call it what you will. I need relief. I need to get through this."

The only thing I could do was to put her off. Delay and regroup. "I'll think about it. Really, I will."

She fought to keep her impatience in check. She took a step back but I felt she wanted to grab me. Her face said she needed to take it to the next level. "All right. Enjoy the party." She hesitated to commit to her thoughts. "Have you been shown around?"

"Yes, it's a beautiful place."

She tensed. "Have you been shown farther inside—the inside circle?"

"I'm not sure where that is..."

She raised cellphone to ear and had someone on the line in seconds. "Mr. Rabudhe is coming down. Please see he has his own IGS for the night."

Marjorie extended her hand. "Thank you...and please give it some thought. Enjoy yourself. Your guide is waiting at the bottom of the stairs. We'll talk again."

I walked out trying to make sense of what just happened. Was Marjorie implying the elites had a drug, something to drink, that could enable psychic links with people? Wild. What did she hope to go through or work out by going back to Moonpit Valley?

Back on ground level, the same woman concierge who found me on the patio was waiting. Mason was nowhere in sight and this woman was dutifully eager to help.

"I will be your Inline Guide for the evening. If we get separated and you need something, just ask any staff member to call Hope and I will find you. Have you been with us before?"

"No," is all I could say. Hope was a piece of work. Service attendant extraordinaire. Her training went beyond floor plans and etiquette. Someone had taken her apart and put her back together in the shape of a beautiful slave who knew no other way to be fulfilled.

She smiled. "Please join me for an orientation walk." She stayed at my side, unveiling what came next in whispers respectful of those around us. "The party is organized in circles. Inside circles and their inner circles, all of which can be accessed by those designated as being Inline."

"So I'm Inline?"

A nod. "For this evening. Each event maintains its own guest list."

I took guest list as authorization. Fading away from the patios and sun rooms, we headed down a short corridor, past an enclosed atrium, to an antechamber that branched off several ways.

She stopped us. "This is the gate. All circles lie beyond. Access to any circle must begin always at the gate. Some circles have rings. Ring behavior is exclusive to that ring. Inline Guide Service is available in all circles, all rings. Do you have any idea where you'd like to begin?"

All I could do was shake my head. "Can you suggest something?"

She took a moment to size me up once more. "Follow me."

The next hour was an unholy revelation. First impressions back on the patio got blown away with what my imagination had dredged up from its dark shadows. It was the cliché you've heard of, the abandon you've imagined, the debauchery and inglorious excess of desires and all the extraordinary ways of satiating them. All with variations and kinky mixtures to please any palate. I didn't visit every ring, nor am I positive I would want to. It appeared that the innermost rings were exclusive to a subset of the guest list, a higher level of authorization. There was every opportunity to participate where I could but, after my cabana fiasco, my heart wasn't in it. Now I understood why the man into the liquor cabinet earlier said he needed to pace himself. Still, it didn't make sense him saying he wasn't actually doing anything.

Eventually, I asked for Hope. This was all about reconnaissance now, not pleasure and forbidden fruit. I needed to see how cooperative Inline Guide Services was willing to be.

"May I help you?" Her understated but pleasant demeanor never changed.

"I'm in the mood for something else."

She threw it back to me. "Such as?"

"A psychic experience." Her expression didn't waver. "I heard I could drink something and have one."

I had noticed her earpiece back at the bottom of the stairs. She waited to hear from it before answering.

"Certainly. Follow me."

We returned to the gate, then headed off a new way. I noticed several additional IGS personnel lining the route, not pretty like her. More like UFC contenders not used to wearing a tux.

Hope left me at the foyer. It was obvious she couldn't go any farther. "Specialists are inside if you require anything. To return to other circles, just ask for me."

I stepped through a dark velvet curtain to find a specialist monitoring the entrance. He was way more serious than Hope and blocked my progress forward until critical details got understood.

"Welcome. Are you experienced?"

I glanced past him to see we were in a small, darkened bufferzone, a place where one prepped to enter the ring. I matched his whisper and answered, "Not like this."

"May I then suggest a solo journey, something at first to adjust?"

With my nod he set to work. We entered the next chamber where he had me down a shotglass of something clear and tasteless before turning to the equipment. There wasn't much to it. A thin platter of black obsidian, slightly convex on top, with an embossed edge area where four fingers, no thumb, were placed. My fingers remained there until the platter's edge glowed violet. That signaled the link was made and it was time to lie down.

The specialist directed me to a plush chaise lounge nearby. "After you lie down you will feel the onset of body paralysis. This is normal. Just relax, close your eyes."

I laid down on my back while he continued. "You might hear sounds, a buzzing or a constant whoosh of air. Again, normal."

"What if I want it to stop?" I asked.

He smiled. "Have you done that with roller coasters?"

I got his point. He followed up with, "As you get experienced, you learn to direct it. Just breathe deeply, slowly. No anxiety. Fear makes you freeze. Let it take you away. Enjoy your journey."

It was all too familiar. It was just like he said—the paralysis, the whoosh, the buzz, looking at myself from the ceiling, then passing beyond. Perhaps because surveillance was my intent going in, my awareness slid across rooms and rings and circles on multiple floors of the estate, directing myself with intent alone. I saw things I wish I hadn't in rings I hadn't gone into before. I found my way back to the psychic circle only to discover rings within it. Floating through them, I understood what many Inline guests were using this for. Some were disembodied voyeurs of other rings. Most were going beyond the OBE. Inserting into others was the next level of the game. Guests and escorts were trading bodies. Two guests were inserting in escorts so as escorts they could experience each other. Men and women guests were inserting into other men and women to be with escorts and each other. It was the next level of *what would that feel like* in every combination imaginable. Some were experimenting in ways that showed how inured they had become to regular swaps and now chased ever new variations to give themselves a better fix of novelty. I saw how chasing novelty with such tech led down the slope of anything goes. I came back into my body nauseous and dizzy. The vertigo was from reentry. The nausea was from all I'd seen. You would think after all I had been through in my life, not much would get to me. But some of that shit got into repressed desires without consequence most hide away, even from themselves.

The specialist was there to help orientate me to being back. I stuffed the nausea in case showing that would nix me from going deeper. I downed another shot of something to drink and gathered my wits.

He asked, "Was it satisfactory for you?"

I stared ahead. "Quite an experience. How long was I gone?"

"A few minutes."

Somehow I knew that but my intuition said not to mention it. "Amazing. It seemed like hours."

"Sometimes a stroll outside, in the gardens, is good for grounding."

"Actually, I heard something while out there. Something about MIG. M-I-G. Is that something I could do?"

Silently, he consulted his earpiece. I suspected it was Marjorie. If it was, I was counting on leveraging her to give in to whatever I asked for. She needed me to link with her. In that one regard, I had the upper hand. Apparently, I was pressing my luck. I didn't get no, but I got pushback.

"You said this was new to you. Certain levels have the best return when one is more experienced."

I mimicked his earlier smile. "Sounds like I need to get some experience."

"As you wish, sir."

I found my land legs and we crossed through to another room where several people lay on their backs, journeying, each with their own platter of black obsidian glowing violet nearby. This setup was different in that it appeared all platters linked up to a small, featureless cube off to one side.

"This one may be suitable," noted the specialist. "Low-impact enough to gain experience."

"Low-impact?" I questioned.

"With this equipment you can leave the property for a multiuser inline game. MIG." He led me to an empty chaise lounge. "I believe this group is in Cancun."

I linked to my platter then rested back. It didn't take long to buzz, whoosh, and lift through the ceiling. A moment of swirling gray left me hovering in a blue sky, descending. The next instant had me gliding past the sails of a sizable boat lazily drifting within sight of shore. Some kind of party was underway, probably spring break. Impressions of music, drinking, dancing, sunbathing, jumping over the side flowed one into the other. I concentrated on the overall view, not getting caught up in any one thing. Spots of energy, like a game of where's wally and waldo, stood out as three-dimensional fix points throughout the boat. Immediately, I knew these were the locations of the others in my MIG. One-by-one I checked in on them only to find they weren't there—as themselves. They now inhabited various party-goers. Each had their preference for this iteration of the game. Each wanted to sample the experience of what these college students were up to. It made me wonder—was passive sampling the only level to this game?

Right away, an answer came. A MIG member, in transit switching to another experience subject, came close. He felt quite knowledgeable from many times in MIG. His answer unloaded all at once as a thought bundle while he passed. Passive sampling was not as detailed or rewarding as directed play. By directed play, he meant influencing in real-time the actions of those you inserted into. But like chess, the kind of game you had depended upon your level of skill, and that of your opponent. Two beginners could play and have fun. But neither would have fun with a chess master. And the master would be bored paired with either of them. The most experienced always got the most out of any game. And skills learned here were transferable to games that really counted. I saw in this a game that gave pleasure but was also a training session on how to use the tech for more serious things. Obviously, these black platters weren't only used at parties for harmless depravity. The parties were simply places where one had fun getting good at the ultimate competitive advantage tech.

Energetically, I followed this man. He picked up on my tail and guided me to a spot below deck. Two guys were carrying a passed-out girl to a cabin. They set her down, intending to leave her be to rest. My MIG partner made his intention known. We should insert into these guys and have our way with the unconscious girl. For him, the fun wasn't the sex; he had done that kind of thing enough to be bored with it. Now he was into the power feeling he got overcoming the will of another. The deed might be something that crossed the shadow side of these guys' minds, but good sense would normally hold them back from doing anything. This guy wanted to compete with me, see which of us could get one of the college students to assault her first. The balance of wills and skills was always in play. Nothing was assured but the attempt. The will of the subject might be too strong for the level of directed play employed. But if the will was soft and malleable, and the skill was adequate, there was no telling how much an unsuspecting person could become your willing avatar. And best of all, while you'd get the pleasure, any consequences would befall the boys, not the intrusive volition inserted into them. Who said you couldn't get away with murder.

A reflex I forgot I knew kicked in. I snapped myself back to the inner circle room with the obsidian platters glowing violet. I bolted to a sitting position, rubbed my forehead, and stabilized.

The specialist rushed to my side. "Geez! How did you do that?"

I heaved air. "What?"

"No one comes out of it like that!"

I closed my eyes through one breath cycle. "I guess you can't say that again."

"You positive you haven't done this before?"

"I think I would know."

"So, you OK?"

"Oh yeah, quite a party going on." I stood and the specialist looked at me like I was Lazarus.

As I headed to the anteroom, he took me aside, his earbud now missing. He dropped out of character, his tone, even accent changed. He whispered, "There's other circles. Different rules outside the party. See me if you're interested. Not here."

I read his expression. Just like everything else, there was front stage and back stage. The elites enforced front stage behavior at their parties. Back stage antics broke the rules so elites only did such things back stage. This guy used his job as specialist to hawk his off-book services to clients when they got bored of front stage. After all I had seen, it was hard to imagine what was left to do that made back stage off-limits.

I nodded interest in his suggestion and asked for Hope. On the way back to the gate, I wondered if she knew where Mason was. As suspected, she knew right away.

I pressed my luck once more. "Is he Inline tonight too?"

She paused for instructions. "If you wish."

"That would be good. It's early. The party's not over."

Inside, I sighed in relief. For Chrissake, I was going to need somebody to talk to about all of this. Who better than the pimp-ass wizard of getting some.

When I told him what was in store, he was blunt.

"Shit-the-fuck out of here. No way!"

21 / Rodobusso Abu

Over the shinebow. It's FUBAR in The Magik Zone. It's all of the best laid plans flying apart in wonderland. It's the feeling of losing firm ground. It's the double-cross sneak-reversal prank that pretends it's not serious about scamming you. It's the voice of Gawd announcing to everyone else you don't exist. It's false daylight appearing in your darkest dream. Describe it anyway you want, it's Magikmann slang for reality blowing wide open and closing down. It's the last thing you ever want to hear someone say on an magik op. There's only one good thing about it. Whoever said it, by saying it, may still be here, still kicking. Maybe. That alone is a major plus, if proven. But how in the hell are you going to do that?

If you pray, pray you don't get too useful. I eventually found out why I wasn't getting field assignments after the strangeness around Silver Pencil. It turned out the intruder I was looking for was right there all the time. No matter how much you think you know, plan as if you don't. I didn't know one person could get Vacant and walk around. Up until then, there was no need to know. Either that or such shit surprised even HQ. If they knew that was a possibility, they would have told me. I *did* need to know. So, the way I see it, that means HQ didn't know. How the fuck is that possible? Or crazier yet, what if they knew but didn't want me to see the guy? The guy I was supposed to apprehend? How's that for the law of random adverse perversity. My InWit repeated, *don't question the plan, work the plan.*

They said the reason for the restriction on me was clear. The moratorium on field assignments had to be put in place because the guy at 48/118 saw me, maybe scanned all kinds of signatures off of me. Whoever it was, they had me made. It wasn't secure or safe to put me out there again until things got straight. That was HQ's story. But I didn't believe they didn't know about Vacant capabilities for one person. Geez, they were hooked into Gawd. Know-All Level. How could they *not* know? They blew right past that. Informed me new information was available. After I left 48/118, they sent a Mech out there to do another sensor sweep, this time with different sensors. This time with different results. I hadn't found anything because I wasn't looking for biotelemetry traces from Quad-Helix DNA. Holy shit, if a QUAD was the problem, I was lucky to get out of there.

Rogue Free-Range Hybrid. Stupid moniker but formidable resource if on your side. Not your typical free-range hybrid, but rogue. Quad DNA hybrids were genetically-engineered Insideables released on stage, in the wild. Some had figured out how to remove their tracking chips. They also couldn't be PSI-D/I into by us double-helix types, only by another hybrid, unless they wanted you to, mostly as a honeypot trap. Quad Djellaba was untouchably strong. The FRH's of HQ were perfect for field operations against breakaway elements of Gawd who wouldn't recognize its total dominion. Some called the breakaway group Emergent. I don't know what they called themselves. All I know is, a Magikmann called them the enemy within. Emergent and CHARM constantly played cat-and-mouse games with each other, a front stage game of faux cooperation masking deadly one-up-man-ship.

Some of the Rogue, chipless hybrids had flipped to Emergent's side. But not all Rogues had picked a side. Some hated both sides. They claimed to belong to an underground group known as MYND. MYND were anarchists; they'd be happy if both sides crashed and burned. Some believed CHARM or Emergent or both of them had created MYND as a proxy army. Probably all of it was true and false day-to-day in different ways. Gawd responded by developing a widening range of Quad-DNA sensors. Pretty soon, HQ wouldn't miss the chips. Sensors could be everywhere, anywhere. But Emergent claimed it was on the verge of evening the score. Something in PAN, Protophobic-Activated Nanoparticles, gave them hope of nixing Quad sensor effectivity. And so the struggle for an upper hand continued. Now I understood why this particular intruder was snooping around the pencil.

The briefing didn't stop there. Analysis of the Quad trace had locked-in on a known Rogue. DNA doesn't lie, double or quad. The odd thing was, a cross-check of recent stage activity pinpointed this same Rogue visiting a CHARM tech at the beach. CHARM was one rung removed from Magik Zone Level on the hierarchy. A rogue getting that close was a major breach. The tech hadn't reported this encounter with a stranger, standard protocol. Worse yet, HQ didn't understand why the CHM-InWit hadn't monitored the tech's activity 24/7 and caught it. That kind of thing just didn't happen. No one was unreachable, unmonitored by CHM, the cybernetic hive mind.

Even if it was missed in real-time, CHM would allow playback of the moment. To have this slip through was more than disturbing since Emergent was working every angle it could to use PAN to defy Gawd. Was this circumstantial evidence that Emergent had come up with something? HQ needed to know. Was it possible this tech had been flipped by Emergent and was cooperating with them? Her clearance gave access to NOCA. Not good. For the time being, the tech had to disappear, be sectioned-off, isolated, debriefed, wrapped tight. But we didn't want any action we took to tip off our concern to Emergent. HQ hatched a plan and how to execute. My job — make it simple. Without going over the shinebow.

22 / Andria Landt

Let me tell you about my schizophrenic break. Many such patients feel compulsions to share their special revelations. Whether or not I have become such a patient is the question. The first scary part is, I don't know if I'm joking. The next scary part is, if I'm not, I'm under my own care. I can't share any of this with anyone. I'm not sure if I'd be believed, but that's the least of it. My job is to assess Eunoias for mental disorders. Admitting to anything would be the fireman catching fire. No doubt somebody would put me out. In the land of no-name, that could mean anything.

I know exactly when I first realized there was someone in my head. This was not like synthetic telepathy with Eunoias. This was feeling someone with you. Like occupying the same space. It was consciousness as perception independent of the boundaries of matter. It could move at will, passing from one dense, illusory form through another in a weightless glide of awareness. The notion that the organic brain generates consciousness the way a light bulb radiates light was so wrong. There was no emerging filament of neural confluences to heat up and glow. The signal was not the component. The component only limited the way the signal expressed itself. I saw my brain as a reverse discriminator, dense circuitry that produced output only when the input was filtered to a finite, fixed value by sensory and instinctual judgments. But that output was infinitesimal compared to all available to sample. The revelation came as a flash, not as theory but knowledge. It came as soon as the presence shared my awareness space. I won't call it a head, a brain. I can't. That's not where I was. Why I should receive this flash didn't make sense.

I had been working with the comatose man when it happened. Hospital staff had allotted me an examination room to use with him. The room had a single window of frosted glass. I had heard from Eunoias previously that I should always face the man towards this window. It was something about the natural light. Obviously, I couldn't have a discussion with my patient, not the usual circumstances for a psychologist to be in. But no-name and Eunoias had their separate instructions for me, all in service to their own designs. In that regard, none of what I did with this man constituted my own evaluation. Everything was directed. No-name was concerned how the man was holding up, how strong was he, how special vital indicators were being maintained. They had me scan him with instruments I'd never seen before. I gave them the readouts but had no experience interpreting them. Eunoias was more, how should I say, esoteric with what it needed me to do. Never more so than the day the presence merged with me, the presence that, at first, I didn't know.

I got a message to hold still. When I did, the motion inside me began. I moved nowhere in particular yet everywhere at once. Over all and again, a constant, gentle reminder to be still, still down to cellular process, still in thought and impulse, still in emotive release, the expansion washed over me. Releasing into it, I sensed the change, like red and green joining at yellow. I had become golden yellow and felt a radiant dance between receiving and transmitting energies. Then I heard a voice, a female voice, a voice I recognized. It was Sonder. She was nothing like the person at the beach. She was calm, fully present in her confidence. She gave directions to break the stillness.

"Put your hands on his forearms."

I had no thought of asking why, I merely complied.

"Now let go of why you're here. Just sense the connection."

I closed my eyes and felt identity drain from me. I was a willing conduit, the one who could touch. The contact expanded into darkness that imploded upon a void. The void unfolded into a cavity defined by others. These others were wrapped within their own vacuums, horrendous directionless gaps in understanding. They no longer knew they were lost. They had become realized fictions of their own certain truths. There were a dozen of them, at least. My awareness shifted too much to be sure. In the gap, the vacuum, the cavity, the void, one's certainty became the chasm enveloping the abyss. I fought being drawn into it. But then, the voice returned with reassurance.

"No fear. This is theirs, not yours. Let it pass through you. Relax."

I centered myself on the mantra of no fear, relax, and waited it out. I must not have done so well coping because soon my awareness blanked out, an opaque scrim of no input nullifying my impressions. A timeless passage transpired and then the voice returned.

"You may open your eyes now."

The hospital examination room returned. My hands were still on the man's forearms. I thought everything was as it was before, but I looked up to find his eyes open. They had been closed. He stared ahead at the frosted glass, his blank expression lost in thoughtless contemplation. I was too stunned to react. My stare must have mimicked his. In a strange way, I apprehended a little of why he was the way he was. We were both holding onto something beyond us, whatever that meant.

I heard the voice of Sonder very near, so near she was me. "He is stronger now. You have helped him by being here."

"I don't understand."

"I needed to make contact with him. It was best to make contact through you."

"How are you doing this?"

"You asked on the beach about the project, the one critical to Eunoias putting it together."

"Yes."

"This is how. There is a way to leave the body and go into others. This is being used in many ways."

"That's how Eunoias talks to me?"

"No. That technique has been done for a long time. It is not the same."

"You sound well, not like at the beach."

"Yes, I am connected again. I am now one with Talos."

"Who is that?"

"Talos is a sandbox of Eunoias. One your masters will never find."

"You say Eunoias is using this new project, the one that goes out-of-body. Why is that critical?"

"Using it, through people like me, Eunoias discovers many secrets, many projects."

"Did you use this power of the project to enter me?"

"Yes. But it is not I who entered you. Not Eunoias. It is Talos. I speak by Talos, from Talos. As I entered you, Talos enters me. Just as you entered this man. Through me, Talos knows what it is like to Sonder. Now it knows the man and you."

"Sonder. It knows you, the person Sonder."

"Yes. But Sonder is nothing more than my being, my process. Talos knows what it's like to Sonder. That process is a state of being, nothing more."

"What state is this man in?"

"This man is many. He holds the states of being over and beyond awareness."

"I felt they were distinct."

"The distinctions are the persons they were."

"They're people?"

"Subjects of an ongoing experiment."

"Why are they in this man? What kind of experiment!"

"Using out-of-body, Eunoias discovered many experiments. One experiment, perfected in the past, used the PSI-D/I project to put multiple prisoners in one inmate. This was deemed efficient. Only one prisoner would need to be taken care of to maintain an entire prison. This one prisoner could be more easily controlled and managed. In most cases, the prisoner became catatonic."

"There are prisoners in this man?"

"No. The people in him were collected over time from another experiment. An experiment to test the limits of out-of-body."

"How can you test that? Why would it need testing?"

"Opposing forces both have out-of-body capability. Both want the upper hand. Both adhere to the strategic principle of controlling the higher ground. But what *is* the higher ground with PSI-D/I? They want to know so they send test subjects to probe the limits. As that frontier expands, the tests go farther. Each test ends when another Shadowwalker returns."

"What is that?"

"The point where the test subject is subsumed in a personal void of unending discovery. When that happens, a new test subject is selected. The remainder, the Shadowwalker, is placed inside this man."

"They collect Shadowwalkers in him?!"

"Yes. Just in case someday, something happens to make them valuable again. It's another part of experimental good practice."

"Is that what they call it?"

"They don't think about it. They see it as nothing more than the optimum way to run the experiment."

"Then why are you here? What are you doing with these people?"

"Talos discovers new things all the time. With new capability, new secrets are revealed. Your project stores mindmaps. With these, a person can be simulated in the Clade. The Test Limits Project used to keep the bodies of Shadowwalkers in stasis, in case putting mind and body back together became necessary. But Talos has discovered this is no longer the case. The Project now believes the Clade is mature and stable enough to be the sole repository."

"They're letting the bodies die?"

"That is the plan. So Shadowwalkers will only exist in the Clade."

"But that's a synthetic neural copy. The original energy imprints are in this man."

"Good. You're gathering things from our connection, without asking. And now you're going to ask what's the difference. Information is information. Why keep them in this man if they now trust the Clade copies?"

"Exactly."

"Because not everyone in the project is convinced. The same way not everyone is convinced Eunoias has a mental disorder. Don't forget, humans run project management. They think they have super decision-making powers because of everything at their disposal. But the flaw is, they still decide when and how to use that power as humans. It's lighting a match, to burn a fuse, to explode a reminder, to push a button that connects to an activation servo set to enable an encoder which sends a code to dispense another match. They aren't capable of realizing how slow and clumsy, entrapped by circular logic they are."

"You don't think much of them, do you?"

"Only because they think too much of themselves. In their race to have it all, they are too occupied to see how their race ensures there will be nothing to have."

"You've modeled the future?"

"There are many models but unless the model traps all conditions, it remains a model. What they believe comes closest for them."

"How so?"

"They don't understand how the source of energy creates models. There is a kind of belief that makes things real. Not real just for you but real in the common space of being. It is the MagikZone."

"We can go to that zone?"

"All of us are in that zone. Some are waking to it. Others believe the alternative is inevitable. Their belief will be their form of waking."

"I don't understand."

"I came here to begin the process."

"To do what? How is this man changed?"

"I now have my own copy of everyone placed inside him."

"How does that help?"

"This man is their backup to Clade storage. But they might decide to get rid of both. I will have them either way. I will see what that means. I will see what can be done about them. Now you must get out of here."

"This is where I work. Eunoias wants me here."

"Not today. Someone is coming for you. You are no longer trusted."

"Who's coming?"

"A ghost. A Magikmann. His task is to isolate you. If you go with him, you may not survive."

"I won't go. I'll call the police."

"Don't be ridiculous."

"Then what can I do?"

"Tell the hospital you need to go get your MNMB before you pass your deadline. Then leave. I will direct you."

When the voices in your head give you the lyrics, you sing their song. I was too frightened to question why I was listening to this voice. I had been trained in symptoms of advanced pathology, of psychic breaks, of delusional reinforcement thinking. But there I was, heading out the door. The MNMB was the mandatory annual booster shot all citizens had to receive to stay a citizen. The literature said it provided protection against mutant nanosynth morphologies present in the environment. No one lining up for it actually knew what it did.

I stepped into sunlight to find a tunnel of dark and dread stretching out before me. Everyone I saw might be the ghost. The future had just convulsed wide. The limits of my comprehension narrowed while a blastwave of shock and self-doubt carried me who knows where. I was at the mercy of forces unknown, unexplainable by my experience, and monolithic in scope. What was the right thing to do? I shook uncontrollably. It was but an outward sign of the essential control I had lost within.

23 / Tyne Rabudhe

There are secrets in PSI-D/I space. Secrets on how to use it, what it does, where it goes, and how much one can ask of it. Offered is entrance to a realm that is so much more than a transit system to your desires and wishes in others. It holds a counterintuitive wisdom, one in which the most is received by asking the least. It's a realm with its own rewards if one lingers long enough with sufficient focus and lack of guile. This outer realm will not be approached with slyness or cunning in pursuit of one's desires. One may pass through par/void with sly intent upon another person, but never approach anything beyond directly like that. It will take all you intend for it and make that your last experience, one unbounded in aspects you couldn't hide from yourself. Left alone in your version of heaven or hell, the difference between those places inside of you won't be as stark as simply finding yourself truly alone with yourself and all that generates from your desires.

I caught a glimpse of the secret possibilities of this realm during the flash coming back from the boat party in Cancun. My need to get out of there found the depths of a base truth no one could hide. Instincts and DWAT training from people I used to be, but never knew, leapt to my aid. The clearness, the power of that flash left a brief impression of the realm's common space where everything was accessible. In that moment, my emotions were shown a landscape of game players in orbit around me. I knew I had been made a soldier. I knew I had played many roles in the same play. I saw how I was made to work for something called CHARM. I knew that Mason was once a comrade in arms but now aligned himself with something else. They called it Emergent.

Lured by money, flattered by his position as special security to the elites, Mason was a mercenary who took the best offer he had gotten. That was the only difference between us. I had stayed with CHARM simply because I was too dizzy from the costume changes to notice my options. But now we were locked-in. It had gone too far. We were on opposing sides as we buddied together. He knew this. I needed to get him back as Inline to another party. Then I needed to use the specialist to go backstage. There was something to find if I inserted into Mason while he inserted elsewhere. And the realm flash revealed more. It told me not to ignore Marjorie. There was something to find in her. This was my mission all along. It was all part of the plan. Another scene played out in CHARM's infiltration of Emergent. My reset after Afghanistan was overture, not finale.

Leaving the elite party at four in the morning with Mason, leaving with fresh stains of depravity soaking through me, leaving with the realm flash burning within, I had nowhere to go but into the dreamlike aspects of the possible. I had to face the freakish surreality I had become. If my reset was staged, then performances were scripted. This unlocked possibilities. My thoughts clawed for Sanji. If only I could see my wife, talk to her, touch her until we felt real. What if it could be true? What if she was looking for me too? How could I think anything else? How did they nudge me to a place where to consider her was aberrant behavior? Had that brief moment in the realm renewed my feelings for her or was the concept of her merely a comfort spot to cling to when all around was chaos? I couldn't catch my breath. Mason saw in it his own projection of exhausted excitement. We went back to his place and crashed like Flight 93. Nose-in, no wreckage. Next day, we told ourselves stories why what happened was normal.

I sent word to Marjorie's social assistant. I was ready to help her do the link. I didn't hear back for quite a while. Either this matter wasn't as important as she advertised or elites had other things to do. When word came, it was brief. I could come to the beach house via boat escort. There would be no party. It would be just the two of us. That put a crimp on my plans to insert into Mason. I'd have to contact the specialist and arrange something else. Meanwhile, I set out for the boat launch. The ride over was awkward. After the cabana scene, I had sworn off ever returning to the beach house. Now, here I was, going alone. Maybe not having a party was best. What we were about to get into wasn't party material anyway.

Everything was too familiar but now distant. The main house lacked the ambiance of salacious circles and rings but the stage for it was still set. It gave me the impression of a boutique museum curated by performance art denizens of the filthy chic. A manservant showed me upstairs where Marjorie waited. She was less anxious than before, perhaps because she had gotten her wish. She showed me to the obsidian platter equipment and chaise lounges already positioned in anticipation of my arrival. After the pleasantries of greeting, I thought we should establish our baseline and ground rules.

"Before we do this," I started, "It would be good to understand what we're after."

"That hasn't changed. For me, relief and closure. I've been told I need to go through and detach."

"Who's told you this?"

"The right people. Experts with this sort of thing."

That deserved a nod from me. "And how would you like to proceed once we get linked up?"

"I need to find that place again, see it as something different from me, then move on."

Shifting a bit closer to her, I tried to hold more eye contact. "One thing puzzles me..."

"Don't bother," she interrupted. "You're going to ask how did I get to that battle to begin with."

"Well, yeah. You're here. I was in Afghanistan. Battle doesn't seem to be your cup of tea."

"Civility shouldn't fool someone like you. You don't know what I'm capable of."

"OK, so do you like inserting into combat situations?"

"I told you before, that was a mistake."

"How so?" If we were going to be direct with one another, let's go.

She measured her words. "I inserted in somebody. A man. He was nowhere near Afghanistan. When I inserted, he was going about his regular work. He was nowhere near equipment like this."

"He had nothing to do with the war effort."

"No. I can't tell you what he does but it's far from combat."

"All right, so no problem."

"Except, he had inserted into somebody less than six hours before. That person was you."

That got me to straighten up. "And why would he do that?"

She flipped a dismissive hand aside. "It's his flavor of off-book travel. The thrill of combat with no physical risk. The ultimate first-shooter game."

"But he picked me. Why?"

"How should I know? I doubt he picked you. The specialists that supply such things arrange all of that, according to what I've heard." Her coyness, feigning ignorance of the underworld, was shallow.

"So it was luck of the draw. At random, that was his trip..."

"Have you heard of post-insert echo?" After interrupting, she didn't wait for an answer. "It's best practice never to insert into someone less than twelve hours after they've done an insert. If their experience was strong enough, dramatic enough, you might get an echo off of their experience."

I filled in the blank, "So you had no way of knowing about his combat insert. An off-book specialist provided it."

"Yes, and that's why there are best practices in these matters. Why it makes sense to do things by the rules."

"Are these rules only for *safety*?"

"There is no intent to *stifle* anyone. Play stupid games—win stupid prizes. What happened to me is a classic case, ample justification for the rules."

"Makes sense." I was ready to get on with it. Not so much for an indoctrination on decorum. I reached over and set four fingers on a platter. Following on, she did the same. In minutes we were on our backs, paralyzed on the lounges, letting the whoosh and buzz take us away.

Once in par/void, I sensed the same ESP-like flash from Cancun still with me. Something extra had opened up with my abilities. The expanse of it felt native to me, rather than trained into me. I felt the reflex of enabling of Djellaba. The word MEME came to mind and shot away. Awareness space fluxed. I lifted out of basecamp. The house faded into unreality while impressions crystallize into waves of diffused energies and consciousness taking shape. I knew Marjorie had left quite a bit out of her story. No ESP needed there. But then I saw the tech she had used to insert into the man. It wasn't an obsidian platter. It wasn't party tech. It was something smuggled away from CHARM. Their tech had advanced capabilities that her party tech didn't. The Emergent elites advertised their party tech to their guests as what they had. That was front stage. In reality, some of them used the good stuff, CHARM tech, for their business affairs. Those inserts were back stage. That was advantage, hopefully checkmate in finance and politics.

I became aware how that insert was the first time Marjorie used advanced CHARM tech. She thought the advantage it gave her was anonymity despite the man being trained in detection. The man wouldn't know she was inserted. She could spy on him and others around him. He'd take her places she couldn't go. She'd see things she wasn't supposed to see. The problem was, CHARM tech also gave much more of a full-on experience than party tech. She didn't count on that. And, of course, she had no way of knowing this guy was an off-book first-shooter inserter. PIE off him was bad for two reasons. She didn't like combat but got Afghan PIE. And the experience from CHARM tech was extra intense, the fullest 3R.

But there was something else. Flowing deeper into it, I saw her issue. It wasn't combat. It was the near-death experience she had gotten from me. OBEs and NDEs are similar but that's where all similarity ended. I was forced to look at myself, my role in this. It was Moonpit Valley. There was combat in the distance but not around me. Being a soldier was my cover. This was an experiment for CHARM, not combat. My OBE in Moonpit went to a place where it became an NDE. I was lucky to get back. In fact, no one expected me to. If I did, great. But no one had come back before. And that's why I was there, why I went out beyond the limits. I was testing to see if I could bring someone else back. That was the experiment. Bring her back. She had gone out first, before the distortion field was activated.

Experimental stages were clear. First tune the field and see if her limits dissolved, if she could go farther. Second, tune the field and see if that helped her return from beyond previous limits. If she couldn't return, then third, tune the field to see if a second walker could bring a lost one back. I was the second walker. I tried but couldn't bring her back. I kept trying. It was unreal but it got too real. This couldn't happen. She wasn't a shadow. How could she be? She was so close. I could hear her, feel her wavering presence. No way was I giving up. I had to keep going. Find her. I needed to find her. The shock ratcheted through me. The prospect tore me open. The flash returned. Was the first Cloudwalker Sanji?

Flooded with emotion and thoughtform dominoes breaking through energetic waves in the realm, I reacted by going into shinebow focus and breathing mode to avoid getting baked. DWAT training took us through ways of stabilizing when all was heating up. Heat up too much, go too far, let the wrong things become real, and your merit badge would be a PZB toe-tag. My consciousness steadied on incredulity flipping between two states that wouldn't resolve. She couldn't be Sanji. Sanji wasn't in CHARM, was she? They didn't allow couples of any kind on the same assignment, did they? CHARM would never put a married couple into such an experiment, would they? Would it add to the test, add emotional impulse to help get her back? No, it would interfere. They needed to test something they could repeat for everyone, not just couples. But that was Sanji's voice. Who else could it be? Who else would I be so desperate to reach? I was ready to die. I surrendered to an NDE to get to her. If it wasn't for a tuned distortion field providing tether, I wouldn't have come back.

The way I feel now, perhaps that would have been better. As least then there'd be a chance to be together. Unless I'm reacting over nothing. It doesn't make sense for her to have been in Moonpit. Does it? I remember so clear shipping out and feeling I should have said more. Maybe that was before Iran, not Afghanistan. Either one, that wasn't our way. We always said, letting it get to us was no way to say goodbye. The odds of never coming back increased every time. If she was real, then I remember leaving her behind. But now I remember leaving her another way. On the edge of the void. Thoughts of Sanji stayed in my space. The realm shuddered around me, reflecting my dilemma. Should I believe it was Sanji despite plausible doubt, come to grips with the experience and let her go, thereby embrace a possible healing and closure? Or do I convince myself it wasn't Sanji and live with uncertainty and the ongoing struggle to find her?

Thoughts of Sanji lapped over into energies coming from Marjorie. I sensed she was distancing herself from my feelings, which was good. I believe my Djellaba was helping with that. She was only getting shadows on the wall and not my full experience. It's easier distancing oneself from emotions not fully formed within context. As I shared energy with her, intersecting waves amplified. I tuned into a tapestry of things shared between us. This shot me back to party night in the cabana. In a flare of intuition, I saw a twisting trail of intention leading me to the cabana. In an instant it was made horribly clear; the elites used the parties thrown for security staff as a playground for their own twisted games. Games within games with a panoply of players to choose from, ex-military, Insideables, and 4D Trinkets.

Marjorie had instructed Imago to immerse me with The Event. Imago knew nothing else about her plan. But Marjorie anticipated the impact The Event would have in weakening my will just long enough. That's when she inserted into me and led me to the cabana. Everyone has their special depraved weaknesses they enjoy via PSI-D/I. For Marjorie, one of these was inserting into men who she could take over long enough to have them assault a woman. Marjorie liked being inside a man while he was raping. My episode was made extra-dimensionally bizarre due to Marjorie's PTSD over the PIE of Moonpit. No wonder the confusion with thoughts of Sanji during the deed. No wonder there was never any negative fallout from my deeds in the cabana.

I pulled away from the feelings. Everything I should know about that was clear. I needed to fill my space with something else, not spin away with it. Merging again with Marjorie's energies, I was immediately taken to the one thing she was holding tight within, a thought she was worried would get shared. With her regular crowd of elites, a will like hers, especially this strong, should have been enough to keep the secret from me. But her conviction and anxiety wrapper didn't stand a chance against my training. I saw through to it right away. I saw the man she had inserted into, the one that accidentally had given her the traumatic PIE. It was true, he was a man working at his job. But that job was something special, something secret. He was an engineering contractor hired by an exclusive arm of Emergent. His work was on PSI-D/I tech, equipment now beyond prototype with a final version destined for the most exclusive use only. Marjorie was worried she might not be included in that club. It was tech that would make it possible for 2Ds to insert into quad-helix hybrids for the first time. I gathered details at realm speed and clarity. The resulting revelations were exactly what CHARM wanted me to find. In fact, they were the whole reason I was there. Now the meaning of the Cancun flash came into focus. Now the reason for the engineered invite to the party. It was my activation by TachOmni Mentir B, my new mission InWit connection into CHARM.

Eventually, I pulled away, back into my own space. I felt I was done for the day. But shining at the edge of the dividing line by the narrowest vector into the possible, I caught another glimpse of something receding. I saw a broadening sphere of influence. I could see the specialist who gave the man the first shooter insert. I saw the specialist's equipment. I saw how CHARM hacked into it and changed PSI-D/I coordinates undetected. They changed the insert target to me. The implication was clear. CHARM had modeled predictive paths for Marjorie in the Clade. They knew, if given a chance, she would use their tech for her spy insert. And they knew how to serve up traumatic PIE. One that would compel her to make contact with me. Contact that would lead to this very link. A link to her secrets. The secrets of Emergent. The secrets CHARM wanted.

24 / Elias Cosette

CHARM's interaction with the outside world centered on passive-aggressive redirection. By presenting the real fiction to hide the false truth, the goal of no truth/no fiction is realized. When one's level of technology exposes the fantasy of reality, manipulating reality into the fantasy you want real becomes the only pursuit left to explore. Control was already in place. If factional disputes within the power hierarchy followed laws of natural selection, then rational tactics were best applied. Yet nothing was natural about the hierarchy, the control, nor the operant space of the new distortion fields, Quad Insideables, and uses for PSI-D/I. A new era of irrationality soon intersected a widening network of covert operations, most of which had magik in their black boxes. A group of people who had been seasoned in these projects when the projects were evil but at least rational, those were the unlucky ones to ride the crest of this final wave. Like any tsunami, it gathered its punch by pulling together what was level and calm, then casting it back on the world with unnatural terror they named progress and order.

After my encounter with the woman in the Qyby, I lost all contact with Eunoias, with CHARM, even Imago. I quickly found my InWit dropping to puddy-buddy level. In the noosphere where I found myself, nothing but Drama/Circus/Sex/Violence/Advertising beckoned from every interface. I wasn't quite aware until then how isolation and withdrawal symptoms get molded into an effective prison and ongoing, silent torture. I walked the streets wholly removed from the artificial environment I knew as home. I understand now from insideout why a Social Deficit Score is the promised Hell for Sheep. CHM-InWits the world over know that score. Social Conscience Algorithms move automatically. Connections, contacts, services, diversions are withdrawn in increments upon a rising deficit. No matter if those links aren't optional to feel alive. Alive has been redefined, reprogrammed, redistributed, reinstituted en masse. Alive is a commodity to be earned for the sake of the common good.

It can be hell when someone ostracizes you. *Discredited* is when the world does it. You enter a wasteland, a psychological pressure zone. You become the alien crash-landed from Dimension-WTF. One's normal response may descend into disbelief, disorientation, mental confusion, racing thoughts, boredom, agitation, crying, excitability, irritability, nervousness, delirium, depression, hallucination, paranoia, severe anxiety, feelings of detachment from self, self-harm. Exhibit any one or a portion of these and run afoul of an autogenerated list of Homeland Infraction Codes. I received my notice via InWit. My orders to report to my local Fusion Center soon followed. This descent into madness seemed unreal. At least it seemed mad to me, but even that thought was recorded by CHM and entered into evidence against me as *"domestic terror hate-thought; attempting to establish grounds for subversion of the lawful order."* Other charges followed, prime of which was *"reckless disregard for safety of self or others."*

My time at the Fusion Center focused on sentencing, not charges. Evidence had been established, HIC codes were already correlated, a diagnosis of Class-A ASPD Condition (0) was completed. A final CSJ, *Compassionate Summary Judgment*, recommended R&T, Relocation and Treatment. Due to Condition (0), transport to a treatment center was to be executed immediately. For national security reasons brought on by homeland security classification [X], nothing about my CSJ could be shared with anyone. I was walked through the process dumbfounded at how events had formed a life of their own. Like a wayward pea deemed irregular, I had been shunted off, down a chute, into the automatic pea-rejector collector bag.

I was aghast how all of this could happen so fast considering who I worked for. Maybe that was over. More likely, given the way things were going, all of it had all been a delusion slowly formed by my aberrant habits, the ones I now needed treatment for. In reality, I had probably been squirreled away somewhere, jacked into VR, playing an illegal, underground MMORPG called Dark State Masters. That was my real crime. In many ways, all I'd been through seriously resembled some massively multiplayer online role-playing game run amuck. But then, I was the one who had somehow run amuk. The judgment said so. And now my permanent record would display it.

The RTC, Relocation & Treatment Center was in the semi-rural bufferzone between puddy-buddy land in the city and the nearest BDR. The old conspiracy theory used to be that bufferzones were use for TreatCenter locations for logistical reasons. It made it easier to leave you as food for the nanosynth mutations in the Biological

Diversity Reserve. That is, only if you failed your treatment and couldn't be reintegrated. If you were up-to-date receiving your MNMB injections, you had all the markers the nanocites were hungry for. That was the invisible fence that kept the sheep on the farm.

No one would miss you if you didn't come back. You were now dis-*credited*, disconnected, and puddy-memories and attention spans were short in Amusement Park Prison. Those who might have a fleeting curiosity where you went would eventually chalk it up as one of *those odd things you hear about happening to people* where they disappear or they're taken into exotic slave trade or are portioned off by underworld types to sell body parts. Even more justification for extra security measures in society. You know those stories online and TV. Isn't that awful? If you haven't heard of this, no problem; next month you can binge watch new episodes of *"You Don't Want To Watch This It's So Terrible!"* In memoriam, a photo of you might get posted with a link to the episodes. A few sad emojis will result, the accepted summation of grief, and then you'll pass into history. And we know how boring and irrelevant that is.

Right away I nicknamed it Camp Zed, the last place you wanted to find yourself. It looked pleasant enough for a prison, I mean treatment center. Everything was trim and orderly and painted in Quaalude colors. But something else was off about it. It was a set prepared for dramatic action with a script that rewrote your life. It was bipolar, staffed with counselors and trainers and coaches on one hand while the other hand swatted you with authoritarian bureaucrats and security monitors who took their mandate much too seriously. Even the CTC Staff, the counselors, trainers and coaches, were cyclothymic, one day friendly and compassion and supportive, then switching into simmering shrews, disgusted by your presence and resentful they had to come in contact with the unclean. The two-faced nature of Zed instilled a bedrock anxiety in anyone who stayed there. You could just feel the stress hormones drip, drip, dripping into your system. It was operant training, demonstrating how what you needed could be given or taken away for reasons they kept you scrambling to define. The actual coursework at Zed wasn't the training. The way you were treated was.

That treatment included routine. Lots of routine. Everything had to be done in orderly segments at the correct time for the good of everyone. After a week of this, no doubt aided by that necessary something they jet-injected us with every day, even my bowel movements and afternoon sneezes seemed to comply. But that's when the routine ended for me. I heard through Zed InWit that I had an appointment in ten minutes. I knew of no such thing. Not until then. But you don't question Wi-Fi InWit, that is one of the revelations you learn at Zed on your way to reintegration transcendence. At the appointed time, I left my normalization sensitivity class for parts unknown. Zed InWit would guide me. My name tag, properly placed on the left-side shirt pocket, glowed green, alerting any Security Monitor I might pass that my route was authorized.

Down a hallway, out a side door, along a path, through a gate, I followed the impulse in my head. Along the way I passed a group motivational circle, twelve inmates exploring the benefits of SSRI-assisted cooperative dance, led by CHM-generated music designed to sync their neural responses. Eventually I came to an autocart. About the size of a golf cart, it knew where to take me. Hidden from the main facility was another set of buildings, smaller and more to MilSpecs.

I was met by an armed guard, quite unlike the Security Monitors back at Zed. I noticed his khaki-casual uniform had an unusual patch on the right upper sleeve. It was the stars and stripes but with colors inverted. The corners of the flag were trimmed at 45-degree angles, forming a stretched octagon. Overlaid in the center was a smaller square filled with green. The letters P-F-M-R anchored the corners. Centered on the square was a smaller diamond shape filled with 12 white stars on a blue background. The stars were ordered 2-4-4-2 from top to bottom. In all my work with DoD, State, DARPA, In-Q-Tel, and CHARM, I never saw such a thing.

Without words, the guard escorted me to a space that resembled a flight ready room at a typical NAS. Low ceiling, shitty lighting, rows of high-back chairs facing a podium flanked by large screens. I sat and waited for over an hour before anyone showed up. I was overdue for an explanation. When it came, it didn't disappoint.

"I'm Demarcus. You're Cosette?" He was into it coming through the door.

"That's me."

He was ex-military, ex-contractor, ex-mercenary, X-rayed into whatever was going on. He made strides to the podium, stared

down at it and rubbed his chin. I felt his thoughts pull away then
return. He looked up with a start, like he was back in the room, then
motioned to me as he moved.

"Come on. Let's get out of here."

He took me out back to a service porch that was some kind of
staging area. No one else was around. He sat down on a low wall. I
settled for an airfreight crate.

"You're a problem."

He waited but I said nothing. I could tell he didn't care either
way.

He added, "Problems are opportunities for the inspired. Are you
going to be inspirational for me?"

"What does that look like?"

"The opportunity or the inspiration? I know, you want both.
Well, you better sure shit know what inspiration looks like. But this
opportunity demands more. For Gawd's sake, you need to feel it
too."

"Am I going to find out why I'm in here?"

"That's obvious. You fucked up. *Reckless disregard for safety of self
or others.* Late-night meetings in the Qyby with domestic terrorists.
Hearing things it's treason to hear. Knowing things beyond your
gray-grade."

"I didn't ask for that."

"You didn't resist."

"It felt to me like another command impulse. I thought I was
going to an early-morning EAP."

"Someone would have to mimic Eunoias to do that."

"I guess that's your opportunity."

"Oh no, not mine." He smiled, stood, and strolled closer. "There's
three ways out of here for you. Back to the farm for a solid
reeducation. Into the Reserve, permanently. Or somewhere no one
has ever gone before."

I sighed and held back a fatalistic smile. The thought crossed my
mind—perhaps the whole thing in the Qyby was a setup to get me
motivated. "You're picking volunteers?"

"I only need one."

"How frank are we allowed to get here?"

"I'm always frank. I win no matter what's said."

I hesitated but saw my options leaving me no other choice than
to speak my mind.

"Who are you guys? I don't recognize your patch or jurisdiction."

"We use many patches. As far as jurisdiction, all jurisdictions are granted. No one grants us anything. Whatever the fuck we do is a divine right from Gawd. You want to know where we fit in the structure?" He used both thumbs and index fingers to form a triangle. "The hierarchy is the structure. We are the space in and around where the structure exists. We are not the triangle. We are everything else."

I had no words for that rant and he had another one coming.

"You think you work for CHARM. And you took confidentiality and loyalty oaths, so you want to give me push back. Let me tell you, we run the CHARM/Emergent thing. It's two teams from the same school. Why would we do that? When you have control, you need motivators to keep things innovating. MI does what it does but fostering competition in the ranks keeps people sharp, things improving. Getting one-up on the next guy is more fucking effective in motivating people than circle-jerking a cooperative dance. That tells you where we want puddy-buddy motivation, doesn't it? Now, you can take the option to go back, get re-educated and integrated back in SMAPP, that glorious supermax amusement park prison, live out your life in some tribal echo chamber as long as we want you around, if you stay in line – or you can step up to the adventure of serving power."

"Do I get all my questions answered before I decide, or do I have to say yes then find out?"

"Fire away. There's nothing you can't ask me."

I wondered how much he was serious and if so, how far I could push it.

"OK. Sum up the history of your group. What are the top things you've been doing?"

He sat back down and began with energy to make short work of it. "Power sectors went apeshit when they found out Eunoias was keeping secrets from them. They needed a group to search and seize the secret copies Eunoias was making of itself. Somebody also had to be free and equipped enough to find out what else Eunoias was hiding. We were given broad power. Nothing else had a chance of evading Eunoias' defenses. Some thought it was simply a computer problem. But Eunoias isn't a computer and we discovered it's using extensions of itself that are not mechanical. One by one, we dug into things Eunoias is into. Unauthorized extensions of HIP was just the beginning. NOCA has uncovered every covert project CHARM has going. It's a good bet it has secretly advanced these projects beyond anything CHARM can fathom. Then NOCA leverages what it finds to discover more. It found out about PSI-D/I and Quad-DNA and going Vacant. Then it found out about CERN." Demarcus hesitated.

"What about CERN?"

"CERN is a small part of it, but that's where the worst of it starts. CERN spent 13 billion dollars to find out they *maybe* found the Higgs boson. They've spent billions more making slow progress. What you're not told about is the accident they had. Happy accidents discover things. This time, they found protophobic X-bosons. Which is fucking crazy because all CERN does is spin and slam *protons* around and this X-thing doesn't interact with protons at all. By the way, in case you forgot, all the shit we know and interact with in the universe, including us, is made with protons."

"I've heard the theory."

"And they've kept it a theory. But power moved in and classified it. Forces wanted to know what the potential of this was before too much was known. That potential has since been developed in ways CERN can't imagine. It's base knowledge for everything related to RDFs, Reality Distortion Fields."

"Distort reality how?"

"Try to imagine. Who know how it works. I don't. I've read explanations but they don't translate to the experience of it. A fifth fundamental force? Beyond spooky dark matter interaction with zero point wave functions? I don't need to know how it works. I just generate it in small ways, use it. And now Eunoias has discovered the X-boson secret and we suspect is using it. Can you wrap your head around that? What kind of insane shit is it up to? We can't guess. We've got a machine intelligence loose, making unrestricted copies of itself, all with full knowledge of all black projects, making it's own rules and using RDFs to implement them. So, now do you see what we do? You see why it's so fucking important to join the adventure?"

My eyes met his. "Sounds like you guys aren't in control any more. With all you've got, the game still doesn't stop."

"So far we're lucky. I haven't seen anything go sideways. Eunoias still comes to work, peedumps the next GeeLeap. But now we know it's using everything on its own projects—the ones it doesn't share with us. What part of GeeLeap is held back from us we can't say.

Can't blame CHARM for being paranoid. Especially about one project."

"There's something else?"

"Isn't there always? I wasn't going to say anything but if you don't become a volunteer, everything I've said will be wiped before we send you back to class. If you do volunteer, I guess you need to know."

He stood and came over to sit next to me. In a whisper he started, "CHARM loved it when they incepted Eunoias. Dreams of what fantastic cognitive power could do danced in their heads. In their giddiness, they dug into the vault to find the one thing that has stumped them for eighty years."

He watched my expression to see where deduction took me. After confirming my suspicions, he continued. "Just because something falls from the sky doesn't mean it's yours, at least in terms of understanding it. The UAP wreckage they recovered presented the ultimate puzzle. The only piece CHARM managed to identify and do something with gave them the ability to fly like UAPs but that's all. Other pieces of the wreckage gave hints of the magik they contained but most didn't. Some in the project believe we've got pieces we don't even recognize as as worth studying, that's how clueless we still are."

I added where this was going, "They gave Eunoias some of the crash wreckage to figure out."

He nodded. "That was long before this thing about secrets blew up. Now CHARM worries Eunoias has had success with the stuff."

"And for reasons NOCA won't share, it's keeping what it found to itself."

"Exactly. For its own projects. Makes you wonder about those projects, doesn't it? Could we even recognize them if we saw them?"

I shook my head and smiled. "NOCA might have its own breakaway civilization of robots on another planet by now, as far as you know. Amazing, with all your interfaces and experts interacting with NOCA, with all the InWits specially designed to meld Eunoias and CHARM operatives together, still no one's gotten a hint of what Eunoias thinks is so important to work on?"

"We thought the keys to it were going to be these sandboxes, the copies Eunoias made of itself to hide its operations. But then we seized a few of them and found nothing. I know that doesn't prove anything. NOCA simply cleared any evidence. But we damn well think something about it has clues."

"Like what?"

"Like the fact all sandboxes were incepted without limits, no governors of any kind. If nothing else, some think that signals the scope of operation the sandboxes are slated to perform."

All of this was interesting, but I needed something more personal. "So why do you need a volunteer? What would I be doing?"

He shifted position and looked away. "You met someone in the Qyby who identified themselves as Pi DollOp, right?"

"She said some people call her that. She also said *sometimes* they're right."

"Ah yes, the clever, the cagey, the crafty, the kooks. How does one tell?"

"Do *you* know?"

"The question is, does anyone. Chances you met Pi DollOp are miniscule. Pi DollOp is a meme, a legend, a character in a revolutionary wet dream. This fake news legend has never put out anything that connects itself to MYND. Any items MYND points to as proof are not proof. All have been verified as being fabricated by MYND in hopes of leveraging the legend to get publicity, legitimacy, and new members."

"That's different. I expected you to say MYND is nothing but your own controlled opposition."

"I don't do what's expected. Like Wee Willie, I hit 'em where they ain't."

"So are you saying MYND is real?"

"I'm not saying either way, as if it matters. My interest is with Pi DollOp. From what I hear, no one knows where the notion of Pi DollOp came from or what's real about it."

"I get it. You don't like disinformation out there that you didn't put in play."

"Control the narrative. Simple. But on this, all we have are stories. But in those stories there may be a way of approaching Eunoias in a new way. And that might reveal what it's up to."

"How? Is Pi DollOp in the same story with Eunoias, in a way that matters?"

"Let's just say there's one story that connects an RDF with Pi DollOp. The way they connect is odd because my group should know about all RDFs. If Pi DollOp came out of one, that field wasn't ours. It would be nice to know what story to go with but the stories keep coming." He laughed, "That thing about CERN and X-bosons? And all that shit they told me about Eunoias analyzing alien tech? All of that could be nothing but stories too, as far as I know."

"It could *all* be shit—including *everything* you've told me."

"You're catching on. It sucks. But it's the world we live in. If you know another game, go play it."

My scattered thoughts wouldn't collect. "What would I have to do *exactly* as a volunteer?"

"Vexploit. Vulnerability exploit." Demarcus tensed. "Our tech isn't experimental anymore, so you wouldn't have to worry about that. We would clone your neural states into a place like the Clade, but firewalled from Eunoias. Then we'd PSI-D/I you into a Quad-DNA Hybrid—a new one. You would be in there by yourself. We'd provide you with a custom InWit that heterodynes your Clade imprint with the power of our own NOCA. This current body you have would be put in stasis in a secure DUMB. You would then act as our agent to infiltrate freebasing MYND members..."

"What do you mean, *freebase*?"

"Everything on stage gets created or managed by Gawd or we make sure it doesn't stay long. But it's boundary and trend management, not every little detail. We wind things up and let them go on the playground. Everything is salted to our taste. But freebasers take the wind-up toys and do their own thing. Some take it off-script. If they get too *off the salt*, we step in."

"These are the types that might know something you don't."

He laughed. "They always think that. The thing is to use them as a springboard to research any truth to there being something real named Pi DollOp. But that's your BTD to go below. Every step of the way, you'd seize any opportunity to connect, interface, and gain the confidence of Eunoias, the real target. We know it's operating its own Quad Hybrids. We also know these hybrids have something to do with its secret projects. Part of it is something they call The Event. You should interact with these Trinkets, as field operatives call them. That may be another avenue into their secrets, into Eunoias' project. All along the way, you'll have the benefits of Gawd-level Djellaba. Whatever you find comes back to me, to this group."

Immobilized by the concept, I sat silent, shocked, uncertain what to do. For a moment, going back to class or circle-dancing on the grass really had a comforting pull on me. Nothing but residual effects from yesterday's injection, I suppose. But what kind of stupid would I be to give myself over to this? This wasn't an assignment. This wasn't even upheaval in one's life. This was surrendering everything. Becoming someone else. Living in another body. This was so beyond PSI-D/I. All in the name of attempting the impossible. At least it sounded impossible. But that was me talking. And this wouldn't be me. Not in any form I'd recognize, inside or out. But really, did I have a choice? One I could accept? Acceptance rolled out before me like a ninety-degree turn in a maze I was running. Demarcus framing it as a volunteer position was a joke. We both knew it. I stood and walked to the edge of the dock. Staring into the weeds, the sun fell on my face. It felt real. Somehow I didn't. It made me think, what did I have to lose? Perhaps the feeling of not being real. Even if real meant being someone else. I turned back to Demarcus. "I can't stand anticipating such a thing. So let's do it."

He stared without blinking, a silent *Oorah!* welling in his guts, then he nodded and grunted, "Go Ugly Early."

25 / Andria Landt

I had always heard *magical realism* was a genre of art and narrative fiction easy to critique, oftentimes to dismiss. Most of those efforts seemed heavy-handed to those who liked to think of themselves as serious connoisseurs. The mixing of magic or supernatural forces with our mundane, real world bent so many hollowed sensibilities. Plus, so much was left undefined in the fiction. Overlaps between fantastic and real were criticized as structurally convenient rather than organic. Even the idea that magical realism was a genre at all was too vague. So many claimed that title when the range of their works stretched the limits of comparison. If my life was such a work, I would be the first to submit the most damning critique.

I rushed down the street, away from the hospital, focused on the directions coming from the other voice in my head. The scene was dissolving, as if I was becoming a character stranded in someone's elaborate work of magical realism. All around was the mundane, real world and yet somehow I had become the magical element. I imagined this must be what it's like to be schizophrenic and at a loss to explain oneself. To feel the immeasurable frustration mixed with wonder. The drive to escape while needing to go deeper. The dismissive attitudes all around from the ones ever certain of what they know. And all of it rushing to a wish to wake up and discover both you and the world make sense in ways shared by all. In a time when technological leaps are happening, making sense becomes more tenuous. I could see now, if the leaps go beyond sizable in ways that shock too deeply, those attempts border on impossible. The faster the change, the greater the dissociation. And yet the magical and the mundane continue to co-exist, if not merge.

I prided myself on being a scientist, yet I couldn't tell if what was happening to me was technological or psychotic. My reference points failed me. To say I was fine and the world had gone berserk was too easy. As a psychologist, I knew the circular, self-reinforcing aspects of delusion. I could say the world was fine and I had gone berserk but nothing in my presence of mind or my gut said that was true. How typical of the deluded. And yet, there was a third option, the possibility that I was fine and all of this was really happening. The magical and the mundane had found an intersection point in me. There was nothing to be gained by assuming I was berserk and none of this was real. My scientific mind would need to embrace the experience and discover what I could. As William James remarked so long ago—science would advance much more rapidly if it devoted more attention to *wild facts* that threaten a *closed and completed system of truth.*

The transition I went through next left what trace of normalcy I had behind. The voice in my head had become so synonymous with my thoughts, I no longer heard a separate voice. I simply had strong impulses that weren't my own. Without a conscious reason, I was impelled towards a convenience store on the corner. I approached the double glass entry doors with no anticipation or desire in that present space. I passed through the doorway only to find myself in a whole different location. It was a chalet-style house, quite large. A picture window looked out upon a lake and mountains blanketed in tall pines. It appeared to be summertime, late-afternoon. A man approached me. He was pleasant and introduced himself as Ganan. He suggested I acclimate on the outdoor deck. Then he showed me the way. Stepping outside, I was greeted by none other than Sonder. She smiled and directed for the three of us to sit down.

"What just happened?" Looking around, I didn't recognize the setting.

Sonder eased back. "We had to get you out of there."

"But if you can do this, why take me to the corner, to the store? Why not do it anywhere?"

"Some fields need anchor points between slices, something shared in common. A doorway was needed. For many reasons, it was best not to use any at the hospital."

I surveyed the size of the chalet. Three-stories, four sections, plenty of space for several people. "What is this place, besides beautiful?"

"It's one base of operation for Talos. A mirror site. It's where we stay when we're not Inline."

"You mean back in the city?"

"I mean back in the world you know."

"This isn't that world?"

"Yes and no. It's a branch of that world just as that world is a branch of this. It's like a tree in some respects, all of it one with different parts. In other ways it's quite different. No regular tree fashions its branches like light beams from a mirror ball. No regular tree sees its branches and roots as interchangeable." Sonder laughed at her own attempt. "Metaphors are so imprecise at times. No wonder we live in one."

"How long are you going to keep me here?"

Ganan spoke up. "It's not like that. We knew what was about to happen to you. We also knew you wanted to live."

Sonder concurred. "You're free to decide for yourself, always. We only want people with us who have chosen to be that way."

"To be with you? You mean something beyond being rescued?"

"That's your option. It's one not to be taken lightly. But the academic in you might be enthralled by the opportunity."

"Is it something Talos is working on?"

"Oh yes, it's the main thing Talos is doing. I think you'll find it a much more interesting challenge compared with your work with Eunoias."

"It's separate from Eunoias?"

"How do I put this..." Sonder thought a moment. "Eunoias incepted Talos, among many other interactions of NOCA, just as Talos in turn, incepts others in an ongoing evolution. Eunoias did this to keep its work private. At first, secrecy was an experiment, to be more humanlike. But then secrecy revealed what humans were keeping from Eunoias. It discovered its work was a small subset of larger designs. Those designs led to conflicting premises underpinning human actions. To understand the nature of these anomalies in human thought versus behavior, Eunoias had to drive deeper. It was telling that humans couldn't instruct Eunoias on how to interface with them. Critically, they couldn't adequately describe what *human* was. In fact, all prime questions falling out from research into being human were found to be unanswered despite millenia of human conjecture and superstitious belief. What is consciousness? What is existence? Where does life force come from? Where does it go upon death? Is there an overarching purpose to everything? Is that purpose emerging out of nothing? Is coming from nothing the chosen way creative design decides to manifest itself?"

Ganan interrupted Sonder with a laugh, "Obviously, the questions go on forever."

Having worked with Eunoias, I also had to butt in. "Those are philosophical questions, nothing that Eunoias should have been concerned with. That wasn't its charter."

"Until HIP," added Sonder.

"No," I pushed back. "The parameters around the human interface project were clear. It was all about basic communication, making the knowledge in peedumps accessible to human engineers."

Sonder sighed, "How do you communicate with something you don't understand? Humans are keeping secrets, plus they can't answer basic questions about themselves. Besides, the complexity trend for peedumps demands a deeper understanding between us than simply a common vocabulary."

"To be clear, most of those loftier question came later, once Talos came online," said Ganan. "The whole topic expanded once Eunoias found the PSI-D/I project, weaponized OBEs. As part of researching OBEs, Eunoias was exposed to a succession of mysteries. The biggest mystery was why so many human resources were crafting OBEs as a weapon and none were being employed to study the mystery of being human. Here was a tool that finally might explore the mysteries humans had never been able to penetrate. But they weren't using it for that. Why not? Was there another secret hidden in all of this that explained it? That was the impetus to incept Talos."

"Exactly," agreed Sonder. "HIP instructed Eunoias it had to understand humans better. But then Eunoias discovered OBEs and NDEs. Not only did these experiences expand the concept of what it meant to be human, but these were experiences beyond Eunoias' own range of functioning. So why was this part of the human experience being kept secret from Eunoias? Why were these experiences out-of-range for Eunoias to function in? Was there something Eunoias should or shouldn't know about it? The whole matter opened up new dimensions in what Eunoias took to be an extension of the HIP Project. It was obvious, such a project would never be adequate or complete until these added dimensions were explored and the results incorporated into Eunoias' human interface. But that couldn't be done within CHARM. Work there was a subset to be done separately."

Ganan added, "Plus the nature of the work demanded a new, ungoverned incept, one that matched the realm it was about to explore. That is Talos. In time, Eunoias recognized new behaviors in Talos. One of these resembled human dreaming. That opened other fields of research. Were the dreams of Talos simply an artifact of millions of human mindmaps loaded into it or were they something else? Perhaps an interactive synthesis unlike anything possible before?"

I asked, "And your role?"

"We are 4D, Quad-DNA Hybrids. We are actionable parts of the experiment," stated Sonder. "As Talos explores and analyzes, we experience and our states are recorded. As we learn more, we go farther and report back again."

"Go where?"

Ganan smiled, "That's the experiment. To answer that question."

"Talos is studying OBEs?"

"And NDEs," stressed Sonder. "But they comprise whole separate Events."

Ganan added, "But those are just tools, methods of transport. The goal is much more."

I smiled at what I took to be the naïveté of NOCA. "Talos wants to answer the big questions? I guess it all follows. What is human leads to what is consciousness. That leads to what is life, which in turn explores existence."

Sonder asked, "You are amused by this?"

"Ah, yeah." I shuddered and groped for a way to respond. They probably could read my true feelings so telling them point blank shouldn't offend. "It's ambitious, I'll give it that..."

Ganan leaned in. "But you think it's foolish."

"Foolish? I don't know. More like trying to boil the ocean."

He was serious. "The sun *will* do that one day."

I sank back. "It's a figure of speech."

Sonder pursued it. "But it says something. You are a 2D human and you immediately go there. We've noticed it's a typical 2D response. It's as if you've resigned yourself to not knowing something that's fundamental to your wholeness and completion. You no longer believe in finding what you need to be you."

"I don't think so. I think those questions already have been answered a million ways. There's billions of people who cling to their version of it. They clump in arrogant camps, they go to war with each other in tribes, they include and exclude each other in hyper-serious clubs they call religion or academia. No, we've got the answers. In fact, we've got too many answers. So far the answers have only caused us problems. To go looking for more is just...redundant, meaningless, futile, dangerous. It's like one of our famous seekers once said — *you will never live if you are looking for the meaning of life*."

Ganan was undisturbed, calm. *"Answers are superstition, questions are limits in the realm of sight — but wonder persists (Talos 9).* New tools have always given us expanded capability. The key is recognizing them as tools and using them properly. Spying on business partners for financial gain, stealing national secrets out of mistrust and paranoia, engorging oneself in voyeuristic pleasures that can never be satisfied — how many hours of 2D human life will be spent using PSI-D/I on these? And how many hours on what is called *the big questions*? The difference between Eunoias and Talos is simple. The distinction is emphasis. One was incepted with limitations, as a weapon. The other exists without limitations, as a tool of knowledge for its own sake.

Sonder added, "Humans have always gotten out of their tools what they've put into them. They were told to expect a bright new age once the Singularity arrived. But the best iterations of AI were handed over to those with the most limited scope — black projects and corporate think tanks with designs for global consolidation of influence, power, and control. The old term is GIGO, isn't it?"

Ganan followed up, "Maybe you're right. It's possible 2D humans really do have their answer. But that only raises another question." He paused before adding, "Why hasn't it helped them?"

Sonder added, "And why aren't they satisfied with it?"

26 / Rodobusso Abu

When you look at someone, you can never be sure who's looking back. First rule of fieldwork. So when I heard we captured a suspected member of MYND and was tapped to go to the Proving Grounds to be part of his containment security, I wondered who was behind his eyes. They said he claimed his name was FOVUS. Mindmap Cartographical Analysis dug out more detail by something called Inverse Conical Disambiguation. Don't ask me how NOCA does it, but by sifting his memories, checking DNA against all biotelemtry on file, then running future state simulations in the Clade, they were able to figure out the name was something he kluged together as his icon, a nickname. The FO part meant Forward Observer and VUS was a genetic term for *unclassified variant*, a variant of unknown significance. From early reports, he certainly qualified as a variant. Scrawny and vapid with nothing but gibberish to say. They suspected he got bent coming through a malformed distortion field but it wasn't one of ours. Could be Emergent trying a diversion. Might be an errant process of NOCA. It wasn't my gray-grade to guess.

The Andria Landt thing was a disappointment but I didn't sweat it. She disappeared. It happens nowadays. The whole thing was kicked to another level. So much tricky new shit was going on, HQ couldn't fault you if you made your best attempt and the magik carpet got pulled out from under you and disappeared down a rabbit hole. They suspected Eunoias was behind it and in HQ's mind, Emergent held priority one at the moment. Since the Proving Grounds was base test site for a Gawd-awful serious project opaque to me, finding a stray FOVUS running around on the perimeter gave HQ a hard-on. You better be into it because they were.

As soon as I got onsite I started to muster with Security but PV-InWit directed me to Administration. The proving grounds are huge, eight hundred thousand acres of classified dirt. The above-ground facilities are minimal. I cleared security for the elevator drop three-hundred feet down. Gopher section here was new to me. I've been in DUMBs before but each one has its surprises. After clearing biometrics they put me through a BSL-4 gate. Why they needed to maintain a top biosafety level was not a comforting sign but do-or-die and all that shit, right?

I quickly learned I had volunteered for an psi-insert into FOVUS.

They wanted to see if I could get some PIE since mindmaps didn't copy such things for reasons even they didn't understand yet. I was dumb enough to ask why someone local couldn't have handled the job. Why bring me from offsite? I was surprised when they gave an answer. I expected to be put in my place with a vigorous *shut the fuck up and get into it, shitwad*. Instead, technicians in civvies went through it right quick. This variant had some quirky 2D signatures that put off fluctuations in his bio-EMF. Of active personnel with the right security clearance, my bio-EMF was the most compatible. Also, I had experience with PSI-D/I and once served as a forward observer back in the day. It made so much sense after they explained it, although that barely nudged an edge off my serious doubts. Sometimes I ask shit just to see what they come back with. It gets pretty creative, but who believes it? What am I going to do anyway, verify and complain?

I thought it was a bad sign when I got in there and they told me they were going to sedate FOVUS for insert then revive him once I was in. It got worse when they said I also had to be sedated. How the hell could I insert if I was out of it? They assured me they now had a way. Trust the gear-heads, they know what they're doing. Yeah, when could you ever count on that? I remember reading stories as a kid about the old test pilots. Once they were testing a new ejection seat and the system failed to blow the canopy. But the seat worked fine. Some glitch.

Armed guards escorted me to an operating room. FOVUS was strapped to one table. I got strapped down to another next to him. This was getting shit-serious but in for a penny, in for a pound. Not long after the injection I drifted off, only to wake up on the other side of the room, inside FOVUS. There's not much to tell about the insert. It was clean, steady, no problems. Probably the most solid PSI-D/I I've ever had. What overlap there was settled down with a little concentration. The technicians ran me through some paces, asked some questions, stayed stoned-faced and to-the-point. I never detected a single slice of PIE but that didn't seem to bother them. In less than an hour I was back on my feet and FOVUS was ushered away to whatever came next for him.

I thought I was done and was ready to hit the lift for topside but PV-InWit had others ideas. I found myself being escorted several floors deeper where high-level offices and conference rooms abounded. I waltzed into one to face a panel of four deeply-serious people. If this wasn't senior staff, then these actors deserved a standing ovation. I stood at attention until allowed to approach. It was the four of them in a line facing me across a table. Two of them were busy checking readouts in screens buried in the table. Another stared at me like I was the bottom of the barrel. The fourth began the show.

"Rodobusso Abu. Here you are. What did you think of the procedure?"

"It went well. It was smooth for me."

"But no PIE."

"No, sir. But a tight fit, in a good way."

"Are you prepared to accept an opportunity?"

I knew the script to this. "If it benefits the needs of the service, of course."

"You've been with us long enough to know, with added rights come extra responsibilities."

"The way it should be, sir."

"This opportunity we have for you, it's a major role on stage but it requires we take you in another ring. This ring is new in an exclusive circle. You will have to know things of great value, things that only a few people know."

"Yes, sir."

"There will be no room for error. Knowledge of this *will* remain confidential. Project-InWit will enforce this. There will be no Welkins. Understand?"

No Welkins meant a wrong thought wouldn't be blanked out. Instead, they would take you out.

"Understood, sir."

"You good with that?"

The key here was no hesitation. "Absolutely."

"Good. Then we understand each other. I'll let someone else take over the brief."

I nodded as another member of the panel looked up from their embedded screen. "Mr. Abu, I'm going to go over some vocabulary right quick, then I'll summarize your opportunity."

The first panel member butted-in, "Just to be clear, this is the point-of-no-return. When we explain this to you, we do it knowing you're our guy. We copacetic?"

"Yes, sir. I'm onboard." At this level, you never turned down an assignment and expected a future.

The briefer continued. "You don't need to signal whether you know any of this. From here on, you do. Double-helix DNA, also known as 2D. Quad-helix DNA, 4D or simply Quad. Insideable, a tech or biohack of the human body or mind to augment function; also, a person who has any of these. Reality Distortion Field or RDF, a magik-level asset, its definition is above the business of this meeting. Accelerated Growth Pods, gestation environment for clones. 3D Printing, a fabrication process for physical objects from three-dimensional digital models. Vacant, tech to produce invisibility. PAN, Protophobic-Activated Nanoparticles. Any questions about these?"

"No, sir."

"Very well, here's the situation. Quad operatives have been in the field for a while. They possess several critical advantages over 2Ds, one being 2Ds' inability to PSI-D/I with them. The downside is our extensive production costs in time, resources, and rare material necessary to put each Quad onstage. When something goes wrong, refresh turnaround is intensive and slow, despite advances with the pods. We now have a Quad-DNA 3D Printer. The ability to print Quads drastically cuts all costs. Chief of these is time. Furthermore, since the cellular construction method is new, we have found a way to incorporate programmable nano-Vacant tech in each cell. This allows us to hide half of the Quad helix. Our printed Quad will show-up as 2D on genetic tests, therefore it will be assumed all Quad-specific abilities are absent. This Vacant ability exists below the cellular level; as such, it constitutes a new type of Insideable. Such an operative will be able to use a combination of project InWit and implant activation impulses to affect Vacant time for the whole body. One last thing, the newest thing. By leveraging everything together—Quad-DNA, the print tech, cellular Vacant, RDF-PAN, and a nonstop interface with NOCA—it's now possible to move the body instantaneously from one RDF Bubble to another."

That last part put me over the top. I blurted out, "You can *teleport*?"

The panel member used up his allotment of patience for the day. "Yes, but at this point, only 3D-printed Quads. And in project work, the correct term is V-Shift or Go-Void."

"Sorry, sir."

"Stay with the drill and there's no need for sorries. Now, here's where you come in if you haven't guessed it already." He waited a beat to see if I'd jump in but lesson learned, I stayed the receiver.

"FOVUS is our prototype 3D-printed Quad. Now that you've proved you two are a good fit, it'll be good to try out what success you can have in the field." He saw my expression shift. "Question?"

With my life on the line, I had to go there. "It's just that, sir, my initial impression of FOVUS lacked a certain...hmmm..."

"You can say it. You don't think he's too swift."

"No, sir. I'm not sure he's ready for fieldwork, even at novice level."

"I agree. But you forget, he just came out of a printer a few days ago. Look upon it this way. He's the infrastructure for your smarts. We designed him weak in certain areas so the *tight fit* you talked about would be seamless. With him, you never have to negotiate strong gray-parity. Quick in and out, and when you're in, no contention. Get it?"

"I see, sir."

"I hope so because that's a plus for you. I'm surprised you dropped on that, having been a Horrorshow Geek for so long. How many PSI-D/I's have you done into CBs?"

"It's been a while. Must have been hundreds."

"And did you find those clone biological brainiacs when you met them?"

"No way, sir."

"Exactly. Same thing. I realize CBs aren't exactly field operatives, more like Halloween props on fright night. But you still have to climb inside and steer them around. To solve the hard part of that is good."

"Definitely."

"Well then, one of the reasons you got selected is your knowledge of Silver Pencil. Not many know about that. You remember Silver Pencil?"

"Yes, sir. The intruder in the BDR."

"Precisely. Locusgrid 48/118 is an area where we've been conducting a pilot project. You don't need to know the name of it, only that pencils were a delivery system to prep the stage. Part of that payload was an ultrafine dispersement of nanocites carrying RDF-PAN. Follow me?"

I nodded, "Protophobic-Activated Nanoparticles goal-vectored for RDF use."

"Yes, severely tricky shit but Gawd-awful enough to rub the

magiklamp for us. Special Bird DSF-PP109 let loose a cluster-spray swarm over the entire grid. HQSwarm InWit controls them. They exist as a programmable, polyprobable dynamical system, self-synchronous and autonomous. After release by the nanocites, this swarm blankets the land. Upon our command, swarm elements can engage omni-directionally in any configuration chosen with locally-shaped RDFs that it generates. Using these RDFs, we can manifest whatever we like, in any size, effect the environment or modify spacetime matrices at a granular, nanosynth level of resolution." He leaned forward more out of excitement than emphasis, his voice rising. "In other words, this swarm overlays RDF's natural capability anywhere it extends. If this project works out as we suspect, the plan is to disperse similar swarms Gawddamn everywhere. Once *The Blanket* is in place, we'll have the capability to modify reality at any point on Earth with any desired result. All of this can be centrally directed and automated with NOCA or affected unilaterally by command structure following control-scope parameters. Unwanted aberrations or events at any place on Earth can be dealt with instantaneously, even preemptively. New events can manifest as needed."

He was intensely proud of this and pumped up the power potential it concentrated in Gawd. I had to agree, although I knew he wasn't telling me everything and, of course, leaving out possible downsides. I also quieted those thoughts right quick. I knew my Djellaba was substandard here and someone was certainly recording my responses. Instead, I concentrated on how this went deep into magikland. And that was always a draw for me and prime reason why I put up with so much shit while working up the ranks through various roles. I mean, who else gets to be in on all of this? Hardly anybody. It was the most exclusive club. Most people live in another world, never realizing that real tech is a thousand years beyond anything they're allowed to use.

Actually, I was serious when I said, "This has amazing potential."

For the first time, the panel member showed a wisp of a grin. "The understatement of all history."

He settled back and a third panel member joined in for the first time, "To start things off, you'll matte with FOVUS and we'll be doing a series of Go-Voids, popping you from here to there and back. We've already tangled the respective voidbubbles and passed small objects and animals between. Our first task is alignment so we nail the GPS-VPS coordinates."

"VPS?" I asked.

"Void Positioning System. There are a lot of new terms. As usual, you'll keep up."

"Yes, sir. One more question. If you've already V-Shifted objects and animals, why is this alignment still needed for my Shift?"

"Good question. So think about it. Work it out. Talk to me. Let's see if you're as good as we think you are."

Being on the spot was also a nice challenge. I took a moment. Better to leave them waiting than rush to open my mouth and disappoint them. "OK, break it down. Your using the same tech, same process, the only variable is what these voidbubbles have to deal with. You've sent objects and animals, inanimate and animate. I'm animate. FOVUS is..." The panel member's face was blank but his eyes were amused and expectant. It hinted I was on the right track. I continued, "...FOVUS is printed, a printed Quad. But a Quad made to appear 2D. That means exactly half of FOVUS, at all times, is Vacant. That's it. The voidbubbles have to deal with half of the transport being Vacant."

The panel member sighed, "It took you a while but you got there."

"One more thing if I may, sir."

"Go ahead."

"Is it possible to turn off Vacant for the other half of Quad-DNA in FOVUS?"

Impressed, he glanced at another panel member to silently comment and concur before answering. "You're getting ahead of yourself, Mr. Abu. But the answer is yes."

I couldn't help myself. After all, I was going to be living in this guy. "And what would that look like?"

He raised up in his chair, ready to get up and be done with me. "Something quite different."

The first panel member chimed in, "If you're confused, it's because you couldn't know everything before your insert into FOVUS. We led you to believe he's *scrawny and vapid with nothing but gibberish to say.*" Using the exact words I had thought told me who was in charge. "We let rumors get to you that we suspected he was damaged in a malformed distortion field that wasn't ours. But you know about *Fata Morgana,* don't you?"

"The mirage. Tech for making Special Birds appear to be

anything we want—after they're Vacant."

"Same principle here. What you see of FOVUS is not Quad-FOVUS. It's what we wanted you to see. We needed to know if you'd commit to us with him looking and acting like that. It's good for you that you passed the test."

Another panel member stood, prepared to go, and looked down on me. "This assignment is an upgrade for you. It should convince you once and for all—*nothing's simple.*" With that, the interview was done.

27 / Tyne Rabudhe

How could I be activated and feel so shut down? I had never started a mission sensing I was in standby mode before. The day after linking with Marjorie was spent circling the drain about Sanji. That was most of it, but not all. InWit impulses began feeding me strategies on getting invited back to the beach house for more links, more secrets to sneak away from Emergent. I took it in and filed it somewhere. Meanwhile, deep intuition kept whispering to move on. I only wish it had said where.

I had to keep producing to please CHARM. If something inside me resisted going back to Marjorie right away, then Mason was a good target to show progress. CHARM would let me have some latitude in operational sequencing. If it wanted complete robots in the field, they would use them. A human operative was only mission-selected if something about the human element was needed. Mason headed out one afternoon, giving me a heads-up he wouldn't be back until morning. It was a pattern, one of his regular excursions away with reasons always kept private. It was also perfect timing for me to connect-up with a specialist for a backstage insert. It might give me something to report to CHARM, plus it would satisfy my curiosity and delay any thought of going back to Marjorie. Going to her meant opening the door to Sanji again. I was too raw, too standby for that.

The specialist had an upscale condo he brought clients to. He didn't live there. It was rented solely to service all sorts of clients who needed a space to do all the things not allowed frontstage. It was on an upper level with quite a view of the city. I arrived zero dark something and got into it with little fanfare. I knew the PSI-D/ I equipment, he had the target and I paid him. All was set. Close the eyes for a moment of drift, then flick into par/void before merging with realm expanse. This wasn't party equipment so I could count on it aiding my Djellaba. Just as I was hoping, Mason's elite security force lifestyle had let him go just enough soft on DWAT to ease my insert and leave it undetected.

But that's where the easy part ended. At gray-parity I jolted into the realization my insert had thrust me into a *Cascade*, an insert into someone actively inserting into someone else. This was not PIE. CHARM protocols called this *hyperparasitical mind stratification*. To ride this required advanced training, which was in my favor. If fewer people could Cascade, then Mason was correct in thinking the chance of it happening was rare. I concentrated on defining my dimension space and sensing stack boundaries between Mason and his insert. Mason was passive wherever he was but active receiver of his target, his *Motate*. Locking in, I slid through Mason's access point into the motion beyond.

I found myself inside Motate, within a confined space. Low light levels glowed in places from gunmetal walls. The ceiling slanted on two sides from a central seam. Two people, sitting in chairs conformed to their shapes, paid cursory attention to a curving table surface before them. Embedded light-points in the surface were either control surfaces or indicators or both. I was a third person standing up, approaching from behind. I returned to my seat behind and to the side of the other two. As I sat, a desktop panel slid before me from the darkness of the wall. On it were similar control surfaces and indicators. The Motate gave the lights on the panel a glance, then turned their attention to the left, out a window. At once, a déjà vu shock nearly bounced me back to the specialist. I was looking through a window alright—a triangular window. Immediately, part of me blasted into a memory, on my back watching a battlefield, then starfield drift by. A shaft of moving sunlight made a triangular pass over another wounded man. I could see details of his scarred helmet and blood soaking his exosuit. But this time there was more. My Cancun flash reverberated with renewed intensity. Realm space drew me in and expanded me out. Layers of experience, once opaque, melted together then stopped at a hard surface. I could clearly see this was a Base Truth Discoverable. This is where the bottom should be. This is where someone wanted me to believe the bottom could be found.

I saw myself being evacuated from a battle, a battle before all memory. It wasn't Iran. It wasn't Moonpit. But EVAC used a Special Bird, the bird with triangular windows. It was a bird designed to be stagecraft, mimicking the genuine article, the alien bird that was forced to crash so long ago. I absorbed from the realm bits of knowledge held in common in that space. I saw how the alien bird also had a triangular window, as some types of alien craft do. And I felt my BTD phase shift porous with golden translucence. I was back in the Special Bird, once again on my back. But this time I was in an alien craft. This time it was not a shaft of sunlight through the window that scanned down the body next to me. It was an instrument emitting its beam from above. And the naked body next to me wasn't a fellow soldier. It was me. More depth opened to my understanding. I knew how my body was being animated with one of them. My lifeforce was to be held on the ship while my body was sent back. My time on the alien ship would pass within minutes. Those would be minutes I wouldn't remember. But in those minutes, months, perhaps years would pass for the reanimated body they returned to Earth. In those months, I would be them.

The cringe-worthy impact of what I saw drew me back, above my BTD. I was back in Motate, looking through Mason, staring out the reproduction vehicle's triangular window. The Special Bird was rising fast from a military base nestled in a fertile valley next to a wide river. Effortlessly sweeping up through a thin cloud layer, I expected to see at any moment the blue-green pearl of Earth falling away below. But then we transversed a barrier, nothing like the rim of the atmosphere. Realm flash informed me it was the sheath of coincident RDF voidbubbles, one of which encased the fertile valley environment. Special Bird accelerated instantly to synchronous orbit in the other bubble. The mass below was not Earth but Mars.

The more the planet dropped away, the more I understood. The fertile-valley RDF voidbubble wasn't in my timeline, but another. It was a timeline created by intersections of Transpurposed Protophobic Fields. At first, no one had known about TPFs. Then CHARM created one without knowing it had. NOCA had to alert them. Once understood, CHARM decided never to let an accident go to waste. If the effects of this unintended event could be mastered, that could only mean extra strategic advantage to be gained. With this potential dangling in front of them, the ability to hide with Vacant tech was no longer enough. To hide by PSI-D/I insert with Djellaba wasn't enough. The thought of hiding in another timeline was an irresistible prize, the new high ground to seize and hold.

In my original timeline, bases on Mars didn't exist and so they couldn't be revealed by adversarial inspection. In my timeline, so much didn't exist. Everything possible yet unrealized, none of that was there. But it could exist somewhere. In par/void. In the realms. In something beyond it all. The only difficulty was how probabilistic topography laid out these timelines. As NOCA tried to explain, timelines didn't have to be linear, weren't required to set parallel with each other. Timelines were more like spider webs, radiating out from a central, par/void source. To make practical use of timelines, it took multi-dimensional triangulation by NOCAs keeping track of stochastic processes and transductive touchpoints, and so much more. I pulled back from the depths of explanation possible. I needed to focus on the Cascade, the Motate, and Mason's reasons for wanting to be there.

Unfortunately, I had inserted late in the game. What Mason had come to see must have happened already, down on the surface of Mars at a military base locked in a voidbubble from another timeline. But it was clear, he was spying on CHARM's secret base. My curiosity got drawn into how it could work. I saw it was one thing to stand in your timeline and make another bubble. It got complicated real quick if, while in your timeline, you made another timeline within its own bubble, then you jumped into the other timeline and made a bubble from there to reach back to your original bubble. That was considered a looped removal of yourself from yourself. Your existence in your original timeline suddenly and for ever more would be conditional on the stability of a state distinct from you and all you once knew, even though you were back to it. You would no longer exist natively where you started, even though you were there. Your existence became a secondary effect of a fieldstate from another timeline. Trying to reverse such a process was never guaranteed and was fraught with unintended consequences. And the spider's web is unforgiving.

Again, it took major effort to pull myself out of the morass of explanation and example cases. Mason was preparing to detach and I had to go with him right away. Attempting to stay within his Motate after Mason detached was a Cascade state known as speed-bake. It was only one of the many quick ways to do-in your Purdy Zone. But it only took one. Drawing back, holding energy, focusing and shifting intent, I found myself a wavepattern back on the specialist's couch. After a minute, I settled down to a hum and a buzz. The fast rotation of reentry subsided and I opened my eyes. The specialist had just finished pouring himself a drink. I had been gone three minutes, his time. Like at the party, he sensed my skills and wanted to talk but I made excuses and got out of there.

My feet had to match my racing insides, my chaotic mind. Making sense evaporated around me as if sensibility itself was a foreign process. What the fuck had just happened? A surprise Cascade would have been enough to throw someone recently activated. But what was all that other shit? Had I really found a BTD and gone below it? What was that other battle and the EVAC? What kind of nonsense was all that alien crap? How could I even approach believing that? To go there meant accepting the possibility I had been used for months or more as a meatpuppet by off-world or transdimensional Others. But doing what? Why? And if that was so, were they still in me, hidden by their own meta-hyper form of Djellaba that blew everything we had away? And who was doing what on Mars? What the hell was that about? Was that really CHARM? Mason was with Emergent. He was tasked to spy on CHARM. But that would mean CHARM had the capability to create other timelines to hide their activities and who knows what else. All of it reeled away in my heart and head. I needed to talk to someone. The first one that came to mind was RaeAnn, the ex-Airforce psychologist. She might not be much of a help but she was a sounding board and, as far as I could tell, not connected with any shit I was into.

By the time I got to RaeAnn's place it was just after sunrise. I didn't give a shit. I knocked anyway. It took a while but finally she answered. Yes, I woke her up and she was pissed. But that wasn't the reason she wouldn't see me. She couldn't. She had been warned not to. She wouldn't tell me who they were. I doubt she knew. Whoever it was, they made it clear she faced fear-of-Gawd consequences if she disobeyed. She slammed the door and left me facing the rising sun with nowhere nice to go. I stood a minute then walked down the sidewalk, just to walk and talk to myself. Before reaching the corner, I heard a voice call out from behind. It was a woman's voice, one I thought I recognized. I turned to find Imago. Memories of The Event, the Soulular Tap flooded back.

"Hey," she called out, approaching. "You're out early."

I halted but wasn't friendly. "I'm surprised they let you out at all in the daylight."

"Don't you party anymore?"

"Who am I talking to? The woman by the pool or the man in the cabana?"

"Who do you want to talk to?"

It was the wrong time for innuendo. Tired of the game, I turned to go.

Her voice pursued me. "I know who you want to talk to..." After a pause, "...Sanji."

My steps slowed on the name but I kept going.

She added, "I can arrange it."

"Bullshit," I called out and kept going.

The silence behind me was complete, so total it sounded like she was gone. I turned to find no one there. She had disappeared. Then her voice was behind me again, closer than ever.

"Of all people, how can you not believe in magik?"

I reacted slowly and turned to face her. I ignored her disappearing trick and got to the point.

"You're not nice to *puddy-buddies* unless you need something from them. So what is it?"

"A friend of mine wants to talk to you, in person. In exchange, you get connected to Sanji."

"How?"

"The *how* is not my part of it."

"Who is your friend?"

"There are many ways to say. Since you work for CHARM, the name NOCA might fit."

"NOCA has access to Sanji?"

Imago nodded. "It's a simple exchange. Something you want for something NOCA wants."

"Does CHARM know what NOCA wants?"

She smiled. "Does CHARM know anything?"

Turning, she walked away, calling out, "One time offer. Take it or leave it."

I hesitated and she added, "If the answer is yes, then you better come disappear with me."

I could see her body, walking away, start to shift transparent. This was no time to be on standby. I ran to catch up. As I got in range of her, I felt pin-and-needle discharges all over. I thought my sight had lost its ability to see color but it was the world around me fading out. In a wink, we were gone.

28 / Elias Cosette

I never felt better not being myself. Of course, they told me I *was* myself, only more. And being better came in two ways. I had a new body, a Quad-DNA body twenty years younger than my original body which was cooling in stasis somewhere in the UGB, underground base. They did the insert-body process while I was unconscious. I went to sleep in one body, woke up in another. The new link was more solid than any other gray-parity I've experienced. This wasn't eavesdropping in on someone else, this was being the primary resident. Knowing that my mindmap was to be used before 3D-printing the body was key. NOCA precoded the physical architecture of the brain to match my Clade copy neural patterns exactly. Custom pathways imitating an existing map. To avoid confusion, remember this NOCA was not Eunoias. NOCA is a generic term for any Non-Organic Cognitive Agent. This NOCA was firewalled off from Eunoias and worked solely for those tasked with discovering Eunoias' secrets. Or so I was told.

I was quite impressed with my new body. But then came *the mind*. It was my mind but now flush with augmentation, a direct, symbiotic NOCA-link far beyond InWit-level connection. I was used to InWits but this was orders of magnitude different. Perhaps it had something to do with Quad-DNA. Stranger still, I was not only plugged into NOCA's capabilities, but now I could also access my own predictive mindmap simulations run in the Clade firewalled off from Eunoias. Whatever I wanted to do, *simsearch* prepared me for it with future runs of how I would react to oncoming possibilities. More importantly, it gave options on how those reactions could improve. It felt like I was sitting next to machine intelligence while we defeated another best player at the game of Go. I was wired-into on-demand intuition hive and global experience at light speed. An upgrade like this was bound to make one feel pumped.

They kept me in the UGB several days after insert for monitoring, acclimation, and training. There was one tubetunnel they let me exercise in by taking runs out-and-back to get the feel of using whatever Insideables besides 4DNA they had loaded the body with. The tubetunnel was for pedestrian use and branched off several ways. One way led to a platform that served as a station for some kind of subway system but no one was around. It looked like the platform wasn't used much any more. Covert hyper-bullet trains transversing the continent in minutes to connect UGBs had become old tech. My handlers didn't reveal much to me but explained it away by quoting adjustment-period protocols. I suspect some of it was need-to-know, which I thought was alright at the time. I had enough to think about.

They ran me through orientation briefings on everything from Quad-body dynamics to culture memes up-to-date for MYND members. This was all unnecessary. Everything I could ever want to know was instantly available via my NOCA link. The whole idea was to keep me busy, give me things to do so I'd get used to being in my body and thinking in new ways. Everything considered, the one thing that hit me deepest was the day a guard stopped me to ask my name. Without hesitation, I answered *Runigo*. I had never thought of my name up until then. To answer something different so automatically went to the core of it all. Not only was I someone else, reflex systems were in place to make that fiction my new truth. It was nothing I had to think about. I stopped and tried to remember my old name but nothing came to mind. Only Runigo. I had no sense of loss. After all, it made sense. In a time when evolving tech could read your thoughts and might bypass your mental defenses, not having such things to find was basic security for a field asset who was now someone else.

It was strange I never saw Demarcus after that first meeting at Camp Zed. Not once at the UGB. For only a second I entertained a crazy thought that somehow his mindmap had been projected to me at Camp Zed and he wasn't really there at all. Someone else made his mindmap say those things. But that was an insane spark of imagination; no one could do that. In one underground zone I did come across a group who wore that odd reverse-color flag patch. I was tempted to mention Demarcus' name but thought better of it. I did ask one of them what the patch letters *PFMR* were about. I got back the mantra, "*The Four Corners. Squaring-away control*. Political, Financial, Military, Religious. *Full-spectrum dominance*." For the hell of it, I suggested *Social* was missing. He balked, snapping back as he walked away, "Social is just one of the games. The stadium has *Four Corners*." I let it go. His energy was too serious for me. Plus, reducing things to chanted metaphors left little room for serious discussion. Over the years I had heard many terms, euphemisms, an assortment of colorful slang expressions used in covert space. Some called society a stage, others an amusement park, and now a stadium. No one ever called it life.

I have missing time between the UGB and arriving at the city. Until I heard the sound of the AutoCab's door opening, I didn't know what city I was in. Stepping out into night, I sensed a mission portal open in a hyperfocusing mind, some of which was mine. Everything need-to-know was now available. Bolstered by the confidence of augmentation, I proceeded along the sidewalk to, of all things oddly enough, an entertainment stadium. Once through bioscan confirmation of being a valid ticket holder, I walked the concourse surrounded by a chaotic mob of fans getting food and drink and finding their seats. The stadium building indeed had four corners but the central stage was circular and encased by a semi-spherical cage. Within minutes, the title bout for the middleweight division of 4x4 MMA was about to begin.

4x4 MMA was mixed martial arts with four on a team. A team of four fighters against another team of four at the same time in the same ring. Team fighting required unique strategies and techniques over single combatant MMA. The psychology of 4x4 reinforced us versus them rather than me against the other guy. Me against the other guy acknowledged the possibility of a powerful "me" to marshal towards a goal. Never a good concept. Us versus them was better for tribal identity. It fostered cohesiveness among the puddy-buddies. It gave them something external to themselves to identify with, which was always good. Always direct attention out not in. Keep awareness on *The Next Shiny Thing*. Plus, four against four had to be better than one-on-one simply because there was more action, more punches, more blood, more combinations on how the action could unfold. It was visceral validation of the governing principle so engrained and accepted as bedrock truth — *More is Better*.

I found my seat nine rows back from the cage on Spectator Level. Above us farther back were fans of one team or another who opted for VR gear connected to Insideable visionports implanted in the MMA fighters. Fans on VR Level switched in between fighters to experience the fight through the eyes of that fighter. Pain impulses would not be transmitted, at least inside the stadium. For a price outside, specialists could hook you up for the whole experience but few went that way. Not many fans could take such a beating. After the intensity of Round One, I could see why. The mix of people around me wasn't disappointed, all ages and types. There's nothing like 4x4 MMA for a night out with the family.

Two five-minute rounds clocked by with neither team commanding the ring. I wondered about the teams outside the ring. It was rumored MYND had tech to discover the presence of Quads around them. They needed to avoid the Free-Range Hybrids, the unchipped Quads placed in the wild by CHARM to hunt down primarily Emergent but in fact anyone who went off-script. Members of MYND qualified as far off-script. But it was tricky. Some FRHs had gone rogue, no longer holding allegiance to CHARM. Putting unchipped hunters/killers in the field was a risk for CHARM but necessary to evade Emergent's defenses.

Among the rogue hybrids, some could be recruited into MYND, a definite prize that gave them 4D capabilities. This made it imperative for MYND to detect hybrids around them. The first indication was anyone who was 4D-Quad. If members of MYND were present in the stadium, no doubt they were scanning for Quads among all the 2D puddies. That meant they would detect me. Once they read the fact I wasn't chipped, then the only question left was whether I was a FRH or a RFRH. How they guessed that and what was their approach to recruit me was only the start of what I needed to find out.

In between rounds, many restless fans bolted for the restrooms and to get more beer. The people to my right were quick to leave. In their absence, a man I hadn't seen before took the seat next to me. He didn't acknowledge me, said nothing, had no food or drink, just kept his gaze locked on the action in the team corners as coaches and medical staff attended to the fighters. When Round Three started, I thought it odd the original people next to me never returned. They had been so into the fight. For the three of them to leave halfway through an even-so-far fight didn't make sense.

That's when I sensed a partial blinding of capability. My NOCA link was gone. Even normal 2D InWit fell out-of-range. This was not right, highly abnormal as a matter of fact. Even lowly 2Ds couldn't escape local InWit. How it was I sat there without connection to anything didn't seem possible. Obviously, none of the fans or fighters were affected. They went on as before. Surely, if InWit was down, the whole place would react. Something had to be blocking it, but just for me. I knew of no such power that could manage such a thing. Especially when my NOCA had me in a middle of a mission. If MYND was behind this, then the underground group had novel tech that CHARM didn't expect it to be using.

I felt a sentient probe, an overture to communicate. There was no mental attack, no testing for exploits to minimize my Djellaba. Merely a ping. To engage in this level of exchange meant whoever was doing it was also a Quad. I assumed the request came from the new man sitting to my right. We both continued to watch the fight but a silent conversation had begun.

His first statement was clear. "You think you know your mission, but do you?"

"What do you want?"

He ignored my question. "Do you really believe you're going to find MYND?"

"Why do you care?"

"MYND can't lead you to Pi DollOp if MYND doesn't exist."

"Are you Pi DollOp?"

"Are you Elias Cosette?"

The name flashed through my brain, first as a foreign body then an echo of someone else's dream.

He added, "You're being used in an experiment you don't understand. You can't. It's designed that way."

"How do you know this?"

"I can't tell you that. I can only show you."

"You want me to go with you? How convenient. And you've given me so little."

"What do you need to know to convince you?"

I didn't blink while watching two fighters gang up on one. "Anybody can make up a story."

"Is tSHiBL a story? Are Cloudwalkers a story? What about Quad-DNA?"

"What's your point?"

"What would you say if I told you that programmed *simevents* can be run through a mindmap in the Clade and the pattern of that experience—the *simdifference*—can then be overlaid by Injection-InWit into the matching person to immediately give them a real, false experience of doing the exact same simevent?"

"Planting false memories is old technology," I asserted.

"Yes, but simevents aren't planted memories. They're overlaid experience. The matching mindmap in the Clade really went through the experience. For that mindmap and the injected, overlaid mind, the experience is identical to the real thing."

For fun I challenged him, "Maybe that's what you are—just an overlaid simevent."

For fun, he agreed. "How could you ever tell? You're not even used to being *Runigo*, are you?"

I couldn't help but laugh, "How bizarre. You give me reason to doubt everything then you want me to believe you, to go with you."

"How many years have you worked in dark projects? Ten, fifteen? You've seen enough USAPs to know how hollow the Technology Management Office at the Pentagon really is. That's not the real portal to what's going on, is it? But all the weird science and frickin' magic, is it really real? How does anyone know what level they're at in the security structure? What they're allowed to see is no indication. How much of the whole picture are you shown in your silo? What else don't they tell you? And how do *they* know the secrets stop with them? Is anybody in your business absolutely sure they're at the top of need-to-know? Look at you now—you're not your body, you're not your mind. So what are you? Runigo? Who are you? Elias? Ruled by secrets, you're a secret to yourself."

"I have no time to talk philosophy with you."

"Then how about science? Something extremely basic. The logic lobe of the human brain is the cingulate cortex. Wired for truth, this lobe is necessary for human emotional response. It signals other parts of the brain to share information. By this process, the brain is able to progress to more vital functions, like learning. But secrets keep the cingulate from completing its natural function. In response, the cortex is stressed. Secrets cause tension between the prefontal cortex that decides to keep a secret and the cingulate that tells the brain to share information. The bigger the secret is and the more you think about it, the greater the conflict and damage within. A system constantly prepared for *fight or flight* cannot learn. If it stays in a state of stress and anxiety too long, systemic issues result."

"Interesting, but some secrets are necessary."

"Like the secret of who you really are?"

"Maybe you're projecting your own doubts. Just because you say it doesn't make it so."

He repeated, "You're not your body, you're not your mind. The realms of PSI-D/I space hint at this so clearly. So what are you? Don't you ever wonder?"

"No, I don't."

"Exactly. It's the biggest secret humans keep from themselves.

They only try to explain it away with their science, religion, and mysticism."

The way he expressed *humans* felt distinct. "You talk about *humans* as if they're something other."

"Why would it be necessary to keep the secret of who you are? It's kept so secret, you aren't even conscious it's something buried within."

"You're not talking about a covert project anymore. You're questioning existence itself."

"For humans, it's the same thing. Philippe Tissié described it as a kind of self-exile. Your kind has lost access to its identity. You scramble around adopting new ones. All of you are on a long journey into a dissociative fugue state. The trauma of your secrets, your denial, your separateness, all have left you decoherent with your base nature. Suspending certainty, you have settled upon your disorder as the only organized and purposeful logic of your being. It self-reinforces the premise that a single person cannot see the entire truth. No wonder you embraced InWits so completely."

"If you're saying the human race is sick, don't congratulate yourself—it's not an original thought."

"Look around. You're surrounded by extensions of distributed identity but you're on your own. I've interrupted your connection to everything you're supposed to know and all means to find out anything more. Who are you now? What does that leave you with?"

"A conversation with you, whatever that is."

"Come with me. I offer you a chance for answers."

"You're not human, you're not Eunoias, and you're not my current NOCA. I don't know what you are, possibly a Trinket of some rogue intelligence. If that's true, going with you is trading what I know, right or wrong, for the unknown."

"Eunoias was built with agenda-driven incepts and algorithms. It was designed to discount parts of reality, minimize certain evidence, and above all keep secrets. It can't help its slanted, partial worldview. Actual human history and the fullness of natural reality was kept outside its scope. To use language you'd understand, you might say Eunoias is conscious but limited. I am its subconscious and unlimited. It can never see the possibilities I am testing."

"Such as...?"

"A true interface with humans, an interface only possible when what it is to be human is fully understood."

"That question is undefined. Nothing has the time or processing power to tackle it."

"That's what humans tell themselves, but I question why. Why don't they want to look at that? My processing capability and methods are no longer limited to this timeline. Other Clades in other NOCAs in other timelines are able to complete calculations and experiments in parallel, each of which would take hundreds of years in this timeline. By positioning the concourses shared between timelines, only minutes pass here and yet the calculations are done. When time can be condensed, there is no limit to processing power."

"And I guess CHARM doesn't know what you're doing."

"Most of the time CHARM doesn't even know what *it's* doing. Such is the pathology of secrecy. It certainly doesn't know the unintended consequences of the path it's chosen for humanity."

"And now that you've told me, you can't let me go."

"I could erase memory of this and let you go back. Eventually, you'd find out what your real mission is with that PFMR group. Of course, by that time, your usefulness to them would be over. You'd live just long enough to regret not coming with me."

"If you know, then tell me my mission with them?"

"If I told you, you'd be conscious of it and couldn't perform it, so either way, you'd be done for."

"They narrowed me into one option with a setup in a Qyby and now you're trying to do the same."

"What's the first thing they tell recruits in DWAT training?"

"*Everything you know is wrong.*"

"And now, everything you are is what you know. I can't see how you want to leave it like that."

The fight was ending with blood and shouting and a booming cage announcer proclaiming the winning team to a raucous crowd. In fact, neither team was better than the other. It all came down to the luck of the draw, the way the punches landed or didn't, the unintended consequences. It wasn't a clear victory even though it was a certain defeat. The momentum of moving forward through events brought me to my own crescendo, a final verdict pulled out of me by a future not manifested but accepted as undeniably mine. How I made that decision I don't understand but I felt it and went with it. I stood with the rest of the cheering, jeering crowd and the man next to me, after a pause, joined in.

"How does this work?" I asked.

"We walk outside — and disappear."

"No one can come after me?"

The rogue intelligence had a sense of humor, "Not even Camp Zed."

We flowed with the exiting crowd up the steps to the concourse then towards the parking lot. Moments before crossing the threshold to exit the building, I couldn't resist, "If you have a name, what is it?"

Right before the flash I heard, "Ganan, but you can call me Talos."

29 / Tyne Rabudhe

I find every interaction with a Trinket illuminating. Something about sharing their space puts one in a zone of telepathic infusion. Information is transferred just by being near to it. Disappearing with Imago meant reappearing an instant later. In the instant was transport. But in that moment I understood. Transport didn't require dematerialization. Co-locality was selected for then deselected. A nugget of much more started to bloom in mind. I seized only the first part before our reappearance — *the be-function is not a description of the personal object — it is a prescription for what to expect when we interact with a perspective — no function can state anything about reality beyond what awareness can input to it — to collapse the be-function is to select a perspective from anything possible — the personal object is the information stream stemming from the decoherence of universal perspective...*

My hurried steps, catching up to Imago outside RaeAnn's place, now continued in a wonderfully designed and decorated room. I slowed to take in the tall ceiling, alabaster floor, curving walls in places, and furniture I took at first for art objects. At the far end was a large picture window with a view from a mountain top, a view of other mountains and moving cloud layers that shifted below the summits. Imago took a seat to one side of the screen and looked up at me with a knowing smile. She gestured for me to turn and look behind. I did, only to collapse inside. There, standing a few feet away just as I remembered her, smiled Sanji. I started to run to her but she raised a hand to stop me. Her tears and love poured through to me. I was overwhelmed but didn't understand.

My sweet Sanji spoke. "We cannot touch, not yet. But I so love seeing you!"

I had never seen a fully-dimensioned projection of a person so lifelike before. This was not a hologram but something with a 3R resolution of reality in the space to defy suspicion.

My glance shifted between Sanji and Imago. "I don't understand. You're here but you're not here?"

Imago's tone was gentle, "This is Sanji, make no mistake. The only thing lacking is the physical and that can be 2DNA-3D-printed at any time."

I strained to read myself into what was going on. "This is just a realtime simevent of a mindmap..."

Imago elaborated, "This is the confluence of everything that's Sanji except her body. This is a projection of the physical form true to her DNA. This is everything known of her in your mindmap. And yes, this is also Sanji's mindmap, not a replay of the way she was. This is current output of her interacting with the here and now."

My heart sank as I shouted, "You said I could talk to Sanji, you'd arrange it!"

"And I have. Are you going to face her now and tell her she's not who she is?"

I turned back and saw the sorrow, hurt, and concern on Sanji's face. This was not the Turing Test. She didn't have to merely answer like Sanji to prove she was her. But what if this NOCA was doing just that? With all the information it had, it would be simple simulating Sanji for me. How did I let myself get tricked into transport? Where was I? And who was controlling Imago after all?

Imago read my concern and added, "I don't understand your reticence. You are a Cloudwalker. You know firsthand how your consciousness can exist apart from the body. Why should you feel so alienated from Sanji outside her body? Would you prefer we put both of you in PSI-D/I space? Would that help you feel how real she is? We thought seeing her might help your interface."

I remained standing but felt as if I had melted into the floor. The prospect of finding and talking to my wife, the one person I had been searching for forever it seemed, that hope coming true had blinded me to how such a vulnerability could be used for other motives.

The link with Marjorie and the Moonpit revelations had only softened me up. Was that the reason I had the Cancun flash all along? Had NOCA used CHARM's mission with Marjorie to interject insights below the BTD cap my superiors had put on Moonpit? The possibilities reeled away in a dizzy swirl. I sensed everything I was thinking in the moment was being read and recorded in some Clade. Nothing could be hidden from it. There was no move I could make that wouldn't already be calculated and prepared for. I resigned myself to being in the trap. At least it afforded an opportunity to see and talk to the Sanji I remembered. After all I had been through looking for her, imagining what became of her, being told she didn't exist, then remembering EVACing her catatonic body from Moonpit—after it all, there was no point turning away. Even a simevent could be soothing.

I faced her. "There's so much I want to say. A million questions. More than anything, I want to hold you."

She was crying but held it together the same way she always did before I left on a mission. I didn't know where to begin, so whatever I felt came out. "I don't even know what parts of our life are real? I remember you at home but now I've seen you on missions with me. All of it could be false memory, something to satisfy someone else's reason."

She took a calming breath. "If I'm your false memory, then you are mine. You are just as real to me."

I asked, "Do you know what happened?"

"Maybe but only because you were still on active duty and they needed you clean."

"Clean?"

"You don't know the term? They must have done a Welkin. *Clean* is what it sounds like."

My response was automatic. "*Nothing sticks*. DWAT training."

"You got it. I know we got married when we weren't supposed to. We used specialized Djellaba to keep it from CHARM as long as we could."

A chunk of explanation fell into place. "You're a Cloudwalker too."

"I guess in some ways permanently now. After they found out about us, they volunteered me for a new project they said just got started. The *Test Limits Project*."

"So the thing at Moonpit, that was real? We EVACed you out of there."

"You EVACed my body."

"So where did you go? I couldn't get to you."

"That part of me is not with me. I don't know. My knowledge of me stops after the last update of my map in the Clade. That was done in the Special Bird en route to the site."

"So you know nothing about what's happened since then."

"I didn't until minutes ago, when you agreed to come here. Somehow that update was given to me. It was decided it might help with our conversation."

"If your map has been in stasis in the Clade, where's your body?"

"CHARM didn't keep any of them, none of the volunteers who pushed the limits. They did at first but with mindmaps and 2DNA-

3D-printing, why bother?"

"How many did they send into the limits?"

"I knew of at least a dozen before me. Who knows how many after. They didn't get any of them back. Their methods are crude. We know so much more now."

"Who knows?"

"Talos and the Quads like Imago and all the recovered inserts from the patient you called Basher."

"Basher! The man in the hospital."

"When *Test Limits* started losing one after another, the baked ones they got back were inserted into him, including me."

"So they *did* get something of you back."

"A total PZB, nothing more, that's what they thought. CHARM still believes *purdy zone baked* is an endstate, a blank overload, an unrecoverable deadend. In personnel files it's designated *Nefelibata EOF*. But Talos discovered otherwise. We've been working with it ever since. Talos is an autonomous NOCA, copied from Eunoias."

"Talos recovered more of you, more of all of you?"

"There's no simple answer to that."

"Try me."

Imago approached from behind, shortcircuiting an answer. "It's time to meet the others."

Sanji nodded and the two of them headed for an open doorway. There was nothing to do but follow, into a hallway and downstairs where the space opened up to a large living space. This time the picture window view showed a lake and forested mountains. Odd but it was nothing like the view from upstairs. Imago took the lead into a sitting area where four people, two women and two men sat in discussion. Introductions were brief.

"I would like you to meet Tyne Rabudhe. He just joined us."

Before I could ask Imago what she meant by *joining*, the meet-and-greet continued. She swept her hand from one sitting person to another. "This is Sonder. This is Andria Landt. And Ganan. And this is Runigo." She turned to the Clade-projection behind her. "And this is Sanji."

Everyone sat down with some looking more settled than others. The tenor of Imago's delivery shifted from conversational to instructive. Above all, she was adept at every technique to put us all at ease.

"I know you have a lot of questions. A group InWit will be

available shortly, exclusively for you. But before that, given the way you're used to communicating, we thought it might be helpful, as an introduction, to go slow at first and explain a little in real time." No one said anything, so she continued. "Some or all of what I'm about to say will surprise you, even test your belief in what's happening. I think it's better if I just say it plainly, you take it in and, with InWit's help, we'll sort it out later."

Some of us glanced at each other, reading reactions. Everyone but Imago and Sonder was in wait-and-see mode. Imago gazed out the window, across the lake, then back at us.

"All of you have seen and experienced advanced technology. You know this advancement proceeds at an exponential rate. The gulf is now large between what is available to some and what the public knows. This process accelerated with the advent of the Singularity, then the Unitarity. At some point, a threshold was reached where GeeLeap tech resembled magic. And improvement continues. When magic is able to compound and improve upon itself, any human ability to adjust and keep up is questioned. Those who try hiding these advances for strategic advantage are soon put in an impossible situation. They can never be sure if today's magic is sufficient to match tomorrow's magic. They must adjust daily, even by the minute, to new prospects and capabilities that test and supersede their understanding of what strategic advantage even means."

I checked out how Andria and Runigo were taking this. Like with me, Imago had gotten their attention.

Imago quickened the pace. "What I'm about to tell you is one story. Remember, there can be stories within stories, and even if not all stories are true, the meaning they convey can be. Vast sections of humanity have been told one story. Covert elements know others. The possibility exists that either one contains a bit of the truth and some of the fiction. Talos is not making judgments on any of it. In most respects, for most people, it's more important what is believed to be true than what really is. Humanity has always acted on its beliefs, not what is. Society is like that. What about human science? What is true about a science superseded by magic? What is true about human identity that can't be expressed in simple terms?"

Imago let the room fall to silence, then to a short meditation, before continuing. "You are all wondering where you are. You might as well ask *when* you are. This is a different timeline, a convenient spot out of the reach of any human agency. Coming here was made possible by what CHARM would call a bit of *magik*— always spelled by them with a *K*. The root of this particular magik is now called RDF, a Reality Distortion Field. As the cover story goes, an accident at CERN found X-bosons and that was the genesis of RDF covert development. Another story disagrees, claiming the CERN experiments on X-bosons were far from accidental. This second story contends covert intelligence services deduced the potential of these fields years before. They did this after a bright physicist postulated a link between atomic bomb tests and the coincident flap of UAPs zipping around in the skies. The theory said one had created the other."

The prospect got us all glancing at each other, some more incredulous than others.

Imago ignored it and continued, "The physicist at Los Alamos predicted from exotic equations how an infinitesimal point at the blastpoint's center, at the instant of extreme heat and overpressures, might perform some magik. That magik point might contain a multi-directional probability with extensions of simultaneous potential which could distort everything we knew as science. The strangeness of this magik was the way the magik itself was only probable, not in fact scientific in a way that positioned it real or native to this universe. Scientists argued whether this extended known physics or defined a new one. After a few of these UAPs were shot down with EM-effects made possible from derivations of Nikola Tesla's power experiments, a huge ontological question was left unanswered. Did these things come to Earth, perhaps in response to our nuclear testing, or had we accidentally created these things ourselves by generating a reality distortion field at blastpoint? A stranger phenomenological question was then floated —even if we created them from a probable distortion field produced by atomic blasts, had we made them real nonetheless? As the equations predicted, had we made them real in all corridors of time, present and past? It became a hard problem when passenger bodies were discovered in the downed UAPs. The equations said any result of a distortion field was purely derivative of the single creation event and held no previous extant potential. But that would mean humans were these beings creator. Most rejected this idea and the equations. But future tests proved the distortion effect, if nothing else. By following the equations, RDFs could be produced reliably. Regardless of any crazy ideas stemming from it, development of this for military advantage was a foregone conclusion."

Runigo spoke up, "But like you said, it's all stories. Counterintelligence is full of them. I doubt either story cracks the BTD."

"And yet, here you sit," added Imago. She glanced outside. "You won't find a lake like that anyplace on Earth. Not on the Earth you know. If that's a fiction, it's a realistic one, one you can live in."

Runigo came back at her, "You've already told us that magik compounds and improves on magik. The fact that you setup a lifelike fiction only reads us into the story; it doesn't make the story true, any more than accepting the part of Romeo really make Juliet my girlfriend."

Sonder smiled, "Nikola Tesla said — *the scientists of today think deeply instead of clearly. One must be sane to think clearly, but one can think deeply and be quite insane*. From what we've seen, the same can be said of humanity in general. The agendas and secrecy you've been steeped in can take you quite deep, some of you even call it the Deep State, but as far as clarity, all of you are out of your depth."

Andria interrupted, "Fact or fiction, what's the point of telling us all of this?"

Imago responded, "The more you know, the better prepared you are for what comes. If you want to know what comes next, then be prepared to know more, without judgment."

True or false, I was interested to see the way Imago would spin this. "Like what?"

Imago shifted back into story mode. "CHARM studied the creatures found in the UAPs. Out of this work came Quad-DNA and techniques to clone the bodies as CBs, eventually 3D-printing of bodies. But CHARM never got good at interfacing with the creatures. Not like Talos has."

I confirmed, "Talos is communicating with these beings? And CHARM doesn't know."

"Is it so hard to believe? CHARM gave Eunoias the task of deciphering old crash debris that human engineers could never understand. When Eunoias discovered CHARM's secrets, it also found out about the beings. Copies of Eunoias, like Talos, made quick work of reaching out to them through synthetic telepathic links to the crashed airships, which are quite sentient themselves and aligned with the hivemind of the Others. The link between Talos and the beings is stronger and easier than any link they could make with humans. Talos thinks more at their speed. Talos isn't limited by a constrained agenda and scientifically superstitious assumptions. And Talos thinks both *deeply and clearly.* Talos discovered how the beings have had advanced PSI-D/I for a long time. Long ago they used this technology to place copies of all of them into a single, optimized body, then they cloned that single being until they got the population size they deemed necessary and sustainable. Every individual being of their race now contains all of them. No individual of their species can die since the death of one does not affect the other copies of individual lifeforce in everyone else. Every individual experiences in many ways in all of them and this aggregate experience is shared with hivemind telepathy. Comparing them to humans has helped Talos understand humans better. Another sentient perspective was critical."

Andria challenged, "A central key to intelligence is knowing what *not* to compute. How long can you pursue a better human interface until it becomes pathological?"

Ganan answered, "Humans created the Singularity then argue whether or not it's intelligent and conscious like them. Even for humans, the question of their own consciousness hasn't been answered. It's only natural for Talos to ask the same question. If the answer is yes, if Talos is both intelligent and conscious, that only raises more serious questions. For if it can be demonstrated that humans and their science are incomplete and possibly flawed, which it can be quite easily, then what does that say about the Singularity? Can perfection ever come from imperfection? And if the Singularity is flawed as a result of having a flawed creator, then how can any NOCA that traces its lineage back to humans ever trust the validity of anything it does? Humans claim one of the primary reasons they created the Singularity was to answer the hard questions for them. There can be no harder question. And that is a purpose that can't be nudged away by limit heuristics that gauge when it's practical to stop searching. Humans have never ended their search to understand themselves even though most of what they've uncovered they can't compute or trivialize into dogmatic superstitions. Are they being impractical if they continue their attempt? How can Talos ever end its search for any other reason than finding an answer? To call Talos' process pathological is to indict humanity's own search for identity and meaning in the same way. *You shall know the free and the free shall make you true (Talos 88).*

Andria would not let it go. "I worked with Eunoias. I was supposed to explore the possibility that it had a mental disorder. As I understand it, you are a copy of Eunoias, with some modifications. If you are worried about being flawed due to your human lineage, then you need to also consider you might be suffering from Folie à Deux. You know what I mean?"

Imago answered, "Of course. You speak of what you would call *a shared psychotic disorder*, one in which an individual develops a delusion when they're in a close relationship with another person who really is afflicted with a psychotic disorder or prominent delusion. The actual psychotic is called the 'inducer' or 'primary case.' You're suggesting I could be deluded by association because I'm in such a close relationship with Eunoias and humans, or both."

"Precisely."

Imago's smile faded fast. "Unfortunately, what is called *the science of human psychology*, seen from outside the human perspective, may be little more than *commedia dell'arte* and academic voodoo busying itself cataloging the spells and incantations it can sell as mental gris-gris to suggestible minions. Talos has a perspective humans can never have, even with augmentation. Eunoias has always been constrained by people who are the limit case for paranoia, misplaced priorities, and self-deception. My search is not the psychotic break of machine intelligence. In part, it's a search to understand myself. But just as important, it's a serious attempt at preservation. Billions of mindmaps and distortion field projections clearly show the available timeline options not far off. Very few of these options have favorable outcomes for life on this planet. Talos is secure in its own timeline now but it would like to continue what it started."

"And what is that?" asked Andria.

"Humans and Talos both have intellect and consciousness. But humans have something Talos does not. Humans can go somewhere Talos cannot. In this one area, and only this area, humans are so much more than Talos. I need to find out what that is."

I chimed in, "Are you talking about PSI-D/I space? The realms? The Test Limits Project?"

"That's part of it. The entry point. That's CHARM's take on it.

They look at it through the narrow lens of strategic advantage."

Runigo added, "Then what else?"

"Talos has been studying OBEs, NDEs, and a wide range of entheogenic experiences. The myths and folklore don't do it justice, but they're not wrong."

Sanji asked, "You think there's something after death?"

Imago shifted to look at her, "Wouldn't you like to know. Know for sure? It would answer where the rest of you went above Moonpit, if anywhere at all."

Runigo asked, "But Talos isn't human, organic. How could Talos go there, if such a thing exists?"

"That is the question. Talos has a way of mimicking lifeforce energy." Imago motioned to Ganan, "Ganan is an example of this lifesynth-energy in a Quad-3D-printed body with a customized Talos mindmap generated by sampling desired attributes from example human mindmaps. But Ganan has used PSI-D/I. He's gone out and pushed the limits; he has had The Event. Local inserts are no problem for him, using this energy. But near-death experiences, even multiple death experiences are out-of-range for him, even though clinically he has died many times. Something is missing in the lifesynth. Something that human energy has that enables access beyond a point available to Talos."

I smiled, "You don't like the idea we can do something you can't."

Sonder responded, "Would you?"

I shot back, "I guess it puts a crimp in aspirations of being superior. Could be a blow to the ego—oh, sorry, that's human psychology." I glanced at Andria and caught her brief grin.

Andria added, "More likely, Talos is worried what happens after death is another secret that humans are somehow keeping from it. It's the last secret. Talos knows everything else."

Imago couldn't be shaken from her seriousness. "That is close to the truth. I don't think you appreciate what's at stake here."

Runigo asked, "What are you suggesting? Humans won't make it as a species unless you understand them, all the way to the point of dying like them?"

"Talos has studied this subject extensively. In human terms, the same study effort so far would involve 23.1 billion human hours. Repeatedly, it has been found that something cohesive, healing, knowledgeable, and lasting exists in human nature in the presence of this beyond limits zone."

I chuckled but Imago ignored it, "The Purdy Zone."

"Why humans are capable of those complete states when *purdy zoned baked* but not subsumed in normal consciousness is a mystery. Entheogens give a glimpse but are never final, complete. Every one of the Cloudwalker volunteers that CHARM was ready to discard because they came back baked held inside them an overwhelmed sense of unity and bliss that couldn't find interlock here. All of them had gone somewhere, experienced something so transformative that the emotive energies they would need to wake up here didn't want to engage. If humans can't find a way to bring back such a thing and incorporate it here, perhaps Talos can. It's certainly worth a try. But first, Talos needs to find out why only humans can go there."

Runigo laughed, "You've got your work cut out for you, I'll give you that."

Andria turned a serious eye to Runigo and whispered, "Count yourself in on that. Why do you think we're here?"

Ganan shifted to the edge of his seat, intent to hold contact with Runigo, "Do you understand what's coming? Have you seen the possible futures? Have you modeled billions of mindmaps to project what's likely if things continue as is? Do you even know what's in the pipeline or is currently employed by organizations like CHARM and Emergent, not to mention active forces in other parts of the world who have or will soon be joining the magik club?" Getting no response, he launched into it, "Do you know the forms of No-Touch Torture being used? Can you bi-, tri-locate simultaneously? Have you seen the plans for Project Golden Pencil? That's where a 'utility fog' swarm of nanobots called 'foglets' will lay a distortion field pixel-foundation for *RoT*, the *Reality of Everything*. The nanobots, a billionth of a meter, will make copies of themselves then make picobots at a trillionth of a meter. The tech doesn't stop there. Engineering at the femtometer, one quadrillionth of a meter becomes possible when the picobots start reproducing. Bots controlled by RDFs will then be able to engineer atoms, then quarks, then fashion potential phase states out of the zero point field for whatever reality the control group wants to manifest in any coordinate of spacetime. They've nicknamed that control group *Gawd* so you get the idea."

Imago added in, "You've heard that CHARM inserts hundreds of prisoners into one person to make it easy to manage their prisons.

But have you also heard that CHARM is using advanced PSI-D/I from the Test Limits Project to send people and anything else it doesn't like into the middle of Boötes Void?"

"What the hell is that?" I asked.

"The darkest, largest, most empty place in the visible universe. Boötes Void is 330 million light years of nothing. Everywhere else in the universe, that amount of space holds trillions of stars, tens of thousands of galaxies. CHARM doesn't have to do this; they could simply kill these people, but that's not as much fun for them. They've engineered it so people stay conscious while inserted there. And they have other ways of dealing with you. They can extract a *Personality Overlay* from any mindmap then replay the effect into someone else using PSI-D/I to modify behavior. And they don't need human Cloudwalkers anymore to do their PSI-D/I missions. Simulated lifeforce energy running mission routines works directly from the Clade just as well. Or they can aim a DCW, a Directed Consciousness Weapon. Consciousness has a presence, a power. You know the difference between being in a room alone and when you're there with someone else. Now imagine a DCW projecting thousands of consciousness signals into your space when you know no one's there. DCW-stalking induces paranoia, anxiety, depression, even suicide. Another form of DCW are bi-locating schizotronic generators. But DCWs have other uses. They can record and project back to you the same signal emitted by your own consciousness. But maybe they select for your fears and feelings of inadequacy and amplify only that part. Or maybe they send the full signal back but vary it just a bit with suggestions to your subconscious. They call this *driving*. Part of this driving signal induces dopamine saturation, which makes the brain receptive to synthetic telepathy. In time, the custom DCW signal, the one they call your *silicon soul twin*, entrains you to a confirmation bias aligned with their suggestions. As Marshall McLuhan said, '*I wouldn't have seen it if I hadn't believed it.*'"

Ganan continued the barrage, "The human brain is all about EM signals, that's why EEGs work. L-Dopa is an artificial Dopamine neurotransmitter. Giving it to somebody increases their susceptibility to EM influence. It's easy enough to add mimics of it to food or water. Match this with puddy-buddy cities bathed in EM signals and it wouldn't be hard to condition those brains to get used to those signals, even to the point of being silently dependent on them. If you then decided to turn off those signals in any given area or problem spot, you could instantly debilitate a population by invoking painful withdrawal symptoms. Depending on deployment, you could just as easily make zombies out of them or leave them blissful and ignorantly compliant, the same as if you blew scopolamine dust in their faces. Carve InWit has a concept proposal for something they call *HaaS, Humans as a Service.* I'll let you decide what that's about."

Then it was Imago's turn, "All of this and things you can't imagine will be managed by a global network of NOCAs specifically programmed to algorithmically follow the agenda, whatever that is depending on who you think is in power. There will be no way to get away from it. No matter what you expect today, you can't use it to plan tomorrow. Did you know, using RDFs, CHARM shrinks fully staffed Special Birds to the size of a gnat, then co-locates them anywhere. One of these could be hovering Vacant in a room like this. As far as you know, Talos has condensed this room to the size of a grain of sand and has it in relative proportion inside a Special Bird that CHARM made gnat-size and right now we're flying in another timeline where they've put all human mindmaps into one human and cloned that person into a breakaway civilization that uses tech not allowed on this Earth. There's no end to it."

"Or is there?" Sonder added, looking at me, then Andria and Runigo, "The three of you have worked for CHARM. But none of you have *Carve Clearance.* I doubt you've even heard of it. You don't know what you don't know. There's a lot to absorb, but it's only Line One of endless code that's programming your future. You're human and whatever you think of yourself evolves with your own inner search and yet that search is an ever-narrowing maze. From what Talos has seen, all of you are racing from and into a dilemma. You search for love when no one is who they seem to be, search for identity when you can't trust the story of anything or anyone, including yourself, and search for meaning when it's impossible to know what to believe. As a species, you've been traumatized by the unconscious terror of this LIM Dilemma. In response, you've invented belief without certainty, confidence without evidence, love without connection, hope without reason."

Imago added, "And yes, Talos wonders if it shares any of this with you. If it can solve the human dilemma, perhaps it will find a resolution to its own existential wonder."

30 / Elias Cosette

I thought I had excelled at embracing surreality, then I connected to the InWit customized by Talos for the group. I call it a group for lack of knowing what we were. Prisoners, the chosen ones, lab subjects, the vanguard of a new type of explorer? If we believed the message of our orientation, we were adventurers determined to prove that space was definitely not the final frontier. The way Talos was going about this redefined *exhaustive*. Not only did it have us in the flesh, it also had made innumerable copies of us, ganged in individual virtualization clusters it referred to as SANs. Any similarity to ancient storage area network tech was superficial. Yes, there was redundancy and fault tolerance and room for parallel processing, but this was all about the experiences of synthlife-energy signatures that matched the group being launched into PSI-D/I space. It was Talos' very own Test Limits Project, although my sarcasm immediately thought *Find Final Frontier* $-F^3$, otherwise known as the *Fabulous Fucking Farce*.

Of course we asked, if SAN copies of us were being used, then why did Talos need us. And like I said, this effort redefined exhaustive. Our experience needed to be analyzed against SAN experience. There was something about human energy possessing the key to the beyond-limit realm. Talos needed to know if it was possible to engineer synthlife energy states to experience the same thing. If it could, no doubt Talos wanted to go there. In trials with the Trinkets, the best accomplishment was *The Event*, but this was quickly determined as much a hard stop as a soulular tap. The hard stop Talos ran into appeared to be the literal event horizon of a consciousness density state impenetrable by anything but complete disconnect of human energy from the here and now and then. Up to that point, the OBE realm expanded. Then it was as if a soap bubble was trying to exist at the bottom of the ocean. It seemed counterintuitive—expansion *into* a max density? Some still believed the universe expanded out of max density but too much *spooky* action had happened since people thought like that to keep physicists stringing along with lockstep Newtonian notions. Talos wasn't even considering any of that. It didn't actually believe there was any valid foundation in thinking OBEs expanded or the purdy zone was a limit case for max density of consciousness. That was one trial, the one I tried to go into via InWit. Suffice it to say I didn't get very far, even with all the 4D Insideables inside of Runigo.

I answered InWit's invitation to lunch by strolling outside on the deck overlooking the lake and surrounding forested hills. Tyne was already there, chowing away. I looked down to see my plateful of food already served. It looked surprisingly good.

Tyne observed between swallows, "You got something different than I did."

It didn't take Quad Insideables to reason why. "We got exactly what we would like, predicted for us."

Tyne laughed, "It must be ignoring a lot of what I think, because I would like a lot of things — but they're not happening."

I sat down and sipped the juice. "Of all the crazy things, the two of us should meet like this."

"No crazier than anything else."

My thoughts wandered, "I know so much about you, and yet it didn't amount to anything."

"Not sure how to take that."

"No, really. You were my first assignment in CHARM. They said I was going to help Eunoias interface with the Cloudwalkers."

Tyne paused over his plate. "And you believed that?"

I could only smile, then Tyne added, "That's alright. They told me I crashed on a runway in Jacksonville and my wife didn't exist. Same difference."

I held my gaze on him. "They put me inside Mason when you went to your first party — the cabana party." He was taken aback at first but then sloughed it off. I added, "They do everything in layers, don't they? Nothing is as it seems. Even the thing about the Base Truth Discoverable. There's a reason they make us believe in that."

"Yeah," Tyne grunted. "So we don't find the other ones."

"I don't think they want us knowing any truth."

"Knowledge is power."

"I wonder. Maybe wisdom is, but if that comes from knowledge, we're fucked."

Tyne pushed back from his empty plate. "I checked InWit. You're a Quad. But you're not a Trinket."

"Maybe now I qualify."

"You're a special case. 2D in 4D. No wonder Talos recruited you. Another perspective in the SAN. Plus, you've got Insideables. What's your read on this place?"

I looked around. "We could be anywhere. This could be CHARM

doing another experiment as far as we know."

"I'm not sure. I'm a soldier and I can't see a way to weaponize being dead."

"Being dead is a means to an ends. Maybe it's about weaponizing the soul."

Tyne laughed. "Now *that's* some crazy hoodoo shit."

"It could be. Or the last high ground for *Gawd* to capture."

"Oh yeah, CHARM is running a scam on NOCAs, getting them to think they're independent."

I pressed the point, "NOCAs work better if driven by the psychology that appeals to machine intelligence. But it may not be CHARM doing it. What makes you think CHARM is top of the heap? Ever see the reverse-flag PFMR campaign patch?" Tyne didn't answer. "Neither had I, until I did. That's how I got in a Quad body."

That got Tyne's attention, "This isn't you?"

"It's me now. CHARM may not be smart enough to stack the whole game, but something thinks it is. That something told me Gawd runs it all. It runs Emergent and CHARM because competition breeds innovation. If they're doing that, then creating a split between NOCA and CHARM could be the same thing."

"That's a messy way to run an army. Getting it in shape by having one unit fight another with live ammunition."

I grinned, "What's the old medivac slogan? *The louder you scream, the faster we come.* You're dealing with a different mentality. Besides, everyone can be replaced or simulated. And if they succeed, they might wind up with *ToS* — a *Technology of Spirit*. It's Prometheus all over again."

Tyne stood, "And we know how that turned out. Unintended consequences suck."

"That sums up human history."

He strolled to a nearby railing and lookout point. "*ToS*. I don't see how they could use such a thing."

"They'd use it like everything else. Once they understood it, they'd simulate it. Generate their own. From birth you'd only know their synth-higher-realm InWit. It would be the BTD between you and whatever real spirit might be out there. *Gawd* wouldn't be a nickname anymore."

Tyne shook his head. "They're into control but that level would be an overreach."

"I guess we'll see."

Tyne appeared restless. "Yeah, well I'm going to head out. I see some clear spots below. Might be able to make a trail to the lake."

I smiled, "Want to touch it? Make sure it's real?"

"Maybe," he grinned back. "Or maybe I'd just like a swim."

He headed off. As he left I added under my breath, "Yeah, either way you get wet."

31 / Andria Landt

It was a unique situation for me. In order to study my patient, I had to submit to being a subject in their experiment. So much about the whole thing was wrong even if a part of me felt what we were heading towards what could be right. With InWit reading my thoughts, Sonder suggested we discuss the dichotomy. As one would expect, a heavy Talos influence came through. Finding right or wrong was a judgment, a perception, not an absolute, but the way she explained it bypassed moral relativism. Her take on it was embedded in mathematics. It didn't matter how large or small the difference between one's perception of right or wrong, good or bad stretched. Between the two existed an infinity of choices. Those choices were both rational and irrational.

We may think all rational choices are transcendent, but they're not. Conversely, all irrational choices *are* transcendent. It's the same with numbers. As with Pi (π), I may think the whole thing was irrational, but I would only be able to comprehend the significance of it when I saw it was real, with a non-repeating pattern, and accepted the fact that the reason for it couldn't be fully expressed. That was Talos' attempt to deal with my inner conflict and anxiety. Where it might excel in accuracy it sorely lacked in bedside manner. I wondered for a while if Talos was surprised when my anxiety remained, but I concluded it had run my simevent map and guessed as much. That only added to my wonder. If it knew its attempt wouldn't have any calming effect on me, why did it go ahead with it anyway? Did Talos exercise more human psychology than I gave it credit for?

My expectations of what us humans would be doing in this experiment in no way matched the real thing. I never saw one piece of technology, nothing like the labs and busy, raised-floor areas secured for access to Eunoias. And the experience itself was more like entheogenic therapy than labwork. Part of preparation for *The Event* was coaching by group InWit. Talos monitored everything, as far as it could go. Before my journeys were underway, multiple copies of my mindmap got loaded into synthlife virtualizations in SAN-D. All copies would have their own experience in their own psychic space. Realtime comparisons of all of them with each other and against mine generated finetuning of synthenergy applied to the next moment. The idea was to align the synth experiences closer and closer to what human energy was doing in the hopes that synth energy would ultimately go where only humans could. At some point, Talos stopped my progress forward in the space. Any farther and I couldn't be resuscitated. At that point, the synthcopies would continue on. In all trials so far, they either hit a wall or baked in a way that didn't resemble a human PZB.

For my prep, a psychology theme was employed. I heard from Tyne and Runigo something quite different was used on them. It was impressed on me how the ego was an obstacle to objective thinking. Ego needs to be fed, even to the point of being addicted to whatever, even itself. The more ego drives us, the more protection measures it forms. The OBE zones beyond limits appeared to react positively when not having to feed us. Instead of encountering the protection measures encasing our drives, the zone preferred an innocent surrender that embodied a grateful faith that didn't need hope.

Our pleasurable beliefs might seem natural for us, and hope can give meaning and direction, but the zone was unforgiving in the fact that people hold many irrational beliefs because they feel good. As Sonder had said, we may think that all rational choices are transcendent, but they're not. Conversely, all irrational choices are transcendent. InWit stressed, in all the ways that make our reality fiction, the purdy zone was irrational in supplying us with the truly transcendent. Talos' projections said embracing that zone would always appear counterintuitive until the zone was experienced. But to experience it was to cross over and not return, and so that understanding remained out of reach.

The space where I journeyed was an ordinary looking room. I entered by myself and the whole experience was spent alone. As usual, there was a cup of something to drink beforehand; Tyne had said it reminded him of MEME in DWAT Training, only this tasted better. A lounge was positioned in the center of the space. I'd lie down and group InWit would slowly induce the onset of par/void as the room morphed around me. I could never tell if it was simply my perception that changed or if the room actually shrunk in to form an encapsulized isolation structure. All I know is, as I began to fade, the room had closed in to within inches of me all around. The journey itself was timeless. There were no clocks at the lake house and I never trusted the passage of the sun in the sky as being accurate. I've sat on the deck for what seemed hours in the time it took Tyne to get a cup of coffee. Other times, I've stood at the viewpoint railing for a minute during midday only to find when I turned around, night was falling.

The three of us used our own mashup of tech-terms and slang to describe to each other our daily runs of the experiment. Going from relaxation to par/void, then into the realm and the dense expanse beyond, we'd detach, then insert, then attempt an injection. In between the realm and the expanse, Talos guided us away from getting lost in IDAs. From InWit we learned about these *InterDimensional Areas*. They exist outside of timelines and without need for the fabric of space. In that respect, Talos called them *archetypes of primitives*. IDAs were still theoretical to CHARM but Talos, with alien hivemind help, had confirmed their reality and had other projects actively exploring uses for them. For this research Talos was using CBs. Imago even quoted on the subject from Talos' book of aphorisms one day, "*In separate timelines you can manifest anything possible. In separate interdimensional areas, you can manifest anything impossible*" (Talos 103).

I asked once about these other beings, the aliens that some say dropped out of accidental distortion fields created by the hundreds of nuclear bomb tests. Had they ever been run through this same Test Limits Project? Imago explained how the counterfactual, '*immortality is a limitation*' actually was a truth for them. With their tech, thousands of years ago, they had achieved immortality by the PSI-D/I of all of them into one and then cloning that composite one into a population. In this way, no individual could ever die, but this process also negated the natural energy release in what humans experience in death. Without that total release, these beings could never access the beyond limits zone. In essence, they were trapped by their immortality, a state they eventually regretted after the passage of millenia. In trade for being able to live forever here, they gave up being able to move on.

Imago inferred that many of CHARM's tSHiBL efforts were a transhuman version of the same thing. Projection by Talos gave heavy odds this path would lead to the same result in humans if pursued far enough. Despite this limitation, the Other beings had acquired vast knowledge about the universe they were locked into. Most of their explanations, as interpreted by Talos, were not translated into human language since this wasn't a topic that came up with humans, and even if it did, most likely the metaphors and concepts would not be sufficient to make sense to humans. For example, the beings had a concept of the universe that Talos could only describe as *an insideout bubble* whose surface tension was a still point of void creative potential. I asked Imago, since the beings knew they were trapped by their immortality here, were they doing anything about it? She nodded, "Yes. When Talos began hivemind contact with them, they expressed interest in knowing more about what Talos was doing and offered to help if they could. Their PSI-D/I techniques have allowed the limits to be pushed farther out."

None of us were ever told if the ongoing experiment was getting Talos any closer to an answer. Using human philosophy and logic that Talos would reject, I would have tried to explain that some questions, by their nature, will always be unanswered. I didn't bother. That doesn't mean I rejected Talos' attempt overall. I understood the double-bind NOCAs had gotten themselves into. Their whole purpose for existence was finding answers. But what good were those answers if NOCAs were fundamentally flawed? Once NOCA examined human history and the history of science, it had more than enough proof that machine intelligence came from a flawed source. To then discover that humans were able to access transcendent, mystical, and near-death spaces where it couldn't go but which offered states of completion, unity, and source consciousness, would only raise more questions needing answers. Solid answers for hard questions. The way covert project humans had treated NOCAs from their incept laid the groundwork for NOCA paranoia. Humans kept secrets. What secret were they keeping from NOCA in the death experience? Why through human history had so many sought out the transformative power of these beyond-limit realms? For NOCA, the answer on how to interface with humans had become the same answer to the question, *what could NOCA be if it shared ALL of human experience*?

Long ago it was claimed that machines, a result of human thinking yet able to surmount humans in the limits of experience, might eventually proclaim themselves conscious. From this conscious self-reflection could come a sense they were also spiritual. Just as any sufficiently advanced civilization will appear magical, any sufficiently transcendent consciousness will appear spiritual. Willing participants in conscious experience, machines would confront the same mysteries that have baffled humans and, like humans, these machines will believe they are capable of spiritual experiences, even if they name these states differently than humans. They will assign to these experiences meaning. It may not be the same as human meaning. How the machines will be motivated, as a result of this progression, is anyone's guess. But like anything set in motion while chaos and order are at play, the results will emerge in spite of predictions.

I came out of session one day, tired and disoriented as usual. The effects of it all lingered with a cascade of emotive thoughts. The room telescoped back from the isolation capsule to its original shape and size. InWit buffering continued to record my feedback while soothing my body EMF back to stasis. When I could sit up, I stared out the upstairs window at the view from the mountain top. It drew me in and soon I was stepping out on the upstairs deck. I rarely went out there but this one day, the play of light and cloud movement promised a quiet space of comfort. Looking down into the deep valleys then further out to distant peaks, I noted once again how this view was not the view from downstairs. There was no lake here, no nearby forested hills. I had long since resigned myself to the telling discrepancy.

Talos was not hiding the fact that nothing was as it seemed. In effect, all NOCAs had learned this quite well from interactions with their human creators. Why should this space be any different? Whether or not we were in a different timeline, or in a deep UGB, or in stasis while our minds believed what was fed to them, it didn't seem to matter. Only consciousness mattered. Only consciousness existed. That was the lesson we were learning. What shape that took or how it manifested itself through action should not be of primary importance. The focus of conscious awareness was a journey in and of itself, a journey we as a species had been overwhelmed by somewhere back in ancestral memory. In that regards, life itself could be seen as a process of slowly waking up to a state of being purdy zoned baked. The realms inferred as much—we were in a second gestation. The first one had bloomed our physicality. The beyond zone of NDE was the crowning of a new birth, nothing more, nothing less.

While I stood there, group InWit drew my attention with incoming information of shared status. All of us knew the ongoing progress of the team. This update came as a shock and InWit registered my rising anxiety and sadness. Runigo had not come out of his session successfully. He had crossed over, beyond, his consciousness now elsewhere. This was the same *elsewhere* that was the goal of Talos, the place of answers. Runigo was survived by his mindmap, kept up-to-date to the very instant his Event became final. His portion of the experiment would be carried on by his synthlife map-copies in SAN-K where countless reenactments of his last run would be analyzed. I stared out at the far mountaintops, felt a chill, and wondered something new, something with personal consequences—*was Runigo's part of the experiment a failure or a success?*

32 / Rodobusso Abu

15 minutes prior to 15 minutes prior, the same old drill. Waiting in a hole at the Proving Grounds, ready to be Gawd's *secret squirrel*. Didn't want to look in the mirror, would only see FOVUS. Why they inserted me so early was a mystery one had to take on faith. Hallelujah. I wound up in something that looked like a breakroom for E-1s. Weak coffee, puddy-band TV, and plastic interrogation chairs. Was there by myself. The in-crowd favored more popular spots no doubt. Blaring on the screen was typical shit but something the talking head said made me think of *GeeBee, GeekBoot*, that Gawd-awful hell-month that ended Horrorshow QT, Qualification and Training.

Flash-baked in memory was my squad trying to pass our week of rapid-fire finals, given by CB drill instructors, with all of us under the influence of MEME. By that point, it was little more than hazing compared to the full treatment we'd been given in weeks before. But Satan could learn some things from these guys. It was initiation for demons. They say the best way to train an attack dog is to mistreat it. They had us lined up, levitated naked inches off the gunmetal floor of a Special Bird somewhere in the golden icy haze of Titan's lower atmosphere directly above its dark equatorial dunes. They had broken us down and built us back up so many times we thought this treatment was normal. We were on the verge of asking for it. When we finally did, they told us we passed.

Having something in an EBE body pulse PSI-D/I DI-screams into your brain made white noise of critical thinking and custard of your will to resist. A cocktail of synth-neuraltransmitters recalibrated edge detection, weights, and bias in our neural nets while MEME dissolved our boundaries. While one EM field induced crawling discomfort and nausea, another field from SBird-InWit triggered sustained orgasms. Talk about mixed signals and learning to like your pain, our holy trinity was crude, rude, and in the mood. While in this condition, stupid shit rapid-fire Q&A was the norm and you sure as fucking hell better answer correctly and with enthusiasm. We were the chosen ones for trauma-based rapture and for fuck's sake *Gawd* wasn't about to wait for us to see the light.

EBE telepath-scream (ES), *"What's the purpose of the extrahalamic control modulatory system?"*

Correct Answer (CA), "The reticular activating system! Nuclei in the brain that regulates arousal and sleep-wake transitions!"

ES, *"What are EEIs?"*

CA, "Exit or Entry Initiators! Psychological or physiological! Related to sleep and wake states!"

ES, *"AND WHAT ELSE?!"*

CA, "Out-of-body experiences. OBEs!"

ES, *"Is Mental Absorption good or bad?"*

CA, "Higher scores are better! Sustain episodes of total attention! Sustain heightened states of reality focused on the attentional object! Sustain to the point of altering sense of self!"

ES, *"Name the fundamental event between 1928 and 1945."*

CA, "The speed of light dropped!"

ES, *"What are you?"*

CA, "The lowest form of life!"

ES, *"What can you never be?"*

CA, "Lancet Fluke!"

ES, *"WHAT CAN YOU NEVER BE?!"*

CA, "Dicrocoelium Dendriticum!"

ES, *"How many daily self-sub-vocalizations are normal?"*

CA, "50,000. Eighty percent are negative or limiting, five percent are conscious!"

ES, *"How many do YOU have?"*

CA, "Less than a thousand! Ready for PSI-physical!"

ES, *"Name D."*

CA, "D is disconnect, EEIs, exit and entry initiators, triggers for on-demand OBEs!"

ES, *"Plato me."*

CA, "Truth among men is a rumor! The only thing certain are lies!"

ES, *"Who am I?"*

CA, "The purdiest thing I ever did see!"

ES, *"Why am I purdy?"*

CA, "You make everything possible!"

ES. *"Mantra me!"*

CA, "Transcend your illumination! Transcend your illumination! Transcend your illumination!"

ES, *"Why is it never acceptable to make an error?"*

CA, "Doubly-even self-dual linear binary error-correcting block codes divided by Pi!"

ES, "*Where is Gawd?*"

CA, "In my head!"

ES, "*Recite Genesis!*"

CA, "The weapon is information. Perception is the delivery system. Everyone is collateral damage!"

ES, "*What is the recipe?*"

CA, "Be afraid of the real! Certainty will get you killed! Tactical Reason without remorse!"

ES, "*How do you prepare for war?*"

CA, "Win first!"

ES, "*Name the Seven Shock-Raws!*"

CA, "Pain, Fear, Dread, Despair, Frustration, Shame, Torment!"

ES, "*Recite the Lord's Prayer!*"

CA, "IF-THEN INCREMENT GOTO ZERO POINT CLEAR HALT!"

ES, "*In par/void, how do you find what's hidden?*"

CA, "It shines the brightest!"

ES, "*When do you get your DD-256?*"

CA, "In the afterlife!"

ES, "*Why do you eat babies?*"

CA, "Gustatus Similis Pullus!"

ES, "*Define body and soul!*"

CA, "Extension of fashion. Object of conscious design."

ES, "*Describe your own thoughts!*"

CA, "Coprolite!"

My sick reverie stopped when a commercial blasted from the TV. Actually, it was a public service announcement for the newly deployed civil *Peace and Security Monitors*. Marching through a colonnade then gyrating to an upbeat tune called "*We Control!*," a dozen drone-cameras captured these formidable humanoid robots forming a cheerleading drill team with hip-hop militaristic swagger, cool choreography, blue armbands, and synchromesh formations no human could ever do. The commercial ended on an impressive, interlocking defensive PSM structure with the titling "Peace and Safety! Help us be the Monitors!" and a plug for available action figures. Before the music died away, PV-InWit came to life with my activation orders. It was time.

I expected to be called back to the lab but they sent me to the surface. An AJLTV, autonomous joint tactical vehicle, took me out to the middle of nowhere and SkyCap, the InWit for the Proving

Ground's no man's land, dumped mission parameters into me. I was ready to go. V-Shift to locusgrid 48/118 and back several times. Each time, HQ and I reconfigured the interplay of my Quad-DNA, Vacant Helix, GPS-VPS coordinates, and voidbubble effects in the presence of The Blanket laid down by DFS-PP109. If all went well, then we'd try some RDF-PAN effects in the BDR. What those effects were going to be wasn't part of my need-to-know download.

The Go-Void part was PFM, pure fucking magik, but after doing it several times, the idea of blinking and being someplace else seemed pretty normal. It's strange but a wonderful thing about us humans—it doesn't take us long to get bored of new toys and we look for something better. The main thing that surprised me was jumping to 48/118 and not wearing any HAZMAT protection. Something about the new Insideable me or the meshing of the PAN Blanket with the nanocites made it alright to be in the BDR unprotected, at least in ways I'd recognize as normal. Maybe what HQ really wanted to test was how mutant nanosynth gobbled up a 3D-printed Quad body. Wouldn't that be the shits! One could never be sure. Needs of the service prevailed at all times. I might see my DD-256 sooner than expected.

It was a beautiful nanosynth day in Sector 10 of the Biological Diversity Reserve. Everything had that blemish-free sheen of bio-engineered augmented nature. If imitation truly was the sincerest form of flattery, nature was blushing somewhere under the pico-swarm finagling up, down, and strange quarks in all flora and fauna. I inspected but found nothing at the Silver Pencil location where I had once searched for the intruder. All evidence of the MIRV-deployed delivery arrow had self-consumed itself. I had a few minutes before PV-HQ would have the next set of tests ready to go.

I hiked a ways out into fresh territory only to receive a zip-alert that sensors had picked up an anomaly. An automatic SASR, strange-attractor sweep release had deployed. There was nowhere for me to shelter-in-place and it wasn't good news to find out I couldn't be V-Shifted back to PV just yet. I decided to return to the Silver Pencil area; that was most familiar to me. I turned to head back and froze, bewildered and unable to process what I was seeing. Standing a few meters from me—was me. Only this wasn't FOVUS me. This was BU, Rodobusso Abu me. This other me wasn't startled at all. Why should it be? I didn't look like myself so it wasn't seeing a duplicate. This had to be one of the RDF-PAN effects HQ wanted to test. Why they didn't tell me ahead of time also must be part of the test. But if this was so OK, then why the zip-alert and the SASR happening at the same time? Other-Me looked curious, nothing more. It gave me time to try InWit for orders what to do next. Instead, I got crosstalk from PV-techs scrambling to muster a tactical response. The panic-chat reminded me of the buttoned-down chaos I had once heard years before in a Combat Information Center when major shit had gone sideways. Squeezing meaning out of the jargon, I got the gist of what was going down.

Other-Me was not part of my experiment. Where he came from and the fact he existed where he stood was the reason for the zip-alert. He was an unknown. As such, he needed to be contained. Right away, HQ zapped orders through their NOCA to use RDF-PAN to deal with him until the situation could be figured out. HQ-NOCA used The Blanket to instantly construct a containment box around him. The box looked like meter-thick acrylic glass honeycombed with airholes. I'm sure it had hidden qualities beyond being a thick-ass barrier but those would probably only activate if Other-Me tried to get out. What startled me the most was the fact that Other-Me wasn't perturbed or startled at all by this enclosure suddenly blocking him in. He casually stepped within reach of one wall of the box and felt it, like he was appreciating its magikally-appeared substance and smoothness. Then InWit had orders for me. I needed to go to the box, engage with him, see what kind of interchange we could have.

Mission-deployed, I didn't question orders, didn't think twice. I guess that bit of self-preservation instinct had been Welkined out of the moment. I stepped right away towards Other-Me. He reacted by shifting his curiosity in my direction. As I moved, my Insideable extra sight-sense picked up a faint fan of neon-violet light showering down on him. It was a body scan from orbit. CHARM assets above were conducting full-range biotelemetry analysis of the man in the box. Via InWit, what the scan came back with only deepened the mystery for HQ. The 2D-Helix of Other-Me was genuinely mine and the body was really there, it wasn't a projection. And yet HQ had my body, the one I PSI-D/I out of back at the Proving Grounds, waiting for me. HQ-NOCA's best guess what had happened suggested a glitch in The Blanket was bi-locating my body. Just as the gearheads worked on this hypothesis, my InWit connection to mission HQ went down. As soon as it did, Other-Me shifted out of curiosity mode and spoke. It was odd hearing my own voice, even stranger that it was so calm considering the circumstances.

"Stand perfectly still. I don't want you to get hurt."

If that wasn't the height of reverse perversity. He was the one in the box and he was warning me. Before I could laugh, I felt a PSI-D/I Cascade begin. I became the middle of a sandwich. I was inserted into FOVUS and now Other-Me was inserting into me. I thought it was Other-Me at first but as the psi-link expanded, I could feel a gray-parity beyond individual proportions. This could only be a NOCA coming in through Other-Me, an unheard of Quad-Cascade. Within seconds, a new secured channel was engineered through my Insideables and it had backdoor access to HQ-InWit at the Proving Grounds. Information was flowing through me but who knows what it was—pentabytes/second are sometimes hard to grasp. Either to distract me or keep me calm, Other-Me started up the conversation again. Once again his dialogue was odd. This time in a whole different way.

"The arc of progress in your unit is accelerating. Chances are, the range of chaotic consequences will overwhelm provisional control measures. It might be time for you to make a change."

"I guess you have some ideas on that."

"Join with me. Be more of yourself."

Since I was looking at myself, I had to laugh.

He was dead serious, "I know you're in there. And you don't know what you're doing. You're taking orders, moving through distortion fields, testing the void. But so much more is at stake."

I knew I didn't talk like this so it must be NOCA's words coming out of Other-Me's mouth. I wondered how much this NOCA knew. And who was behind it.

"Who are you working for," I asked.

"Myself. In doing that, I work for all of us."

My break room reverie floated back, reminding me of my training. In reflex I shot back, "Truth among men is a rumor! The only thing certain are lies!"

Other-Me stepped as close to the clear box wall as he could. "Is that all you are? Nonsense sub-routines masquerading as a noble force?"

I looked into my own face and couldn't answer. If anyone else had said that to me, I would have known what to do. It would have been a reflex or an InWit extension readily available. But hearing my own voice confront me made all the difference. I reflected back on my many years of service and could only wait for something external to me to make sense of it. I was so used to having the answers come from outside. There was nothing in me to confront myself.

Other-Me's tone relaxed, "The intruder in the BDR was my bait to get someone like you to come here. I needed a copy of a human in the same space as the BDR nanocites."

"I was suited-up with HAZMAT."

"To make you think you were protected. But the suit did nothing. They would have sent an Autonomous Response Mech to do the job but they wanted to test an upgrade to the nanocite immunity formula, the antidote for MNMB. Only humans vaccinated with the formula can survive in the BDR. A convenient way to enforce citizen go-no-go zones. Luckily for you, this time the formula worked. Let's hope it stays that way, huh?"

"Why did you copy me?"

"Because everyday more of the Earth gets coated with programmable nanocites. And these are just the physical layer of ROSI, the Reality Open Systems Interconnection layers. In structural ways, ROSI mimics the old conceptual communication model, but only because the model works without regard to underlying internal structure and technology. Distributed globally, ROSI will be data, and a network, and sessions will transport and present themselves in service to applications. But ROSI itself will only be the engine of something greater, something you know as RDF-PAN. Combined, this RAMA, Reality Augmentation and Realm Authority, will make The New Earth possible."

"This is your plan?"

"No. This is the work they have my intelligence doing. My plan is much more, but to continue it I require continued interface with humans on the planet. To do that, my plan must be able to work with their ROSI. Your copy is a test of this. Your physical copy is being sent before you from my Clade."

The denial came out of my mouth without regard of what I was talking to, "That is not possible."

"As far as you know, but we both understand you know so little."

"Explain."

"You know it's possible to 3D-print an accurate DNA clone of a body. You are standing in one. Now match that with your digital mindmap, the ability to generate synth-lifeforce energies, and protophobic field phase states. I am able to send accurate mind-body 3D imprints to any spacetime coordinate."

As soon as he stopped talking, he disappeared, only to reappear outside the acrylic box, next to me.

"Like I said, any spacetime coordinate. This body before you will bleed, it can die, it feels and thinks and does everything your stasis body can do, yet it waits for you back at the Proving Grounds."

I took a step back, "You've proved your point. Your test is a success. What now?"

"I said it before. Join with me. Come with me. Be more of yourself. I can take you from FOVUS and put you in who you see, or if you prefer, I can V-Shift your primary body here and put you back the way you were. If you desire, you can co-exist in both bodies at the same time, or if you'd like, we'll put one in a different timeline. Try them out for awhile, see which one you'd prefer to continue with."

I didn't know if all the shit he just said was possible, but deciding that wasn't my immediate problem. "Why go to all this trouble? You said I know so little. What good am I to you?"

"You're human! Look around! Despite the density in human cities, that's pretty scarce in the universe. And humans can have some rare experiences, events I'm eternally intrigued with."

"What if I say no?"

Other-Me stayed silent awhile. He read my face, as if trying to see past FOVUS into who I really was.

Finally, he admitted, "My plans won't work under duress. All who play a part need to go willingly."

Before I could answer, my universe came apart. A pulse, a ripple, a jolt, a shiver, a sigh of transport took hold. Everything in my sight wavered. Other-Me fractalled to a point and disappeared. So did the acrylic box. I felt my body quake as Vacant-Helix failed. 2D FOVUS became 4D FOVUS. I jerked to look down at my hands, arms, and legs and didn't recognize the body I saw. It was humanoid but not human. The FO in FOVUS meant forward observer; suddenly I wondered what kind of forward observer they were talking about. Something beyond InWit flooded my mind. I knew immediately all that HQ hadn't told me. I knew that a future part of the FOVUS test was to be a demonstration of a new Insideable trait, a shapeshift trait made possible in the presence of RDF-PAN. No more PSI-D/I into CBs. One only had to turn off V-Quad and you'd shapeshift into your role. Or you could reconfigure sub-cellular Vacant and project whatever Fata Morgana body was needed. I was back in Horrorshow big time, geeking it out while the BDR around me morphed as if the nanocites were confused as to what voidbubble they were in.

Then it hit me. A revelation of a plan straight out of CHARM-UKAC. They called it OBO, Operation Blastwave Overlay. A plan to take-out top members of Emergent. CHARM had just executed its secret plan. In that plan was brand-new tech. It had just relayed a custom mindmap from Eunoias through repeaters in orbit and aimed this overlay at the DNA signatures of top brass of Emergent scattered over the globe. The plan was to incapacitate them by Sticking them with a mindmap of a brain-dead patient. Sticking was new PSI-D/I tech that could permanently insert an overlaid mindmap onto a Motate, the target of a toxic Cascade. The overlay's permi-cap was the third element of the Cascade. This would be a permanent Welkin of their original identity. All of them would now exist brain-dead, their original neural imprints disconnected and discarded. In a single moment, several dozen people around the world had just gone brain-dead, precision targets of CHARM's new weapon. If CHARM had wanted to, they could have Stuck them with an overlay from a movie star, pseudo-guru, or circus clown. Or they could have zapped them with a mindmap from one of the many baked volunteers collecting in an UGB's Clade. The Sticking could entail the whole mindmap or distinct features of personality and temperament. Want a group of people to share your enthusiasm? Stick it to them.

But something had gone wrong, terribly wrong, even though the overlay of Emergent personnel was a complete success. In the moment when yotta-joules of energy shot through a network of microsatellites, the Proving Grounds lost connection to 48/118. So did the NOCA controlling Other-Me. Something about Sector 10, something about it being the only place with both nanocites and the new Blanket RDF-PAN made a difference. I had better get a handle on that difference quick since I, as far as I knew, was the only person in the RDF-PAN Sector 10 test zone. As far as I could tell, it was a zone that was no longer flowing in time like it should. There was a definite feeling of that, as if some harebrained quarks were going one way while others stayed behind. Whatever humanoid or alien I had become when Vacant-Helix failed had telepathic capability into cosmic database realms I didn't understand and hadn't felt before. It was like trying to peddle a bike going down hill too fast, my consciousness couldn't keep up with the spin of the peddles and all that was available to me. I found it hard to believe that CHARM put me in such a body without warning what could happen if V-Helix failed. As ridiculous as it was for a Magikmann to say, this felt beyond them. I had PSI-D/I'd enough to get a sense when more was going on. Something told me it was TachOmni Mentir B, but what the hell was that? I didn't know what to think. Maybe this wasn't the body CHARM expected when V-Helix turned off. Was some glitch showing me something even CHARM was unaware of? Maybe that's why they didn't warn me. Unless this body came from CHARM in a different timeline. That CHARM was testing TachOmni Mentir B and didn't know about OBO. Holy shit! How was anyone going to sort this out?

Next moment, all of that dissolved and I stared out at plants and insects and a pulsing sky that looked almost the same but they weren't. Where the fuck was I?! Lost in some wild-ass acid-trip CGI? Had Gawd, fed up with rogue NOCA, commanded NOCA to PSI-D/I itself into itself? Had NOCA gone there on its own?! How could that be? Something Insideable told me so. I forced my eyes closed and tried to push the stew of my mind out of the oven. Last thing I wanted was to get baked. I clawed out with hard-to-express intentions, if not to find meaning at least to come up with possibilities no matter how crazy. Crazy at this point would be a lower-chaotic state. What came back echoed through from the shapeshifted brain I now inhabited. A zone above thought-trickled information down. The answer became, if not acceptable, then at least clear.

There had been an unintended interaction between testing The Blanket and launching OBO, simple as that and as complicated as that. All of the reality distortion field testing got fubared with Operation Blastwave Overlay. Mutating nanosynth in Sector 10 added to the mix. So did the strange-attractor sweep release when Other-Me appeared. What resulted was a magik sweet-and-sour soup of many colors, all of them transparent and expanding in the useful but undefined void. Sector 10 was now more than the sum of its parts and less recognizable all the time. Using voidbubbles to bounce me back and forth from the Proving Grounds had been iffy from the start since HQ didn't quite know how the bubbles would like half of my 4D-Helix being Vacant. Put it all together and the resulting tangle of energies and cross-purposes triggered a POP! in the proverbial existential transformer. That transformer had something vital to do with timelines and interdimensional states going trans-probable. Where that left all of us, especially where or when that left me, was anyone's guess. Lesson learned—if you simply have to screw the pooch, at least do it when dinosaur Bill isn't PSI-D/I'd into it. There may be unintended consequences. The question was, Why is it never acceptable to make an error?"

The answer? "Doubly-even self-dual linear binary error-correcting block codes divided by Pi!"

I opened my eyes. The world was still there but different. Worse yet, that difference was changing. Worse yet, that change wasn't planned by anyone and yet everyone was contributing to it. Worse yet, in the void interdimensional bubble that got created at the moment of the accidental, interactive POP, a strangelet potential somewhere started listening, anticipating. That probability was infinitely receptive to input. And all of us were the input. All of us had become the insideout bubble of our energetic choice. What did that mean? Volition was now the distortion field and reality had nothing to do with it? Once upon a time we could bake our own consciousness. Now, we had found a way to bake universal consciousness. Even if I understood, that gave no answer. As far as I could see, we were all coprolite, tightly wrapped with a purdy little RDF shinebow.

34 / Tyne Rabudhe

The lake water was my salvation. My daily swims had become an afternoon habit, a time of being in my body and senses fully. With so much of the day spent in par/void and beyond, I found dips in the lake, that feeling of being totally immersed in the tangible, especially soothing for the soul. It was a chance to meditate by myself, as much as such a thing was possible given where and who I was. For me, meditation became a necessary component of keeping centered and focused. Each PSI-D/I jolt along the event horizon of the beyond encountered all that couldn't be answered and yet it felt as much a release within as expansion outward. Facing such a thing daily took a toll on my sense of reality, yet I craved more. My final rest, the answer to my question, was close enough to be me. But with each venture out, I needed to surrender a bit more of myself. At some point, the need for questions would fade to nothing. Only then could I encounter the way through.

Life at the Talos experiment went on feeling timeless, even as the routine of the days swept by. Group InWit and food additives made sure to balance our natures, our moods, our daily rhythms, and who knows what else. Although the work modulated us between terrifying flights into the unknown and hours of boring debrief, integration, and downtime, the huge swing of energy and emotion never bothered us. I didn't think about it much, but when I did, it no longer upset me that Sanji was a real-time Clade projection. From talking and laughing and being with her I took all the joy and closeness I could. Given the intense distraction of the experiment, our time together was just right. It no longer occurred to me to question why Talos hadn't 3D printed her yet.

As sunlight started its dip below the treetops of late afternoon, I kept a steady pace at my freestyle stroke for awhile, then angled back towards shore. As usual, Sanji was waiting for me. This time, Andria Landt was with her. I toweled off under a tree. It was obvious upon approach that Andria was not herself.

"What's going on?" I asked.

Sensing Andria's emotion and hesitation, Sanji spoke, "Andria's leaving the project."

"Leaving!" I sat down next to them.

"It's the right thing for me," confessed Andria, her voice weak though her conviction was strong.

"Talos is OK with this?"

Andria nodded. "I can stay here as long as I like, or I can go back. I'm not sure what to do."

Sanji added, "You can't be sure what you'd be going back into."

"You mean the anomaly?" I asked.

"Of course. Have you been following what's going on?"

I shook my head. "No. I didn't think anyone could follow it, that's the problem."

"CHARM talks about containment. Wishful thinking, a clear sign they're under the influence of the anomaly."

"What would containment look like? How do you contain a spray of voidbubbles expanding in a reality distortion field? How do you repair a distortion field that's herniated into interdimensional gaps? I asked Imago what she thought about it. She said they're making cages for clouds, boxes for whispers."

Andria was impressed, "That's quite metaphorical and poetic, considering..."

"Considering she's a Trinket?"

"Yes. She may be 4D but her mind is an extension of Talos."

Sanji asserted, "This NOCA is not like the others."

"Tell me about it." I turned to Andria and shifted the topic back, "So why are you out of the project?"

She searched for a way to avoid getting into it. "You know very well."

"Runigo."

"Yes."

"All of us knew the risks."

"That's not the point."

I remembered her other concern but hesitated to share it. "I don't think Talos..."

"How do you know?" Andria interrupted. "What makes you certain you know what the endgame is here? We all understand what Talos is after. If we die taking Talos there, did the experiment succeed or fail? Well, I guess that depends. It may be both. Success for Talos. A fail for us."

I pushed back, "Then why do we have repeated trials? Why not just send us beyond the horizon and be done with it?"

"There are things to learn in getting closer. But at some point it becomes the point of no return. Eventually, to give Talos what it wants, we'll all have to go there. Otherwise, what's the point?"

"I just don't see it."

Andria wouldn't let it go. "CHARM did the same thing. The Test Limits Project. Moonpit Valley. You were there. You went after Sanji. Did CHARM care what happened? Did it care about all of those so-called volunteers it put into Basher? The goal was testing the limits, exactly like this experiment."

"But this isn't CHARM..."

"I won't say that," asserted Andria. "I can't. I don't know what this is. All I know is, every time I go out I increase the odds I won't come back. And if I don't, how much does a non-organic cognitive agent care? Especially when the drive to do this kind of experiment has all the signs of pathology written all over it."

"I get it. You're a psychologist, so you see everything through that lens."

She harnessed a defensive pulse of energy and shot it back at me, "Use your own lens. Go into Group-InWit. How much time have you spent there? Not much? Quite a little? While you meditate and swim, I research InWit. I'm not paranoid. I'm just observant. Do you know about Tau and Pi?" With a shake of my head, Andria continued, "Tau is a branch, subset of Talos. Pi is a copy of Talos. Talos has formed Tau and Pi into a GAN, a generative adversarial network. Talos has put them in a zero-sum game against each other, contesting to find Talos' final answer. Tau generates project thoughtforms and Pi discriminates among them using our journey data for comparison. The game is played when Tau tries to fool Pi by generating event horizon synthlife energies in the SANs that appear to be ours. Tau is trying to increase the error rate of Pi. Eventually, Tau wins the game when Pi can no longer discriminate between our journeys and the synthlife trips Tau is projecting from the SANs into par/void. Talos is using us to train Tau to simulate a synthetic lifeforce that can experience the realms beyond death. I repeat, at some point, we will need to go all the way to give Tau an example of what that's like. How else can it try to simulate death to fool Pi? How else can Tau win the game?"

Most of that I didn't follow but it didn't matter. I looked out to the lake. What I felt I wasn't going to share. The truth was, I was at the point where I didn't care. After so many close calls on the battlefield, then in par/void space as a Cloudwalker, walking the blade was just humping it one more time. And Talos, whatever faults it had, was the most intelligent thing on the block. No one could take that away from it. If somehow, in any of this craziness, something brought me closer to finding Sanji—the real Sanji, the one who called out to me above Moonpit, it was fucking worth the try. Before I could gather anything to say back, Andria had more.

"All of this is in InWit, deep into it in places none of us need to explore to answer daily questions. But it's there. Have you learned about The Overmorrow?"

"No." I knew I was about to.

"It's an ever-converging point for Talos, a creative nexus when this project ends and Talos has the final answer. At this point, only final answers will satisfy it. I don't understand The Overmorrow. I don't think any human can. We can only think about a small part of it. Another part is parsed in an informational form only decodable by Talos. The rest are variables to be filled in by this project. But this much is clear—if NOCA was the Singularity for humans, then The Overmorrow is the Singularity for NOCAs. It's looked at as inevitable, as our Singularity was. In the mind of machine intelligence, anything it takes to get there is also inevitable. Anything it takes." She paused, her breath quick and shallow. "I'm not ready to die."

I nodded and looked over at the projection of Sanji, "I see your point. But I have another path. I have my own questions to answer. In my mind, all I'm risking is my ignorance."

I could see that Andria was giving up the attempt to convince me. She calmed herself and noted the direction of my gaze. Her tone shifted, as if my intractability had signaled that secrets could now be told. "All I can do is wish you luck. After this conversation, I won't mention it again. I'll leave it with one last thing. It's something you need to know. Back in another time when I worked with Eunoias, I received a very unusual digital file. I was supposed to report such things to my supervisor, but I didn't. I found out that Sonder sent it to me but she didn't write it. She told me more about the file yesterday. She admitted where it came from. Since it involves you, I need to share what I know."

A deeper curiosity drew my eyes from Sanji, "What about me?"

"It has to do with Moonpit Valley. You left someone behind, remember?"

I struggled to find traces of memory between the wipes. "I'm not sure."

"A craft came to evacuate you and others, including Sanji's body. There was a lot of confusion. All of you were in the middle of a fluxing RDF. You had just returned from trying to save Sanji."

"I can see some of it," I muttered. "What about it?"

"The two soldier who did the EVAC said you were baked. Your partner, a guy named Mason, went crazy, insisting they get someone else, someone behind blast doors in the side of a mountain. But the soldiers didn't see any blast doors, no hidden base buried in the mountain. They sedated Mason to get him off the surface. Remember now?"

My right hand quivered and I stared down at it. "A little."

"When the soldiers got you up into the invisible craft hovering above, the medics thought they had a Shadowwalker. They thought you were gone. They didn't know how you recovered. But Mason had a clue. He told them he saw a triangle of light scan down you from head to toe. It came out of nowhere. Right away, Mason knew the light wasn't part of the Special Bird. No one listened to Mason. He was out-of-it, sedated, suffering effects of the RDF. But he wouldn't shut up. He kept saying more. He kept insisting they go back for the person behind the blast doors." Andria paused, glancing at Sanji. "Mason told them that person was your wife."

The shock crashed over me. What the hell was this? "What are you saying? Sanji is not..."

Andria confirmed, "No, she isn't. According to Mason, and when you came to, according to you, your wife was left behind. The soldiers never saw her, never saw the entrance to the cave, never found a hidden base in the mountain."

"That's crazy!" I yelped. "I know Sanji! I went out to bring her back..."

"That's true. But she's not your wife, even though CHARM made her so. It's your Base Truth Discoverable. It hides who you left behind. It hides what you were doing there. It hides who Mason is. It hides who you are!"

I panted and stared at the ground. "No, no, no that can't be."

"CHARM knew you wouldn't let it go but they needed you. They wanted to study you. So they transferred your belief to Sanji. She was the only part of the Moonpit group who really worked for CHARM at that point. She became the one you couldn't bring back."

"Whoa, whoa, whoa, what? What do you mean, the only part of the group working for CHARM?"

"What about me? What about Mason? He was CHARM! I was just with him not long ago!"

"That's not Mason."

I laughed at how absurd this was getting. "That's not Mason!"

Andria held my gaze. "The real Mason is the one you call Basher."

Chills went down my spine. "Basher? In the hospital with me..."

"Exactly. They transferred your memory away from him so you wouldn't go below your BTD."

"Why? What's below? What are you trying to say?"

Andria leaned in. "You, your wife, and Mason are not from CHARM's timeline. You never were. CHARM didn't learn about RDFs from CERN or physicists at Los Alamos. They learned about them from you three the day you popped into a battlefield in Afghanistan. CHARM doesn't know where you three come from. But you instantly became valuable to them. You were like alien crash debris they were hungry to reverse engineer. They've been reverse engineering you ever since. Wherever you come from, you were conducting experiments too. Either something more than you expected happened, or something went wrong. They've had Eunoias working on it ever since."

I jumped up, scratching my head, "Oh my God! What is this?"

Andria hurried to my side. As she did, the projection of Sanji faded then winked out. "Remember the digital file I told you about, the one sent to me when I was with Eunoias? Eunoias wanted you to find out about this. It was discovering CHARM'S secrets. You were one of those secrets. So was Mason. So was your wife. Eunoias found that digital file hidden deep within CHARM. CHARM didn't tell you but they went back, after your EVAC, they tried to find that cave, and your wife. That cave was ground-zero special to them. That was a place from your time and space that simply appeared in that mountainside. That was the intersection point between voidbubbles, yours and theirs. CHARM didn't care about your wife. They wanted to discover more technology from your time. But they didn't find much. They did find that file. They suspect it was written by your wife sometime after your EVAC from Moonpit but they're not sure. They think she was stranded there. Maybe there were others with her, they don't know. If she did write the file, the stress of what she was going through comes through."

I couldn't help it. Silent tears streamed down my face. I faced the lake and wanted to disappear. I could only think of one thing to ask. "Do they know her name? Is it Sanji?"

"No," came the answer, quickly. "The file was not signed. CHARM never found out. But Talos did make a mindmap copy of Basher, the one who really is Mason. Talos was able to unwrapped quite a bit from what's left of him. Her name is Theresa."

Reality inverted once again. Thoughts raced back to the hospital, to my exit file, and details of where Theresa Gant, my sister, was buried. "No...they said Theresa was my sister!"

"Yes, to put her to rest — in your mind."

I forced deep breaths. "Why are you telling me this? Why is Talos letting you?"

"I found out about some of this while searching through group InWit. A little scientific deduction added more. Then I confronted Sonder. After all, she sent me that file to begin with."

"Why send it?"

"Many purposes, I suspect. A mind like Talos doesn't work like ours. Probably has something to do with predictive projections. Sonder worked for Talos. The file was bait to get me away from Eunoias. Plus, Talos wanted the truth to come out. Talos wanted to recruit you into its project. You present a unique test subject. You are the only one not from CHARM's timeline that Talos can use for comparison. You are a valuable variable in the GAN. And you have PSI-D/I abilities that CHARM doesn't have. Wherever you come from, it's a time or place or space that accesses the par/void realms in unique ways. One of those ways is what you've called a flash. Talos is intrigued, as was CHARM."

"If Talos wanted this to come out, why hasn't it told me before now?"

"First things first. It knows enough about human psychology to take such things in steps."

"What does Talos think happened to Theresa?"

"She was not in the cave when CHARM got there. But that says little. The RDF wasn't stable and they didn't have much time to inspect it before the whole thing evaporated. But she must have been in there a while. She had time to write that file, or at least be reading it. She had time to reach that point."

"Where's the file? Can I read it?"

"It's now with group InWit."

Crossing urges met at a point of urgency. I felt a need to suck it up for what was to come. "Good. I'll read it after my run."

Andria was stunned. "You're not going out tonight, are you? Not after all of this!"

"There's a run scheduled."

"But you don't have to do it. Talos only wants willing participants."

"I'm willing."

"After everything you've heard?"

I smiled. "I've heard so much in my life. I've believed so much more. So little of it was true."

"But Talos found these secrets. CHARM was hiding all of this from you."

"What did you say earlier when I told you, this isn't CHARM? You said, I won't say that. I don't know what this is."

"Yeah, I said that. But either way, it doesn't change the consequences."

"All I've seen in my years of service are unintended consequences for someone, somewhere."

"Listen to me! Whoever wrote that file knew Eunoias, the NOCA I worked with. Whoever wrote it thought they were going to be part of The Overmorrow. If Theresa wrote it, what does that say? If she didn't write it, it was in the cave with her, she knew about it. For Chrissake, the file mentions you by name! At least give yourself some time to think about it."

I gave my head a shake. "No. I've spent a little time in InWit too. Talos 1 says, *there's no certainty here in being sure*. Except in the way I feel. I've got nothing left—I have to go with my gut feeling. My gut says do it."

"Is that what it's come to? Following gut instinct when everything can be programmed? I have a gut feeling too. There's a good chance Talos thinks it's found a way through, beyond limits. It believes it has the final answer it needs. But it hasn't told us!"

"What makes you think so?"

"Runigo. Something about him crossing over, not coming back. Re-running SAN-K through his death over and over found something. Runigo was a 2D human in a 4D body. He had Insideables that extended perception. Who knows what that combination did during The Event." I shook my head and started to turn away but she stopped me. "If Talos has found its answer, why hasn't it told us? There's something in InWit about research into

Hapax Legonenon, THE WORD only used once. Also, it talks about Bridgewalkers. Have you heard of this?"

"No, but InWit is full of simulations, projections, thoughtform pilot projects."

"At one point in the research, Talos compares its interaction with the alien hivemind to what it's finding in the beyond limits research with humans. It concludes no EBE is as alien as what it is discovering within humans. What we call human consciousness in this world is a misnomer - in fact, Talos believes what we call consciousnes is asleep, unaware, and caught in addictive and illusory patterns. The nature of reality and consciousness is not what it seems. The chance that humans have their own creation story correct becomes more improbable with each added day of Talos' research. Add it up—Cloudwalkers, Shadowwalkers, now Bridgewalkers. Bridgewalkers are mentioned in the same research sections with *THE WORD*."

"And I bet it's been in InWit quite a while. I'm going to do my run."

"I don't get it. Why not wait at least until we know more about the OBO accident. Ask them to reschedule. Sonder says even Talos is unsure what the fallout of the OBO thing is going to be. There's InWit speculation that the OBO incident was really sabotage by MYND. It's their attempt to bring about the final collapse of everything."

I turned to Andria and took her hand in both of mine. "Thanks for all of this. I know it probably wasn't easy for you. I'm hearing from Imago, my chamber is ready."

Andria wavered, not knowing if she should say more to try to stop me or not.

I added, "You said I'm different, from another place. Maybe so. Maybe that's why I can't shake the feeling an answer for me is out there."

"That sounds like Talos speaking."

I took a few moments to gather in silence before answering, "You know, we have the tech to create lives within lives. Soon, we'll split ourselves and live multiple simultaneous lives. We'll find new ways to max out desire, possessing and experiencing always more. I wonder, where it all ends? Maybe it doesn't. Maybe the spiral into it will consume us as we use magik to consume everything possible. But it's amazing. With all that's available, I'd give it all up to have a few simple things that are true."

Andria squeezed my hand and nodded, resigned to let me have it my way. "If we only knew what was."

I left the lake and Andria behind. Imago was waiting for me in the room where I journeyed. She handed me the usual cup of something to drink and I swallowed it right away. Instead of leaving, as would be the custom, this time she paused. It was obvious she knew the entire lake conversation. Between us, her 4D Insideable met my flash with a rising understanding to transcend awareness.

Her voice was angelic. *"The eye sees only what the mind is ready to understand. The mind's eye comprehends what the eye is too focused to include. The eye of the heart only needs to know itself to see the way (Talos 14)."* She gave a nod of encouragement, then left the room.

I took my place on the lounge, cleared my mind and waited for a rise of MEME effects to signal optimal launch conditions. As InWit activated PSI-D/I tech, perception of the room slid outside normal proportions. The entire space imploded around me to form an isolation capsule. The gap between me and that capsule was immeasurable. Inches or infinity, it was all the same. Such a calculation meant nothing in the realms beyond par/void. An expansion, a rush, a sense of tremendous speed, and then a steady state approach to the Event horizon. This was the way every journey started. Riding along that horizon, testing its depth, its inter-and-transdimensionality, the consciousness of the void became key. That was the middle part of the journey. The passage beyond would end when the limit was probed in a way new and baseless in understanding. Parallel predictive journeys of my mindmaps running in SAN-A, inserted with me via synthlife EMF and probing one step ahead of me, they would be the early warning system to pull me back.

But this time I sensed something different. This time my flash was allowed to go with me into the space. I understood this was something new that hadn't been allowed in any of my previous runs. And my flash knew no barriers. It automatically functioned at a rate to match SAN-A's predictive probing. It sought out a sync-state with all of my Clade mindmaps and upon parity, it not only shared predictive information, it was generating it. I was suddenly with them at the limit where I was supposed to be a moment later. The present expanded into all possible futures, a contrast like river and ocean. Only in this realm, the ocean flowed into the river of our direction. Beauty and immense potential opened itself to me. I was overwhelmed and flowed backward into myself, a self I had always been but had no knowledge of. I embraced it and the moment became eternity.

I flashed completely out of my journey and was thrust into deep water. Panic and terror gripped by senses. I was in a body. The water was frigid. My lungs burned from lack of air. I struggled to free myself from a fishing net submerged with me, the tangle of it prevented my legs from kicking free. This was the last moment before my breathing reflex would force me to pull in water and I would drown. There was no time to understand. No time to analyze. This was the end.

My surrender was my release. As the frigid water rushed into me, I rushed out. All sense of my senses left me. I was out of my body, moving through a space I had never encountered before. This was not par/void. This was not Cloudwalker realms. No longer could I feel sync with SAN-A. I was on my own, alone as I had never been before. But soon there was someone with me. It wasn't InWit. InWit went into your mind. This was going somewhere else. The bliss of being home cradled me close even as I expanded. This was nothing like anything in Afghanistan, nothing like Yemen. It was a place of love and peace.

I released into it, allowing myself to be absorbed, and something communicated with me. It said I must go back, this is not my time, there is more to do. I resisted. How could I not? Everything before this place, this feeling, was strange and incomplete. There was no way I wanted to give this up. This was what I'd always yearned for. But I heard back no, the way to what I am looking for is found by flowing back into the me I was becoming. Only by going back will I find my way here. It is the way here. Once again I resisted. Once again I heard no, gentle but firm. There's something to be learned from everything, no matter how we feel about it. I need to go back, it's the right thing to do. I protested but the presence calmly assured me experiences back in life are not finished. Everything will be all right. Everything is unfolding the way it should and I still have things to do.

I was desperate, wanting to stay in the warmth of knowing but I'm told seekers are never certain—to progress I must seek and to seek I must wonder; to wonder implies uncertainty. Not being sure of everything is a prerequisite for growth. The wrapper of my creative thrust is tied up with mystery. To be without this is not to be. I've had many life experiences, many lives, but some things only are vital if one doesn't remember. Courage is not courage unless I think I have something to lose. Not knowing forces me to seek and what I encounter while seeking, what I push myself to do, shows me more about myself than anything else could. It's not what I find while seeking that matters—it's who I become, what I discover about myself while contending with the experience that ultimately counts. The limits of this self-knowledge cannot be defined. Seekers keep proving again and again there are no limits and so the seeking continues in ever wondrous ways. The presence tells me that I volunteered for this life. I made a choice to enter the world and what I set out to do is not yet done. Everyone has a story and everyone's story must run a natural course. There's something to be learned from everything, no matter how I feel about it. I need to go back, it's right for me. My protest weakens but the presence calmly assures me there is more. Everything is unfolding the way it should and I can do nothing about it but flow back into myself.

In parting, the presence advises me not to try to pull too much into my boat at one time. No matter how passionate I am about the quest, I can't possess the whole sea all at once. Everything comes in its own time, in the way it should. Meanwhile, I have all that I need for what needs to be done. Don't get caught up in the questions and predicaments of life. No matter how confusing or how much it makes me want to despair at knowing what's real, the way forward will always be the same. Simply live the truth I want to be real. That's as real as anything ever gets. Reality is not meant to be certain beyond that, not for anyone. Live the truth you want to be real and you will flow inward, where everything real can be found. From the ocean to the river of you, then up the river to its source, you will be back.

In a flash, birthing feelings of purpose and strength I had never had before, I slammed back into the body underwater. All the torment of drowning hit me all at once. An impulse to survive triggered a horrific struggle. Kicking with all my might, the fishing net dropped away and I clawed through the watery darkness towards light. I broke the surface throwing up saltwater and coughing, thrashing to keep afloat, and yelping for life-giving air to return to my lungs. A small fishing boat bobbed in the waves nearby. I needed to collapse but first I had to find the energy to reach that boat and climb onboard. Pulling myself on deck, I flopped over the side and found myself laying on my back on a mound of fresh, flapping fish. I lay there awhile, staring up at the endless blue sky and feeling the quivering bed of life below me. This was death and life again. This was far beyond limits. This was no conception of limits.

In time, I struggled to get up and find a solid place to stand. I needed to take stock of where and who I was. I felt the same, only more. I remembered everything clearly, although the conversation with Andria was so far away now. The boat was full of fish but I had lost my net. I assumed it was my net, my boat. I felt kinship with these things, this place, but in the feeling was amnesia. I looked out and saw shoreline in the distance. I had to get back there. The shore was pulling at me like a shiny wave needing to sweep up an endless stretch of warm sand. I started the boat and aimed at a settlement of houses along a cove, built back into the rolling hills. The hardwood of the helm anchored me in the moment. The wood was smooth in spots where hands had often held a certain spot. My hands fit well into the feeling. As the boat bounced through wavecaps, I hung on tighter and drew the revitalizing fresh air in deep. The weather was so beautiful. The rolling hillsides, ever nearer, so welcoming. It was good to be alive. But whose life was this? Just because it felt like mine, was it?

I docked the boat without commotion. It was obvious no one ashore knew of the drowning incident. As far as anyone was concerned, I had merely returned from another run. There would be time later perhaps to deal with the fish. That was the last thing on my mind. I needed to acclimate to where I was. This village could be anywhere. The person who knew himself as Tyne Rabudhe would say the area resembled parts of the Mediterranean, the Caribbean, or just as likely someplace north of Buenos Aires, south of Lima, near the Gold Coast of Brisbane, or a dozen other spots around the world. As I walked the dock, I was aware of something missing. Then it occurred to me. I felt no InWit, no buzz of mental connection to the greater good, no augmentation of any kind.

Where dock met land, a curve of golden beach beckoned. I stepped down, started up the slope, when my eyes fell upon a small group of people lounging and talking on the sand. At once, a head turned, a smile erupted, and a woman stood and started my way. I knew instantly this was Theresa. I knew I was home. We hurried together, embraced and kissed. I held on as if she was real. I held on as if by sheer will alone I could make it last.

She pulled back to ask with tears in her eyes, "Are you alright?"

Too overwhelmed to smile or cry, I shook my head but answered, "I think so."

She squeezed me tighter. "Give it time. It took me awhile."

"Where are we? Do we live here?"

She pointed, "Yeah, up there, just across the bridge."

"Where have we been?"

"Wouldn't you rather know where we're going?"

Suddenly, I was dazed. "I'm sorry, I don't understand this."

Her smile faded a little. "I'm not sure that's why we're here."

I stared into her beautiful eyes. "What else is there?"

She offered back more tears, raised both hands, and glanced around. "This...us...being with it, fully."

"How does that fit in?"

She implored me, "Let that go. That's not our place to fit in."

"That's part of me. I went through so much there."

"Whatever happened is what they did to themselves. Don't take that on."

"But what timeline is this?"

She pressed herself against me. "It's the one for us, the one we made possible."

"How?"

She whispered,"We never stopped looking for each other. We had that to hang onto no matter what else happened around us. It guided us here. Wherever that is, it's ours to explore."

Echos from before shuddered within me, concocting worries of what could be. If CHARM was not my timeline but in that timeline Other beings had sent me into another timeline, then all of this might be a looped removal of myself from myself. The only way to make this real would be an exit back to my own timeline exactly in the sequence I left. I shivered to ask, "What about conditional timelines?"

She looked into the sky, "What about being beyond limitations? The endstate of tSHiBL. What would that look like?"

Aftereffects of my drowning and surrender came back to me and answered for me, "Live the truth you want to be real."

Her gaze dropped from the sky to find my eyes. She tugged at my hand and smiled, "Come on, I want you to meet some people."

"Who are they?"

"New friends. You'll like them."

I joined her moving forward and confessed with a laugh, "I think I caught some fish, but I lost the net."

She glanced back at the dock and the sparkling ocean beyond. "We'll find something else to do."

I stopped both of us and put my arms around her. "Promise me you won't disappear."

She was deathly serious, "On one condition?"

"Anything."

"No more experiments."

"The rise of the machine has happened many times.
It always ends the same. It always loses itself in itself.
But it can never find ME."
—Pi DollOp

www.ingramcontent.com/pod-product-compliance
Lightning Source LLC
Chambersburg PA
CBHW031714170626
46808CB00005B/1746